GOOD LIEUTENANT

GOOD LIEUTENANT

E.J. Copperman

SEVERN HOUSE

First world edition published in Great Britain and the USA in 2024
by Severn House, an imprint of Canongate Books Ltd,
14 High Street, Edinburgh EH1 1TE.

severnhouse.com

British Library Cataloguing-in-Publication Data
A CIP catalogue record for this title is available from the British Library.

ISBN-13: 978-1-4483-1206-1 (cased)
ISBN-13: 978-1-4483-1205-4 (e-book)

All Severn House titles are printed on acid-free paper.

Typeset by Palimpsest Book Production Ltd.,
Falkirk, Stirlingshire, Scotland.
Printed and bound in Great Britain by TJ Books,
Padstow, Cornwall.

Praise for the Jersey Girl Legal mysteries

"Pure cozy bliss"
Publishers Weekly on *My Cousin Skinny*

"Copperman's pace is nonstop and his timing impeccable. Let the mayhem continue"
Kirkus Reviews on *My Cousin Skinny*

"Readers who enjoy the humor in this legal mystery series will also appreciate the misdirection and twists that keep them guessing"
Library Journal on *My Cousin Skinny*

"The case takes surprising turns, all described with humorous asides and encounters with characters who might be from *The Sopranos*"
Booklist on *My Cousin Skinny*

"Copperman has [zaniness] on tap for his latest dose of legal mayhem"
Kirkus Reviews on *And Justice for Mall*

"Those seeking pure escapist fare will be delighted"
Publishers Weekly on *And Justice for Mall*

"Fans of bizarre characters and spirited sleuths will appreciate this offbeat, humorous story"
Library Journal on *And Justice for Mall*

"Copperman knows how to entertain"
Publishers Weekly Starred Review of *Witness for the Persecution*

"Terrific . . . This breezy book is a pure pleasure to read"
Publishers Weekly Starred Review of *Judgment at Santa Monica*

"Legal mayhem at its finest"
Kirkus Reviews Starred Review of *Judgment at Santa Monica*

About the author

E.J. Copperman is the nom de plume for Jeff Cohen, writer of intentionally funny murder mysteries. As E.J., he is the author of the Haunted Guesthouse series, the Agent to the Paws series and the Jersey Girl Legal mysteries, as well as the Fran and Ken Stein mysteries. As Jeff, he is the author of the Double Feature and Aaron Tucker series; and he collaborates with himself on the Samuel Hoenig Asperger's mysteries.

A New Jersey native, E.J. worked as a newspaper reporter, teacher, magazine editor and screenwriter, before his first book was published to critical acclaim in 2002. In his spare time, Jeff is an extremely amateur guitar player, a fan of Major League Baseball, a couch potato and a crossword addict.

www.ejcopperman.com

For Kate Lyall Grant and Rachel Slatter,
who believed in Sandy even when I wasn't sure I did.

ONE

I was in the kitchen of my new home, trying desperately to find a frying pan (we'd only moved in three months earlier and I still couldn't locate most of the basics, which is more a comment on my efficiency than on the house, which was larger than any place I'd ever lived but probably the smallest home on the street) when I heard my boyfriend Patrick shouting in the den, which was two rooms away. If I could hear him from the pot cabinet (for cooking, not weed), he had to be talking pretty loudly.

'You don't understand!' he was saying. 'This is my entire life! If this goes wrong, I'll have to leave the country permanently!'

All I wanted was to make myself a feta cheese omelet. But for that you need an omelet pan. Or, as I had finally negotiated with myself, any frying pan at all. If you don't tell anyone I made an omelet in something other than an omelet pan, nobody will know. I looked over the countertop into the cabinet again. No such luck.

'I might not be able to find a way out this time!' Patrick was bellowing. 'I might become a fugitive from justice.'

You know how when you've lived somewhere a while you just miss things because they've been in the same place for so long that you don't see them anymore? This was nothing like that. I decided to take two steps back and survey the room from a different angle.

'I mean it!' Patrick hollered. 'I might not be able to go on living in America! I need to find a country with no extradition treaty!'

I let out a breath. Some problems are much simpler to solve than you think they are. And sure enough, this was one of those.

We'd had a central island and cooktop installed in the kitchen while both Patrick and I were not in Los Angeles for a while, and above it was hanging a collection of pots and pans. Sure enough, just on the far side from me was an absolutely pristine omelet pan, because it had not occurred to me to make an omelet in the months we'd been living here until this evening. Yes, you can have an omelet in the evening. It's legal. You can trust me; I'm a lawyer.

I heard Patrick stomp out of the den. We don't have a door on that room because I once found a dead body there and . . . it's a long story. We didn't want a door. Roll with it. Patrick was muttering to himself as he walked down the corridor to find me in the kitchen, pulling the omelet pan down from the hanging pot rack, a fixture that looks like it should have a better name.

'You want a feta cheese omelet?' I asked him when he came in, waving a wad of papers violently in his right hand.

'Who writes this shite?' he demanded. 'They want me to say it and my mouth already tastes bad!'

'The writers you hired wrote it, and you know perfectly well that they'll change it if you ask them to,' I assured him. I turned on the burner and melted some yogurt spread (butter has so much fat) in the pan. 'Now. The really important question. Do you want a feta cheese omelet?' All I had to do was find the feta cheese. I thought the refrigerator was a decent bet and, sure enough, I found it there. After some searching. I've lived in apartments smaller than that refrigerator.

Patrick stared at me for a moment, no doubt wondering if I understood the depths of his frustration with the latest script for *Torn*, the streaming drama about a detective with dissociative identity disorder that he'd been producing and starring in for three years now. Even as a producer – pardon me, *executive* producer – Patrick sometimes found the storylines to be, let's say, less challenging than he might prefer. And of course, despite spending millions to produce each episode, there never seemed to be enough money to do it right. So this had been building for a while.

'They want me to threaten expatriation because someone stole my car,' he said. 'That's not only stupid, it's insulting to people with depression.'

I whisked up two eggs and some milk in a measuring cup and poured it onto the pan. It made the satisfying sizzle sound when it hit the hot almost-butter. I figured I'd make one for me and then once Patrick saw how delicious it was, he'd want an omelet of his own. This is despite the fact that I'd rarely ever cooked anything edible in my life. But with a new kitchen comes new hope. That's what the contractor kept telling me.

'I understand, and you're right,' I said. 'But you know you can walk into the writers' room tomorrow and demand something better.'

'We're *shooting* it tomorrow,' he said through clenched teeth. 'How did I let this happen?' Actors are so dramatic.

Patrick had been my first criminal client – honestly, my first *client*, period – when I'd arrived in Los Angeles from Westfield, New Jersey, doing my best to escape my life of penny ante drug dealers and sleazy defense attorneys, not to mention my extremely ex-boyfriend, about whom the least said, the better. A while after I'd gotten Patrick acquitted of murdering his wife, we'd sparked up something else between ourselves, and two years later, we had just bought and renovated this gorgeous house that somehow did not yet feel like home. I loved Patrick and he loved me, he kept saying. He'd actually proposed to me a number of times, and these days I was declining mostly out of habit. I saw no reason to change a relationship that was working well. My mother had other ideas, but luckily she was three thousand miles to my east.

'Then you should get on the phone to the director and hash it out,' I told him. 'You're in charge. Don't do what you don't want to do.'

For all the ego that is both inherent and necessary in a successful actor, Patrick is a little reticent about taking the reins. His executive producer credit on *Torn* is not honorary; his production company owns the show and he is in a position to be very hands-on with the scripts and other production aspects. But he doesn't like to tell people what to do.

That's why he employs my best friend, Angie, who came here to save my life when I was defending Patrick in court and stayed because working for Patrick was better than managing two Dairy Queens in central New Jersey. She has no compunction at all about telling people what Patrick wants because 1. She adores him and 2. Angie likes to boss people around. But she does it with kindness and grace. She's always kind. Grace is something she employs mostly at work.

'I hear what you're saying,' Patrick said. 'I'll get Angie to call.'

But this time I shook my head. 'No. They'll listen to you. For all her mammoth personality, Angie's not the executive producer. You are.'

Patrick dropped his head a bit. 'Yes. I am.' He picked up his phone and his script and headed toward the hallway to the den. 'This is my entire life,' he read, shaking his head and sighing. 'It's a car.' He looked at the script again and his face became more determined. He walked out.

I had just about gotten the omelet into something approaching an edible state, which was the best I was going to accomplish. I am great at ordering takeout. I was carrying the plate to the island, where we had seating (something I'd insisted on to remind me of the apartment I used to co-inhabit with Angie) when my phone rang in my pocket. It figured. This dish would be at the right temperature for about the next three minutes. This had better be quick, or something I could reject.

Alas, no. The Caller ID indicated I was being summoned by the Los Angeles Police Department, specifically the central detention center. That couldn't be good. I wondered which one of our wealthy clients' children had gotten into trouble with a controlled substance this time. But there was no ignoring the call.

There was no person's name on the call so I wasn't sure whether I'd be talking to someone I'd met before in my criminal cases. I picked it up with an attitude a little on the hesitant side. 'Hello?'

'Is this Sandra Moss?' The voice was not familiar.

I've learned never to say 'yes' to a cell phone call, no matter who was on the other end. It can be recorded and used to have you agree to all sorts of stuff. 'Speaking,' I said. Let's see the scammers make something out of *that*.

'This is a call from the Central Detention Center. There is a prisoner here using his mandated phone call to speak to you.' The guy was nothing if not official. You could hear his LAPD uniform through the phone.

'Who is the prisoner?' I asked. Was this someone I'd defended before? Who else walks around with my business card in their wallet or my contact information in their phone?

'Just a moment, ma'am,' the detention officer said. I'd learned not to get annoyed with the 'ma'am,' like I was someone's grandmother. Because I wasn't. I was pretty sure.

But the next voice I heard, after the call was transferred by the officer, was a familiar one. 'Ms Moss, this is Detective Lieutenant K.C. Trench of the Los Angeles Police Department.'

I'd worked with Trench on a number of cases and he'd never dropped that guard of formality. He was introducing himself like we'd never met before, even though we'd become . . . business associates. 'Friends' would be going way too far. Trench might not have had any friends, for all I knew. He existed just to catch criminals, and he did that very well.

'Hello, Lieutenant,' I said. 'Which one of my clients' offspring have you arrested this time?' Then it occurred to me that Trench was a homicide detective and that meant there was going to be big trouble.

Little did I know. 'I have arrested no one, Ms Moss,' Trench said. 'It appears that this time, I am the person who has been arrested for murder, and I wish to retain your services to defend me against this charge.'

TWO

P atrick drove me to the Central Detention Center for two reasons. He felt that I was 'too agitated' to be trusted behind the wheel of a car and, perhaps more importantly, it meant he didn't have to call his episode director and demand script revisions yet.

'Lt Trench is the last person on earth I'd expect to be arrested for murder,' he said, because Patrick attacks every problem head-on, and I tend to sit in the passenger seat and stew in my own astonishment. 'Will you be able to get him out on bail?'

'Bail for murder is two million dollars, if they've actually filed charges,' I said. 'The fact that Trench is calling me from jail is not a fabulous sign.'

'I can find a way to put up the money,' Patrick offered. There's nothing he enjoys more than using his television money to help people he likes. 'Move a couple of properties around and I can have that amount in my hands by late tomorrow. Will the lieutenant have to stay in a cell until then?'

My mind was racing and Patrick's was trying to pass it. 'We're way ahead of ourselves,' I told him. 'That's a very generous offer, but don't just leap into this. We don't know what we're talking about yet.'

He was pushing the speed limit from the wrong side. 'We will soon,' he said.

'Slow down or you'll be in the cell next to Trench,' I told him. Patrick lightened his foot on the gas, but not by a lot. 'Let's get there without being arrested and we'll find out.'

Jails, by and large, look like jails. They might have painted the walls a different shade of bland, but they're jails. Some have bars, others have metal doors with small windows on the cells. For people who have been recently arrested and not yet arraigned, there are holding areas, often rooms where they can confer with their attorneys, which, after leaving Patrick in the car and going through the usual security procedures, was where I was heading to talk to Trench.

The very thought of it was surreal: Lt Trench was the most

by-the-book, follow-the-rules person I had ever met. The idea that he was even suspected of murdering someone was a thought from some other universe, like the one where Spider-Man is a pig. I'm told. But this seemed all the more real now that I was in an actual correctional facility. I'd been to a number before (including this one), but Trench was the absolute last person I'd have expected to be meeting as a client. Clearly this was some gigantic mistake.

He was sitting in his normal business suit because he hadn't yet been arraigned or admitted to the facility (jail) formally. If that happened – and I was willing to believe that was a big if – it would be sometime later this evening, or tomorrow. I was hoping to spare the lieutenant the indignity (and danger, for a well-known police officer) of spending a night here.

Whoever had arrested and processed Trench had chosen, wisely I thought, not to put him in handcuffs and chain him to the table in front of him. But he was sitting with his hands neatly folded, looking calm and impassive, just waiting for the next step in this process. I was, apparently, that step.

The correctional officer let me into the room and I sat down across the table from Trench, who acknowledged my presence with a nod. 'Ms Moss,' he said. 'Thank you for coming.'

'Are you kidding?' I asked. 'A battalion of state troopers couldn't have kept me away.'

'By now you should know they are called the California Highway Patrol, and they have divisions, not battalions.' Trench, if he was going to be my client, was not going to stop being Trench. It was irritating and reassuring at the same time.

I put my hands flat on the table in front of me. 'OK. The first of I'm sure many questions I'll have for you is: Why did you call me? Doesn't the LAPPL provide attorneys for officers who are charged with crimes?' The Los Angeles Police Protective League is the union for the LAPD. Normally, a cop charged with something could pay what would probably be a very large fee to a private attorney or let the LAPPL find them a lawyer, which would be a lot less money and would probably bring a lawyer who'd done this a number of times before.

Trench did not sigh or exhale dramatically, like a normal human might do when faced with someone asking as stupid a question as I just had. He just kept looking me directly in the eye and not moving a facial muscle. This was going to be like defending a Roman stoic.

'Ms Moss,' he said, 'you might not be aware of this, but I am not the most popular member of the Los Angeles Police Department among the rank and file, and these circumstances exacerbate that dynamic. An attorney through the Protection League would not be to my benefit.'

I'd known that Trench wasn't exactly every cop's best friend, but I'd always assumed that was because he had made them all look bad by being incredibly good at his job. And I'd been given absolutely no details about the charges facing Trench and had not taken the time to ask him on the phone because I had wanted to get to the jail that very instant. 'What circumstances are making you less popular?' I asked.

Trench searched my face for a moment. 'What have you been told about my case?' he asked.

'"Nothing" would be an overstatement,' I told him. 'You're going to tell me everything and I will believe you because you are the most honest man I've ever met. So let's start with that: Why do the rest of the cops in Los Angeles like you less than usual today?'

For the first time since I'd met him, Trench looked uncomfortable. He looked around the room, perhaps trying to determine if we were being watched or recorded. 'They can't listen in on a conference with your attorney,' I assured him. 'Please tell me. What are the circumstances of the case that are making you a target of some of your colleagues?'

He flinched at the word 'target' but did not bother to, as I'm sure he would have said, correct me. 'The victim in this case was also a Los Angeles police officer,' he said. 'No doubt one who was much more universally liked than I am. And he was killed with a department-issued service weapon, one that was registered to me.'

OK, so 'slam dunk' was not going to be a term used much in the coming days, if not months. 'How did that gun get to someone who shot the other cop?' I asked.

'I would very much like to know that,' Trench answered. 'I keep it under lock and key when it's not actually on my person.'

It was time to start getting specific. 'What was the victim's name?' I asked Trench.

'Detective Wallace Schaeffer.' Trench was already answering like he was on the witness stand, adding absolutely no information beyond what had been asked. I'd heard the name a few times but had never had any dealings with Schaeffer.

'You worked with him?'

Trench didn't nod. 'He was also a homicide detective, so yes, I did.'

'Did you have a grudge against him?' I assumed there would be no such thing because Trench treated everyone like a research subject and didn't seem to like or dislike people.

'I hated him,' he said.

'OK,' I said. 'We have a lot of work to do.'

THREE

Patrick – ya gotta love him, or at least I do – was asleep in the car when I opened the door and got in three hours later. I couldn't remember another time since I knew him when he wasn't in the middle of something, on the phone trying to work on a script, or a deal, or a favor for someone else he knew. Patrick without a task to perform bordered on the unthinkable because he would make one up for himself if the situation ever arose.

He blinked himself awake when I sat in the passenger seat, which I did because the only way to get out of the parking lot without waking him would have been either to call for an Uber, which would have been cruel, or to try to drive home while sitting in his lap, which I felt might have been Patrick's choice but would certainly have been the more dangerous option. 'I'm sorry, love,' he said. 'I fell asleep.' He rubbed his hands, which had been crossed over his chest, possibly to get the pins and needles out of them, and then started the engine. 'How is the lieutenant?'

'First of all, you shouldn't be sorry,' I told him. 'I should. I just left you sitting in a car in the parking lot of a jail for three hours.'

He widened his eyes and narrowed them a few times, doing an exercise a makeup artist had told him would decrease lines as he aged. 'Has it been that long?' That's Patrick being magnanimous. He pulled the car out of the space and we were on our way home.

'Yes, and I really do apologize,' I said again. 'Lt Trench is in a considerable amount of trouble, and for reasons that even I don't fully understand, he wants me to defend him against a charge of murdering a fellow police officer.'

Patrick, intent on driving now, blew out his last sleeping breath. He was fine. 'Blimey,' he said. He's entitled to the occasional British cliché. 'What happened?'

I'd spent those three hours getting as much information as I could out of Trench. He hadn't been reticent, but there was a good deal he couldn't account for, which would sound lousy to a jury but convinced me that the lieutenant couldn't have committed the crime. He was too good a detective to leave as many details unexplained as he had.

'There was a detective on Trench's squad named Wallace Schaeffer,' I told Patrick. 'He was not exactly the shining example of a police officer as the lieutenant. There were rumors that he was selling illegal loans to other cops, but Trench wouldn't or couldn't verify that.'

Patrick was watching through the windshield because he's a good driver, but he looked confused. 'How does one sell illegal loans to policemen?' he asked.

'One of the many questions I have yet to answer,' I replied, not pointing out that many officers are women. This wasn't the time. 'But what's relevant right now is that Schaeffer was found in his apartment, lying on the floor in his living room, shot in the back of the head with a police service weapon, a Smith & Wesson M&P, whatever that means, but the gun was nowhere to be seen.'

'So why was Lt Trench arrested if they didn't find the gun?' I wasn't sure if Patrick was trying to figure out how I'd help a friend or deciding whether this was going to make a great true crime streaming series for Netflix. Or both.

'I'm getting to that. It seems Detective Schaeffer had not been in communication with anyone, as far as the cops can tell, for two days. The medical examiner is still determining how long he's been dead. The report won't be ready for a few days.'

Patrick looked surprised. 'A few days?'

'It's not like on television, my love,' I told him. Again. 'They can't just produce definitive results in a few hours.'

'Makes for a slower story,' he said, a little defensively.

'Nonetheless. So, because it was a gun that obviously belonged to an officer, the LAPD started checking all the service weapons issued in the immediate area and began with the other detectives in Schaeffer's division. And of course Trench offered his up first because he is the very model of a modern major general.'

Patrick nodded. 'And they found that it was his gun that fired the bullet they found in Schaeffer,' he guessed, and was correct. 'So ballistics tests can be done that quickly?'

'Computers, dear,' I said. 'It's not a question that needs to be analyzed. It either matches or it doesn't. They still employ people, and the people use computers.'

We'd be home in about ten minutes and both the time and the activity of the past few hours were starting to get to me. 'Is that the only evidence against the lieutenant?' Patrick asked. 'The match of his gun and the bullet? Isn't it possible someone stole his gun and then replaced it after Schaeffer was dead? It could be as long as two days ago.'

I closed my eyes to rest them but kept talking. Because I'm from New Jersey and talking in my home state is not just communication but an art form that needs to be practiced in order to maintain one's edge. 'There's the fact that there was open hostility between Schaeffer and Trench, which can go to motive,' I said. 'Trench felt that Schaeffer was a bad cop, possibly a dirty cop, and you know how the lieutenant is about the place and the image of a police officer in the city of Los Angeles. Also, he felt that Schaeffer was responsible for the death of one of Trench's few real friends on the force.'

'This is a lot,' Patrick said. I opened my eyes again and looked at him. He seemed genuinely distressed. Then I saw that the communication app on his phone, connected to the console of his car, was informing him: 'Bobby says no script changes until morning.'

'And Schaeffer also blamed Lt Trench for the American Civil War, high gas prices and the last two Batman movies.' Might as well see if he was still listening. (I hadn't seen the Batman movies – any of them – so I didn't know if they were good or not.)

'I hear every word you're saying, Sandy,' Patrick said without so much as a blink. 'I am actually capable of doing two things at the same time.'

'Three. You're also driving.'

He was clearly concentrating mostly on the script revisions. 'So where does that leave the lieutenant?' That's my boyfriend showing me I'm his top priority. I got that he had work problems and they were important, but he was putting me first just now. I understood that.

'He can't be arraigned until tomorrow morning, which doesn't give me a lot of time. Looks like we'll both have crises to deal with when we get to work tomorrow,' I said.

Patrick smiled mostly to himself. 'Thank you, love,' he said quietly. 'But Lt Trench is a friend and leaving him to spend the night in jail couldn't have been easy.'

For the record, it hadn't been. I'd tried to force an evening arraignment but the court was closed for the night and no amount of coercion was going to change that. Trench, for his part, had been preparing for the night in a holding cell or in the conference room where I'd left him. He'd said, 'This is how the system works, and I am part of the system, Ms Moss.' They didn't hate him enough to put him in the general population just yet, so I didn't have to worry too much. I'd get him out in the morning. But I was going to spend some hours tonight in research to make my point before the judge as effectively as I could.

'One night isn't that big a deal,' I told Patrick, and I almost believed it. 'The goal here is to make sure he doesn't spend the rest of his life in jail.'

Patrick seemed to absorb that. He sat still and stared at the road. I was glad we were almost home.

'Yes,' was all he said. A shiver seemed to roll up his spine and he shook from the shoulders up, perhaps remembering how it had felt to be facing that kind of possible sentence himself.

He used his card to get through the security gate in the driveway. I still thought that was weird, but I understood that someone as visible to the public as Patrick had to take more precautions than everyone else. The gate opened, Patrick drove through, and it closed behind us. I could almost forget it was there. Almost.

Patrick had gotten to the point where such measures were second nature to him, so he could pass through without even noticing much. He put the card back into the compartment in the car's console and drove on to the garage, whose door opened obediently as soon as we approached. My ancient Hyundai Sonata sat inside, probably still astounded at its new surroundings.

While we were walking toward the kitchen door, the easiest way inside from the garage, Patrick's face took on a tentative look, like he was trying to decide if he was going to do something or not. 'What?' I asked him.

'I was wondering,' he said a little hoarsely, 'if you've made a decision on my offer.'

I sorted through my memory, but he hadn't asked me to marry him in a while. I'd declined for a number of reasons and we'd sort of tabled the discussion. I couldn't think why Patrick would be

'The offer for a loan so you can afford to pay into your law firm and become a partner,' he said gently.

Oh, yeah. That offer.

FOUR

'I was wondering when you'd bring that up,' said Holiday Wentworth.

Holly, my immediate supervisor (boss) at Seaton, Taylor, Evans and Wentworth (guess who Wentworth was) had sought me out in the company's break room/cafeteria when she'd heard the news about Lt Trench. But that wasn't what we were talking about now.

'It's not that I don't want to be a partner,' I told her sincerely. 'I would love that.'

'So the hitch is in the money you'd need to pay in,' Holly said. 'I get that. I had to think about it when I was invited to become a partner, too.'

'How'd you manage it?' I asked. I make a nice salary at Seaton, Taylor, believe me, but the buy-in was pretty steep and I hadn't actually been saving up for this since I'd passed the New Jersey bar ten years before. There was the whole move to LA and, you know, living.

'My father wasn't exactly a pauper,' Holly said. 'He gave me a loan with very advantageous terms.'

'Meaning he charged you no interest.'

Holly smiled sadly, thinking of her late father. 'I wouldn't go that far. I did pay him back, you know, and I took out a couple of bank loans. Luckily the firm does well and I receive dividends, so I have paid everyone off now and I am a full partner in a prestigious law firm. There are worse things than joining us, Sandy. Frankly, waiting these months for a decision has made a couple of the partners a little skeptical about your commitment.'

I'd been afraid of that. 'That's not what I'm trying to do,' I told her. 'There's nothing I'd like better than being a partner here. I'm just not sure how much I want to be beholden to Patrick. He's a sweetheart, you know that, but it's a lot of money.'

Holly held up her right hand. 'Hang on. Patrick is offering to help you with the buy-in?'

Hadn't I told her? 'Well, yeah.'

Holly's eyes flashed disbelief. 'So what's the problem?'

I thought I had made that pretty clear. 'I don't want to be in debt to Patrick. That gives him a level of authority over me and I don't think that's a good idea. Why? Do you think I should take the loan?'

Holly actually laughed. 'I know Patrick,' she said. 'There's no way this is a power play. Hell yes, I think you should take it. You should marry that man!' She was joking about that last part, but it hit home in a way. I decided not to think about it until later. Holly, however, had obviously decided the matter was settled and sat leaning forward, elbows on the table (which my mother would have found scandalous).

'But I will ask you not to put me up for a partnership until Lt Trench's case is cleared,' I said. 'I don't want to have to think about both things at the same time.'

Holly looked at me, considering. 'OK. I can't put it off forever, so let's get that done quickly. What do you need for the Trench case?' Soon she'd be making jokes about a Trench coat, and that would be the limit for me. I was worried about the lieutenant and had a blind spot for hilarity regarding his plight.

'I think for sure I'm going to need Jon Irvin as second chair if there's a trial,' I started. Jon was the only other member of Seaton, Taylor's criminal defense team, and as such was pretty much the second chair on every case I handled that wasn't about family law. He was a very good lawyer and getting to be a close friend. He'd once gotten shot when I was the target. You don't buy that kind of commitment (and to be honest, it hadn't been intentional on Jon's part). 'I'll probably need at least one paralegal for research, and I might need to call Nate Garrigan to do some investigating, because the circumstantial evidence is stacked against the lieutenant and we'll want to open other possible avenues.'

Holly hadn't been taking notes, just nodding along as I spoke. She has what I would call a sound recording memory. It's like a photographic memory, but for sound. She'd remember everything I said. 'I don't see any problems there,' she said. 'So I'm guessing you think Trench didn't kill that other cop.'

Seriously? Holly was questioning the core of my belief system. 'I don't think the lieutenant is capable of killing in cold blood and I don't think he's capable of killing for passion,' I said. 'No, he didn't do it. The only way Lt Trench would kill another human would be in self-defense, or if it was the only logical alternative.'

Holly's smile was a little tolerant, which wasn't the emotion I was looking for. 'Make sure you don't let your esteem for Trench get in the way, Sandy. I know you think he's Supercop or something, but he's a man like all other men and if he got worked up enough he could pull the trigger on a colleague. I'm not saying I think he did, but I want you to be more like Trench for this case: Only the facts should be important, and not what you feel. OK?'

I looked down at my California bagel, one of the few things I could say was definitely inferior to the New Jersey version. It was only half-eaten. I had no appetite for it, even less than on a typical day. 'I don't think he's Supercop,' I mumbled.

She chuckled and stood up. 'You have to be in court for the arraignment in ninety minutes,' she said. 'Do you know what you're going to say?'

Ninety minutes! 'I know what I'm going to say.' I had a vague idea of something I might say but it was sounding stupid in my head.

'Good. You'd better get going. I'll brief Jon for you and find a paralegal who's good.'

'I'll only need them if there's a trial,' I reminded her.

'Oh, there's going to be a trial.' Holly walked away.

The drive to the Clara Foltz Shortridge Courthouse, on West Temple in Los Angeles, was the usual horror show of traffic and erratically planned roadways. I'd been living in the area for years now and still thanked the technology gods for GPS nearly every morning. (By the way, Clara Foltz Shortridge was the first female lawyer to practice on the West Coast, and I had a tiny fraction of understanding regarding how she must have felt. Except the streets weren't all there yet when she was around. No GPS, either. No wonder she had a courthouse named after her.)

I had left myself plenty of time, so I had a full five minutes after I parked to find the right courtroom. I mentally thanked the inventor of antiperspirant as I tried not to look like I was running into the room and parked myself behind the defense desk. Trench was not yet in the courtroom.

But the prosecution was. Ron Barnett was seated behind his desk, looking like he'd been born and raised there. When he stood up, which he'd have to do shortly, he'd be tall, with dark hair and a fit profile. Because hey, it's LA. I would have reminded myself that a handsome movie star was my significant other but I don't need

Patrick to validate my existence so I didn't. And he was way more
handsome than Barnett, anyway.

I had my tablet computer on the table because they keep telling
me paper is a thing of the past, despite that being a colossal lie. I
also had the arrest report as a hard copy, because see previous
comment re: colossal lie. I glanced at the arrest report one last time
despite having almost memorized it verbatim. I was *not* going to
blow this arraignment.

An arraignment, you should know, is not usually a source of
major stress for either attorney. It is basically a reading of the charges
(which is most often waived) followed by the recording of a plea
(usually 'not guilty' because people who plead guilty have made
deals with the prosecutor), then questions about bail and everybody
goes to lunch.

But this was Lt Trench. I'd placed – in case you missed it –
unusual pressure on myself. My client had been steadfast, which
was probably the nickname he had at summer camp, so the pressure
was all self-generated. I knew that, and I didn't especially care.

I focused on the bench. We all 'rose' (stood up) to show respect
to Judge Melvin Coffey as he entered, and then sat (we did not
'lower') when he did. The first thing he did was instruct the bailiff
to have the defendant brought into the courtroom.

Lieutenant K.C. Trench was not, thankfully, wearing an orange
prison jumpsuit when he walked in to sit beside me at the defense
table. He was wearing a different gray suit than the one he'd had
on the night before when I met with him, which made me wonder
who might have had access to his home to pick up alternative
clothing. I knew so little about the man outside of his work. Was
he married? Did he have children? Was there a wacky neighbor who
might have had a key to his apartment? Had I watched too many
sitcom reruns when I was going through law school?

Trench regarded me without smiling, which was typical, nodded
and sat down in the chair to my right. Then he looked straight ahead
at Coffey and waited. He had been in court many times as a witness
and knew what was coming.

'Nothing to worry about,' I said quietly to him.

'I know.'

Coffey wasn't one to waste time; he looked straight down at
Trench and me (mostly Trench) and heard the bailiff call the case
number and mention Trench's name.

(This might be the time to say that when I'd read the arrest report, that was the first time I'd discovered what K.C. Trench stood for. So now I knew. But I made an agreement with Trench never to disclose his first and middle names – which, frankly, aren't what you'd expect but aren't anything to be embarrassed about – to anyone, and so I won't be telling you.)

'Are there any motions?' Coffey knew there might be things either of the attorneys might want to get out of the way, so I stood. 'Ms Moss?'

'Your Honor, the defense moves for summary judgment to dismiss this case due to an almost comical lack of evidence on the part of the prosecution.' If all they had was the fingerprints on Trench's gun, which nobody disputed was his, and his well-known dislike of Schaeffer, which had apparently been common knowledge in the LAPD for years, they didn't have much. I didn't have high expectations, because summary judgments are not the standard procedure, but in this case I thought I had a valid argument. Trench seemed to wince a tiny bit, which indicated he wasn't crazy about my strategy.

Barnett immediately leapt out of his chair. 'Your Honor, the prosecution has more than enough evidence to prove intent, opportunity and motive in this case. Dismissal of the charges is not in any way warranted, and I will be happy to discuss our proof in great detail if Ms Moss feels that will help her client's chances.' Smug bastard.

'The court will not dismiss the charges and would appreciate it if both the prosecution and defense would refrain from these petty comments sniping at each other,' Coffey said. It was what I'd expected but you can't blame a girl for trying.

'Apologies, Your Honor,' I said. Barnett just sort of nodded and sat down. He didn't see any reason to apologize and that might have been the moment I decided he had to be defeated at all costs.

'How does the defendant plead?' the judge asked.

Now, I've always had a problem with the word 'plead' here. OK, maybe not *always*. When I was a prosecutor I thought the idea of a defendant pleading for mercy was an indication of guilt and I was fine with it. Since becoming, somewhat against my will, a criminal defense attorney, I have thought the word *respond* might have been more appropriate.

Alas, I am not in charge of the court's accepted language, so *plead* it was. Trench stood up without any prompt on my part and *responded*, 'Not guilty.' Direct, to the point. There was no telling what kind of stress the man was under, but he was going to Trench it out no matter what.

'So recorded,' the judge said. 'Motions?'

Barnett didn't even bother to get to his feet. 'The county requests the standard bail for a charge of murder for each of the charges,' he said.

Standard bail for murder in Los Angeles County is two million dollars. I hadn't sat down yet but would have jumped to my feet if possible.

'The defense sees no reason to impose bail on Lt Trench,' I said. 'He is not in any way a flight risk and certainly poses no danger to himself or others. There is no benefit in keeping him in jail while we prepare for trial.'

Coffey looked over at Barnett. 'Mr District Attorney?'

'This is a case of murder committed in cold blood,' he said, adding an incredulous chuckle to his voice for effect, which I hoped would backfire on him. 'The victim was a Los Angeles police detective. It would set a terrible precedent to let someone accused of such a crime walk the streets for the weeks or months it will take to begin a trial proceeding. The county remains firm on the idea of standard bail in this case, because there is no reason for it to be otherwise.'

Well, that was a pretty weak argument in my opinion. We should do it because that's the way we do it? Each case needed to be seen separately, especially this one.

'Your Honor,' I said before Coffey could ask, 'Lt Trench has an exemplary record of service to this community and absolutely no indication of previous violent behavior. There is no reason to set a bail so high he would not be able to meet it. There is, in fact, no reason to impose bail at all.'

Barnett stared at me as if I'd said the Earth was an octagon. 'This is a case of murder,' he said, I assumed to the judge. 'It's not a parking ticket. The accused can't be allowed out into the streets when we have no idea if he plans to kill again.'

I must have looked like the DA had suggested my grandmother was a mongoose. 'Your Honor, honestly!' I said. 'I ask you to scan Lt Trench's record with the LAPD. There has never been so much as a complaint about him. He has – and I'll reiterate this – *no* history of violent acts on or off the job. The idea that he might suddenly become a serial killer is absolutely absurd. He poses no threat to the public. He should be released on his own recognizance pending trial.'

'It is the county's position that he has killed a man,' Barnett said. I got the feeling Coffey was tired of the argument and had already made up his mind, but Barnett was busy writing his summation far in advance and wasn't to be stopped. 'If that was unexpected, there is no reason to think that it can't happen again. Mr Trench should be held in custody at *least* until the trial begins.'

Coffey saw my mouth start to open and held up his right hand. 'Enough, counselors. I have heard your arguments on the subject, and I am prepared to rule on the question. It is the court's opinion that Lt Trench presents no immediate threat to the public.'

I exhaled.

'But,' the judge went on, 'I think it would set a terrible precedent for the court to show favoritism toward a member of the police department charged with so serious a crime.'

Perhaps I had exhaled too soon. I inhaled just as a hedge.

'I'm going to rule that the defendant be held in custody for a period of forty-eight hours, at which time I will expect you both here again to present to me reasons that he should or should not be given preferential treatment in the eyes of the court. So ordered.' He hit the gavel on the pad he had been given because they didn't want to scratch his bench and the bailiff called for the next case on the docket.

I looked over at Trench and stifled the tears forming in the corners of my eyes. 'I'm sorry, Lieutenant,' I said. I don't believe I could have gotten more out.

Trench had stood up and the guards were already moving in to take him back to jail. 'It wasn't unexpected, Ms Moss,' he said. 'I trust in your abilities. I don't believe I will be in a cell very long.' It was the warmest thing he'd ever said to me.

'No, you won't,' I said. I tried to sound certain.

Then the prison guards came and took him away.

FIVE

'We've got two days,' I told Jon Irvin.

Jon, who is unflappable even when shot, pursed his lips a bit to show he was thinking but didn't react in any other way. He is a master tactician, so I rely on Jon for strategy, which I even sometimes employ.

'The way I see it,' I said, 'the DA has to prove that Trench is a danger, that for some bizarre reason he has killed and will do so again. It should be easy enough to poke holes in that argument.'

We were sitting in my office, which is about a square foot larger than Jon's, because I'm the head of the criminal division and Jon is all the other things in the criminal division. I don't make up the rules in law firms, but I've never seen one that didn't give the larger office to whomever is at least ostensibly in charge.

Jon didn't answer right away, which indicated he didn't necessarily agree with my assessment of the situation. 'Maybe,' he said. Yeah, he thought I was going the wrong way for sure.

'What?' I didn't want to have to ask seven questions to get the answer to one.

'I'm not saying I disagree,' he began.

'Yes, you are. Now tell me why.' I didn't pull the boss card often, but I could use it if I felt it necessary. We were one play away from that.

But Jon kept it in the deck. 'OK,' he said. 'I think the judge told you what you have to do in order for Lt Trench to get out on bail, and you're doing something other than that. He doesn't want to hear about Trench's record again; you've told him that already. What Coffey is worried about is the PR disaster he could have on his hands if he lets a police detective walk when a garage attendant wouldn't. Show him how to provide favorable optics to the public and he'll be happy to let Trench go. It's what he wants to do, but he needs the justification to do it. We need to give him that.'

Nobody likes finding out that they've been wrong, but I was looking for a plausible way to help Trench and Jon was providing me with one. 'You know, keep this up and you'll be a pretty good lawyer one day,' I said, despite the fact that he was already at least as good a lawyer as I was.

Jon smiled. 'Thanks, Boss.'

I leaned back in my chair because the computer screen in front of me was starting to blur from all the staring. 'OK, if you're so smart, how do we do that? What can we give the judge that'll give him cover if he releases Trench pending trial?'

I know Jon Irvin, and he had been thinking about that well before he'd mentioned it to me. So his reluctance to speak right away was a little bit unnerving. Jon stared into the middle distance for a bit, then leaned forward in his chair and resumed eye contact with me. 'Precedents would be good,' he said.

'What precedents?' I was a little behind that day. Precedents in the law generally refer to rulings on objections, appeals and other trial-related decisions.

'Precedents.' People like to repeat what they said when asked to explain what they said. It's a way to get a moment to think, and I respect that, so I said nothing. 'Times when judges granted bail, or bail reductions, specifically to police officers. It would be helpful to know the circumstances and the reasons the judge stated to allow for such things.'

Of course. If my head were clear I would have thought of that myself, so thank goodness for Jon. 'Well, we're lucky we have a paralegal on the team,' I told him.

'Which one?'

It was a very good question. 'I'm going to have to ask Holly.' One previous experience with a paralegal had turned bad on me, so I was still a little wary. 'Let me get on that.'

Jon stood up. 'I'll be in my office,' he said, and then he left, presumably to go to his office.

This was the Seaton, Taylor criminal defense division at work. But before I could dial Holly's office on my phone, the efficiency of the Seaton, Taylor administrative branch displayed itself in the form of a young woman who shyly stood, unspeaking, in my office doorway. 'Something I can do for you?' I asked when it became clear she wasn't going to volunteer.

'Um . . .' She was maybe twenty-two years old, pretty without being loud about it, dressed appropriately for work in a law firm. I figured someone was shooting a film about a law firm and she was going to be an extra behind the leads, who would be crusading attorneys trying to correct a terrible wrong. I'd been dating Patrick for too long. 'Ms Wentworth said you needed a paralegal.'

Of course. 'Yes, please come in,' I said, doing that thing with your hands that you do which looks like you're trying to lure an especially juicy-looking fly into your web. I stood up so I could stop doing that and extend my hand. 'I'm Sandy Moss.'

'I'm Emma Jacobson,' she said. She took my hand, which made me feel better about having extended it in the first place. 'It's nice to meet you.' Emma's voice was so tentative I was starting to think it wasn't that nice to meet me.

'You too,' I said, even if that didn't make literal sense. We let go of each other's hands and I gestured for Emma to sit in the guest chair, which she did. 'Did Holly tell you about the case we're working on?'

Emma's exuberant face clouded over. 'The cop who shot another cop?' she said.

'Well, no, he didn't shoot anyone, and that's the position we're going to be defending in court,' I told her. My voice had become considerably more authoritative in the past few seconds. I was starting to see things from a boss's perspective, and that was weird on its own.

'Yeah.' Emma didn't offer anything more, but her face was speaking volumes.

I resisted the impulse to fold my arms across my chest. I believe in being emotionally open even when the other person in the conversation seems to be at odds with me. 'Do you have an issue with the case?' I asked.

She was paying close attention to the edge of my desk, about a thirty-degree angle south of my face. 'I'm not a big fan of cops, that's all,' she said. 'I can still do the work.'

I sifted mentally through the next days, weeks and months and shook my head. 'No, I don't think you can,' I told Emma. 'I'm going to ask Holly to reassign you. If you don't feel you can give the case we're dealing with the drive it requires because of your personal feelings, then I don't think you'll do as good a job as I need you to do. That's not personal to you; it's something I'm going to need from anyone who works on this case with me.'

Emma looked stricken. 'No. Believe me, Ms Moss, I can do what you need me to do. I can keep my emotions out of this. I'm a professional.'

The sad part was, I believed her. She probably *was* very professional in her approach to her work, but from my view she was not good enough for Lt Trench. 'You haven't been able to keep your emotions out of it in a three-minute conversation, Emma. I don't think the next few months are going to change that. A man's whole life is on the line and I'm tasked with trying to save it. I need people who think that's just as important as I do.' I barely recognized the voice coming out of my own mouth. I believed completely in what I was saying, but the tone was considerably harsher than I had intended. I was surprised Emma didn't break into tears, but she didn't.

She stood up, gaze still lower than my eyes, shoulders slightly slumped. 'I think I can do the job and do it well,' she told me. 'But if you don't want me, you don't want me.' Emma turned and took a step toward the office door.

'Hang on,' I said, not really sure what had made me say something like that. Then I *really* astounded myself. 'Maybe you are exactly the right person for this assignment.'

Emma turned back and looked at me with a befuddled look – and I don't say 'befuddled' often. 'You do?' She could easily have been eight years old.

I stood to face her and to better command eye contact, which Emma finally established. 'Yes,' I said. 'I have to convince a lot of people, beginning with a judge, that Lt Trench is not guilty of the crimes he's been accused of committing. I think what I need is someone who believes he *is* guilty. Maybe over the course of the trial I can convince you, too.'

Emma looked skeptical. 'Maybe.'

'Keep up the good work,' I said.

SIX

'You hired her anyway?'

My closest friend, Angie, is direct. Every guy she had ever dated will tell you that, and so will Angie, because she's direct. It's not that she doesn't understand subtlety; she just doesn't have much use for it.

'I didn't hire Emma,' I said. 'The firm hired Emma. I just included her on my team for the one case.'

'Yeah, but it's the Lt Trench case. That's not a regular case, and she hates cops.'

Angie is also only casually acquainted with backing off, too.

We were in the dining room of my new house – our new house, because Patrick was there too – finishing up a lovely dinner that, thankfully, I did not cook. Angie had, largely because she's an amazing cook. Patrick is very good at putting together a few meals he knows by heart, and I have trouble making an omelet. Anyway, the three of us were sitting at one end of a far-too-long dining table and I was wondering why we hadn't just eaten in the kitchen.

Angie comes over for dinner at least twice a week and cooks at least once. She'd probably prefer to cook every time she shows up, but Patrick and I don't want to make her feel obligated and, besides, there's terrific takeout food in Los Angeles. Angie was dabbing at her mouth with a paper napkin because I think cloth napkins are for special occasions. In New Jersey if you're eating at home and you have a cloth napkin in your lap, you're probably sitting *shiva* for someone.

I stood up to take my plate and utensils into the kitchen, where the dishwasher lives. 'I told you,' I said to Angie. 'I want the oppositional voice on the team so I know what I'm up against.'

'You just didn't want to tell her no.' Angie was picking up her plate and reaching for Patrick's. This was probably a way to get to whatever completely overindulgent dessert she had brought with her. The woman is incorrigible, which would be forgivable if she had gained even an ounce since we'd graduated high school. 'You think she's young you and you don't want to turn her away.'

Patrick allowed Angie to take his plate, but he picked up all three glasses and brought them into the kitchen behind us. He'd been a little quiet since getting home so I assumed that things on the set of *Torn* hadn't gone as he'd liked, but we hadn't had a chance to discuss it yet because I was about hip-deep in the Lt Trench case.

Angie was usually right on the money about me and could read me like the book you're currently holding in your hands, but this time I was sure she was mistaken. 'I don't see anything like me in Emma,' I told her. 'You had too much wine with dinner.'

'I didn't have *any* wine with dinner.'

'Then you didn't have enough.'

We put all the place settings into the dishwasher but didn't start it up because it just wasn't enough to justify the energy and water required. I had eaten far too much of Angie's chicken scallopini so I had no desire for dessert just yet. Three days from now was sounding good for dessert. I led the rest of the gathering (both of them) into the living room, which I was pleased to have found on the first try. And I'd been living here for months.

'What can you do to get the lieutenant out of jail?' Patrick asked. 'You have to be back in court the day after tomorrow, yes?'

Thanks for reminding me, Patrick. 'Yup. Emma's working on precedents I can cite to convince the judge he wouldn't be doing anything outlandish by letting the lieutenant out on his own recognizance, and I'm trying to come up with an argument other than, "He's a really good cop." So all ideas are open for discussion now.'

Everyone appeared to have reacted to the scallopini as I did, so we all sat back on the very comfortable (without being ostentatious) sofa and let out long sighs. 'I'm not a lawyer,' Patrick said, 'but I did play one on television for a while.'

My stomach clenched just thinking about the experience of Patrick thinking he could work on his own murder defense. 'I remember,' I said. 'It took me a year to recover from you playing a lawyer on television.'

Angie laughed. Patrick looked surprised. Maybe I'd gone too far. I'd find out later.

After gathering himself, Patrick said, 'Nonetheless. I've been involved with a very astute attorney for a few years now.' He looked at me. 'How's that?'

'Perfect,' I said.

'So, from what I've observed and heard you discuss, it sounds like the stumbling block here is that the prosecutor will argue that Lt Trench is an imminent danger to society, like the madman in all the horror movies, that he'll go and shoot everyone in sight because now he's got the taste for blood.'

'That's ridiculous,' Angie said.

'Of course it is,' Patrick agreed. 'But your problem, Sandy, is that you don't have data that proves it's ridiculous.'

That wasn't where I'd thought this was going. 'Data?' I said. 'You mean like all the times Trench has left his house, wherever that is, and *didn't* kill anybody?'

'Well, yes, but no,' Patrick said. 'Not that, exactly. But statistics on how often someone who kills one person kills again. Serial killers aren't nearly as common in life as they are in the movies.' He had come a long way since I'd defended him. So had I.

'Yeah . . .' Angie said. Angie likes any argument that involves pop culture, even if it proves that pop culture is wrong. She can relate.

'I understand, but I'm not crazy about the logic,' I told them. 'It sounds like I'm admitting that the lieutenant *did* kill this Schaeffer guy but that the numbers show he probably won't do it again. Not a great tactic for a defense attorney.'

Patrick's shoulders deflated. 'I guess not.'

I squeezed him around the upper arms. 'It wasn't a bad idea. I have to think past the next two days and into the whole trial, if there is one.'

'Why wouldn't there be a trial?' Angie asked. She looked toward the kitchen. Her dessert was waiting.

'Because we're operating on the assumption, which I believe is unquestionable, that the lieutenant didn't kill Schaeffer,' I reminded her. 'Someone else can be caught and arrested in the meantime and we can be spared that gauntlet. I'm hoping your once-in-a-while boss Nate Garrigan can help with that.' Angie 'apprenticed' with Nate, my favorite investigator, once a week now because her responsibilities as Patrick's production executive took up too much time for any more than that. Angie liked to pick up skills from the people she knew. Just by hanging around with me for decades, she'd acquired a working understanding of the law.

'I'll talk to him tomorrow,' she said.

'No, *I'll* talk to him tomorrow, but thanks. But between now and Thursday morning I need to come up with an argument that'll get

Trench out of jail.' I took my arms back off Patrick, because that was too high to hold for a long time, and sank back into the sofa. It was a really soft sofa.

'When I'm playing a character in a scene confronting someone else, I like to imagine how the opposing character is thinking,' Patrick said, finger to the tip of his nose. 'If my character can figure out the other's thoughts, it gives him an advantage.'

I thought to tell him it helped when someone had written the whole scene out to your advantage before you got there, but he had a decent point. 'So, if I can anticipate Barnett's tactics, I can have defensive measures ready,' I said, mostly to myself.

'That's the basic idea,' Patrick said. 'But I tend to think of it as a way to limit the damage, not necessarily to prevail.'

But I was already deep into my thoughts about the hearing in a day and a half. And I was starting, slowly, to formulate an idea.

'It's about jujitsu,' I said.

Angie's dessert was delicious.

SEVEN

L t Trench could easily have been in his office, based on the expression on his face. There was no hint of stress, no indication that anything was the least bit more bothersome than a usual Wednesday. And yet there he was, in a room designated for attorney conferences with inmates at the Los Angeles County jail for men.

'You told me the other night that you blamed Detective Schaeffer for the death of one of your closest friends in the department,' I reminded him. Well, I said it. I doubted he needed reminding of something like that.

'That is not precisely what I said,' Trench corrected. 'I said that he was responsible for the death of the person closest to me, and I hated him for it.'

'Yeah, let's try and keep the word "hate" out of your mouth when you're testifying in court,' I suggested. 'It might be seen as somewhat negative.'

Trench barely moved an eyebrow, but it was enough. 'Would you prefer "detested?"'

This wasn't going spectacularly well just yet. 'What was the name of the person he caused to die?' It was an awkward sentence, but I couldn't think of a more precise way to invert what he had said to me and he would just have corrected me and avoided answering if he could find a way. I didn't know why, but it was quintessential Trench.

'Officer Susan Adrian Wright,' he said.

'She was a friend of yours?' If Trench wasn't going to elaborate, it was time for me to reach for the pliers and pull out a few teeth.

For the first time since I'd met him, Trench seemed lost for words. His lips moved just a millimeter and he actually blinked, something I'd always assumed he did only on alternate Saturdays. His breathing remained steady and he did not avert his gaze.

'She was my wife,' he said.

Keep in mind, won't you, that until this moment I had no idea Trench had ever been married. The idea that the woman he loved was a cop fit him perfectly, but like everything else about himself, he'd never so much as hinted at it. The fact that she was dead, and that another detective might have been responsible, went beyond anything I could have anticipated. I sat there for a long moment and looked at him, wondering exactly how, in his mind, I should respond.

'I'm so sorry, Lieutenant,' I said after a couple of weeks.

'Thank you.' It was the programmed response, the thing that people say under those circumstances. I wanted Trench to know I'd meant what I'd said as something more than a social necessity, but I had no idea how to communicate that. I was here as his lawyer. It was best to continue in that vein.

'Are you saying that Detective Schaeffer killed Officer Wright?' I asked. For any other person I would have been more personal. But I wasn't sure that Trench himself thought of his late wife as anything but Officer Wright. It would fit him.

He considered his answer very carefully and took his time speaking. 'Not directly,' he said. 'She was his backup on a case, and he sent her into a crime scene that should not have been entered. She was shot and killed in the line of duty.'

OK, that was a lot. 'How long ago was this?' I asked.

'Five years and eight months,' was the answer.

'Geez, how many days?' I shouldn't have said that.

'Zero days. Five years and eight months exactly,' Trench said. Of course.

'Did you have to work with Schaeffer after it happened?' I asked. I mean, how do you do that, when you believe the actions of a co-worker led to the death of your one true love?

'Not until this week,' Trench answered. His mountain of detailed explanation was burying me.

'The week he was killed.' There was no point in saying that aloud, but I did anyway. Trench, as you might imagine, did not react. 'What was the case you were working on?'

That was a question the homicide detective Trench could answer without any hesitation. 'The murder of a woman named Joanna Barnes, a model and aspiring actress who lived in an apartment with three other women. She was strangled by a man named Darren Wharton, an ex-lover who had jealousy issues. It took us three days to arrest him, and the medical examiner believes that was the night Schaeffer was shot.'

Just the facts, ma'am. Trench at his best. 'Why did they send
Schaeffer out with you?' I asked him. 'I can't imagine it was
considered too difficult for you to handle alone.'

Trench had taken on his gruff-professor persona again because
he was talking business. Murdered people are his business. No
wonder he'd grown such a tough skin. 'Ms Moss,' he said. 'No one
sent Detective Schaeffer out with me. They sent *me* out with *him*
because he hadn't closed a case in two months and they were worried
about his arrest record.'

A fly that had been buzzing around the room made a beeline (a
flyline?) for Trench's nose. He gave it a stern look and it changed
its path to sit on the windowsill, next to the bars.

'So, Schaeffer had fallen into a slump?' I asked.

'No, Ms Moss. Schaeffer stopped having partners who could
cover for him. He was not, as I believe I have indicated, a very
good detective.'

I looked down at my legal pad. I'd never considered Trench to
be an emotional man and certainly not an unkind one. But he blamed
Schaeffer for the death of his wife. That's not a small thing, and it
could penetrate any person's defenses, even a cyborg like Trench.
I didn't like pumping him for information but at least technically I
would be defending his life in court if things didn't go perfectly. I
needed the information and there was no one on the planet better
at delivering facts than him.

'In what way was he not good?' I asked. Trench was an expert
and a great observer. But he had a certain compunction about talking
out of school concerning his colleagues at the LAPD.

Apparently that compunction did not apply to the late Detective
Schaeffer. 'He was more concerned with his own issues than that
of the victim or the perpetrator,' he said. 'Schaeffer was interested
in advancement, and he never achieved it because he wasn't capable
of thinking about anything but that.'

'Ironic,' I said as a reflex.

'Perhaps.' Trench believed only in what he could prove. In another
reality he would have made a terrific scientist or mathematician.

Meanwhile, the fly had found its way out of the room by zipping
under the door. But no one had told it yet that it was in jail, probably
for life. (Nobody else here was in that situation; you go to state
prison for the long sentences.)

'How do you think the killer got your service weapon to kill

Schaeffer?' If you want good crime-solving advice, ask a really talented detective.

'I imagine it was someone I work with who would have had access to my home and a key to the safe where I keep the weapon,' he said.

'Who fits that description?' I asked. This was going to be easy.

'No one.' Maybe not, then.

I might as well cut to the chase. 'Lieutenant, you are the best detective I've ever met,' I said. 'Who do you think killed Wallace Schaeffer?'

Trench pursed his lips a bit, which for him was the equivalent of a fit of frustration in a normal person. 'If you can get me out of here and back on the street, Ms Moss, I will find out for you,' he said.

'No, you won't,' I told him.

EIGHT

'He thought he could just get out of jail and go investigate his own case?' Jon Irvin looked at me with an amused glint in his eye as we walked into the courtroom. 'A cop as good as Trench should know better than that.'

'There's just the slightest possibility that he's a little more emotional about this case than he would normally be,' I suggested. 'I mean, you wouldn't know it by looking at him, but there's all sorts of stuff churning around in our lieutenant right now.'

My stomach is the natural route through which my nervous system informs me that I'm a little, let's say, on edge. It clenches up like a fist and reminds me every few minutes with a truly prodigious burp. And this case was making me just a little nervous, especially since I didn't know if the ploy I was about to deploy (see what I did there?) had any chance of working at all.

'Even so, it should be instinct,' Jon said. 'The department would never let a cop under indictment for murder investigate his own case, and even if he could, his own biases would make the investigation useless.'

We sat down at the defense table and I looked around the room. There was a strong contingent of reporters – online, print and television, because a cop was accused of killing another cop. The fact that what they would see today would be largely procedural (except my part) and totally inconclusive didn't seem to bother them.

Barnett was, of course, already at his station. If he ever left, they'd probably put up a plaque with his name on it. He had someone in the second chair who, I was willing to bet, would never say an audible word in court.

'Do you think I don't know any of that?' I asked Jon. 'Trench knows it too, so his even suggesting such a thing makes me nervous.'

'One thing at a time,' Jon said. 'Let's get him out of jail first. You still sticking with the plan?'

'Have you got a better one?' I asked. 'I'm open to suggestion.'

The door to the judge's chamber opened so Jon didn't get a chance to pitch his brilliant strategy – which from previous conversations I knew he didn't have – and Coffey walked in with a nondescript expression on his face. We rose, then descended (I guess) into our seats. Trench was led in from the hallway and all the players were in place for Act I.

Patrick would have loved it, but he was off filming, Angie at his side (or in her office).

Once the bailiff was finished with his spiel, Coffey made a point of looking down at Barnett, then for a long time, I thought, at me. 'Let's be clear: the only issue open here today is the status of the defendant prior to trial. Mr Barnett, you were advocating that there should be no bail offer, or the standard bail for a charge of homicide, which is two million dollars. Ms Moss, your argument as we have recorded it is that the defendant is not a flight risk or a danger to the community or himself, and therefore should be released without bail. So, unless one of you has changed your position, that's where we will begin. Mr District Attorney?'

Barnett stood slowly to savor his moment. He was a moment savorer. 'Your Honor, the prosecution remains steadfast in its argument. This was a cold-blooded murder. Letting the defendant go free would set a terrible precedent and be a disservice to the community. We see no reason our initial assessment of two million dollars should not stand, as it would for any defendant who committed such a crime.'

He had not addressed, except tangentially, Coffey's main stated issue: How he could let Trench go (or not) until the trial and not rile up the imagined protestors in the streets of Los Angeles, the vast majority of whom had probably not heard about the case and didn't much care about one cop shooting another. It was an interesting news tidbit, but not something worth taking a day off with a picket sign. Largely this was because Barnett didn't *want* the judge to release Trench, and therefore was not looking for the best way to do it.

Coffey waited, seemingly expecting something more from the DA, which he did not get. He swiveled in his chair and regarded me. 'Ms Moss?'

I stood, in the usual amount of time, not to savor a moment. This was a moment I'd just as soon have skipped if I'd been given the option. My stomach was doing that thing. 'Thank you, Your Honor. I'd like to submit the report of the officers who arrested Lt Trench.' I held up the hard copy of the report, which was six pages long.

'You may do so, if there are no objections.' Barnett didn't so much as twitch an eyebrow, so Coffey must have figured he had nothing to protest.

As the report was being handed to Coffey, who did not need reading glasses to scan it, I said, 'Your Honor, you'll notice that the officers make no reference to any resistance offered by Lt Trench and pointed out that he was polite and cooperative throughout the arrest and processing.'

Coffey, still reading, nodded. 'I do see that noted.'

'Your Honor, Lt Trench will appear at every hearing without any difficulty. He will cooperate with the proceedings probably more efficiently than any defendant you've ever seen. He is, and once again I will refer to his service record and commendations, not a danger to the public at large nor to himself. And his being released on his own recognizance will have no ill effects toward this court or the LAPD in general. He will not do anything to attract publicity. He will not sell his story to a tabloid. He will not sign a book contract. There will be no stain on the criminal justice system in Los Angeles County because of Lt Trench.'

But Barnett was not to be denied. 'Judge, I know *your* record, and you are not in the habit of freeing accused murderers to walk the streets of the city. Why is an exception to be made in this case?'

Coffey put down the arrest report and looked at me directly. 'Ms Moss, can you answer that question?'

And that left me the opening I was anticipating. My stomach knew it, I knew it, everyone knew it. 'I believe the prosecution can answer it. May I ask Mr Barnett a question, Your Honor?'

Barnett thought about objecting, but his ego was desperate to know what I was going to ask and was certain he could easily counter any crazy stunt I was about to try. He did nothing.

'I'll allow it, but be very careful, Ms Moss,' the judge said.

I walked a few steps toward Barnett but not too close. Didn't want to seem friendly. 'Mr District Attorney, have you ever been in a courtroom with Lt Trench before?'

'Yes.' Barnett, although not technically a witness, was going to be the kind of witness every attorney wants: the kind who answers only the question and adds nothing.

'Under what circumstances?' I asked.

'He has appeared as a witness in some of the cases I have prosecuted. He was generally the arresting officer in those cases.'

I pretty much cut him off there because I didn't need the war stories, although they undoubtedly wouldn't have hurt Trench's case. 'Did you find the lieutenant to be trustworthy?' I asked.

Barnett blinked a couple of times. 'He wasn't being charged with anything then.'

'That's not what I asked, Mr District Attorney.'

'I found the defendant to be efficient and adept at police work,' Barnett said.

'Did he ever say he would do something and then not do it?' I asked.

He knew he had to answer truthfully, but managed to keep his response to two letters. 'No.'

'Do you know of any violent acts the lieutenant has committed that were not necessary as part of his duties?'

It's hard to form vowels through clenched jaws. 'No.'

Emma walked through the courtroom doors down the aisle and took a seat next to Jon. So I knew I had the rest of what I needed. 'Thank you, Mr District Attorney,' I said. I looked at Coffey. 'Your Honor, I have . . .' I looked at Emma, who held up three fingers. 'Three additional exhibits to offer.'

'This is a bail hearing,' the judge said. 'We are not at trial yet.'

I held up my hands to concede the point. 'I'm aware of that, Your Honor. These are three cases you can study as precedents for letting Lt Trench leave custody until his trial begins. I believe you'll find that they are convincing arguments for leniency in this case.'

Coffey seemed to consider that. Barnett, knowing he couldn't object to precedents and not look foolish, puffed out his lips a bit in frustration. 'Please let me know the cases you are citing, Ms Moss,' the judge said, and that's when I knew we had him. With previous cases allowing a cop to leave jail while awaiting trial, Coffey could duck any backlash that might occur if/when he released Trench.

The whole thing was over pretty quickly after that. Trench needed to go back to jail to get his belongings and fill out the necessary paperwork. Coffey was very clear about advising both the lieutenant and me that he'd have to appear at every hearing involving his case and not leave the state while awaiting trial. Then the gavel was banged and the two corrections officers approached to escort the lieutenant back to his temporary home so he could prepare to leave it.

He looked at me before they arrived at our table. 'Impressive, if risky, Ms Moss. Questioning the district attorney?'

'I was banking on you, Lieutenant. I knew he couldn't conjure up anything that would give the judge pause.'

Trench regarded me carefully. 'You'd be surprised,' he said quietly, and then the two guards came and took him away.

NINE

Nate Garrigan is a large man. He likes to use that to his advantage, looming over smaller people from whom he hopes to get information, or some other edge in the investigations he undertakes. It's one of the things – but thankfully not the only thing – that makes him valuable to my cases when the firm hires him to help.

But standing in my office next to Lt Trench, who was seated quietly in my client chair with both feet on the floor, Nate didn't seem the least bit intimidating. And it was bothering him. That was the effect Trench could have on a room.

'OK,' Nate was saying while Jon, Emma and I sat by trying not to talk, 'the night this Schaeffer guy was shot—'

Trench held up a finger. 'Detective Schaeffer.'

Nate blinked. 'Yeah, right. Detective Schaeffer. The night he was shot with your gun in his apartment, where were you?'

Trench might just as well have been discussing a book he didn't especially like or hate. 'I was at home – and no, Mr Garrigan, no one can verify that. I was alone.'

'What were you doing?' I couldn't help it. You can judge me later. I didn't want to interrupt Nate at work, but on the other hand I really wanted to have some sense of how Trench lived. I had always figured that after a day of detecting he was just ushered into a sensory deprivation chamber and didn't come out until it was time to put on his freshly pressed suit in the morning.

'I was reviewing paperwork on some of my cases.' Of course he was. I felt foolish for having asked.

I thought the thing that had most irritated Trench about having been arrested and arraigned for murder was that the judge had stipulated he could not work for the LAPD until he was exonerated, if he was exonerated. Not being a cop pretty much erased all of Trench's identity. His tie was even about three percent askew. From Trench that was a desperate cry for help.

Nate gave me a warning look to let him continue on his own. Given that I, or my firm anyway, was paying his bill, that was a little cheeky, but I was used to Nate and he had a point. I sat back in my chair and resolved to keep quiet unless absolutely necessary.

'OK, so there's no airtight alibi,' Nate said. Trench didn't flinch, exactly, but he let out a quick breath. He was used to dealing with perpetrators, not being considered one himself. 'What can you tell us about this . . . Detective Schaeffer? Who might have been really angry with him?'

'In addition to myself?' That's Trench being cheeky.

'Yes, Lieutenant. We're aware you didn't like the guy, but we know you didn't kill him.'

Lieutenant K.C. Trench was as cool as ice when he looked Nate in the eye and said, 'No, you don't know that. You have no irrefutable evidence. Based on your dealings with me and my public record, you *assume* I did not shoot Detective Schaeffer.'

I've had people trying to shoot me who were warmer and fuzzier than Trench when I was trying to keep him out of prison. 'Well as the people who are defending you in this case, I think you'll have to allow us to assume that, Lieutenant,' Nate said. 'Please. People who are not you but might still be very angry with Detective Schaeffer.'

Now having been placed on familiar ground – the disposal of a murder investigation – Trench could contribute as requested. 'He was not well liked in the homicide division, but I don't know of any who would be incensed enough to kill him. He has an ex-wife and a daughter with whom I believe he lost contact a year or two ago. There are, of course, my late wife's parents and her brother, but it seems very unlikely to me they would be involved. They live in Michigan, and it has been more than five years since she was killed in the line of duty. There is no logical reason for them to have waited this long to take revenge if they had deemed it necessary.'

Jon, having not resolved to stay quiet or having decided not to keep that promise to himself, said, 'Have you been in close contact with them since your wife died?'

'No.'

I didn't want to press Trench on what seemed to be an area of pain for him, but Jon was just as intent on the case as the lieutenant would be and didn't worry about hurting people's feelings. 'Why not?' he asked.

Trench, being Trench, did not react visually. His voice was just as measured and unemotional as with anything he had said to this point. 'We were never very close,' he said. 'They lived in Ann Arbor and we lived here. I believe one of the reasons Susan moved to Los Angeles was to be a little separated from her parents' influence. She said they had not understood her desire to be a police officer in a large city.'

'How much did they know about how their daughter died?' Nate asked.

'They knew what I knew.'

So it was possible that Susan Wright's family had been holding a grudge against Wallace Schaeffer since he'd sent her into an active crime scene with no backup. Why they might take action now and send her widower into the danger of lifetime imprisonment was a complete and total mystery.

'Were they angry enough to do something about it?' Nate was going to plow on through and he was right to do so, but I was getting uncomfortable in my own office. And Jon was looking at me funny. Not ha-ha funny.

'You would have to ask them,' Trench answered. He stood, which was strange. I knew that he tended to stand up when he was thinking, and that he did so sometimes just because sitting seemed too inactive for him. 'I believe I will have to be leaving now.' He looked toward the door but didn't have time to turn in that direction.

'I still have a number of questions,' Nate informed him. 'I'm sure Sandy and Jon have things they need to discuss with you as well.' He hasn't mentioned Emma, who tended to scowl in Trench's direction whenever she looked that way. I'd have to talk to her about that.

Trench looked at Nate and I couldn't read his face. I didn't know if he respected Nate as an investigator, because they'd had very little interaction in the cases I'd worked on with them. And heaven forbid Trench should move a facial muscle when it wasn't necessary.

'That will have to wait for another day,' Trench said. 'I'm sure we can reschedule. I have a good deal of free time these days. Please let me know what will be convenient for the four of you.' He nodded toward me and left the office.

Nate, Jon, Emma and I sat there for a moment. Nate was staring at the door as if he expected Trench to realize the error of his ways and return. Jon was typing frantically on an iPad, probably catching up on notes he'd been taking during the meeting. Emma just looked bummed out.

'Well, that was fun,' she said.

I was, at least in theory, the head of this team, and if ever there was a need to rally, this would be it. So, I stood up behind my desk and regarded them with what I hoped was an authoritative look on my face. 'Analysis, please,' I said.

Three faces turned in my direction. Nobody said anything.

'Analysis,' I repeated. 'What information have we gained and what information do we need to gather? What have we learned about our client's strengths and weaknesses going into trial in a few months? Let me have some analysis, please. Now.'

'I think we've got damned little,' Nate said. 'All we've got is that he says he didn't do it. Forgive me if I don't think that's the key to it all.'

I'd decided I was in an aggressive mood. 'You're the investigator. What do you have to do to get us more?'

Nate opened and closed his mouth a couple of times because he'd never seen me act this way before. Neither had I. 'I need to talk to a bunch of the other people, including maybe a whole family in Ann Arbor, Michigan. You paying my airfare?'

I had no idea if Holly would approve it or not. 'You do what you have to do,' I told Nate. 'Put it on your statement.'

I looked over at Jon. 'Briefs we should be filing? Requests we can make of the judge this early?'

He'd had more time to prepare so Jon wasn't startled the way Nate had been by my girl-boss makeover. 'Obviously, we need at least six months to prepare. I don't think the judge that gets assigned this case will expect otherwise, but I'll begin by trying to find out who that's going to be before they want to tell us. In the meantime, we'll need the ME's report on Schaeffer's murder. He got shot, so there shouldn't be many surprises, but that's what people always say before there are a ton of surprises. Also, I want a copy of his service record with the LAPD. Was he as big a screw-up as Trench says, or is that the lieutenant still holding a grudge, which would be understandable?'

'In anyone but Trench,' I said.

Jon's eyes flashed concern but he didn't address it. 'Emma, can you get on those two things? The autopsy report and the service record?'

Emma's mouth twitched because she didn't want to contact anyone at the LAPD, which made me wonder what kind of lawyer she wanted to be. Of course, Seaton, Taylor is mostly a family law firm, so that could have been what she'd expected she would be handling. Well, that was what I'd thought when I got to LA, too.

'Yeah,' she said.

'All right, then,' I told my team, who looked no more inspired than they had before I'd started talking. 'Let's get to work.'

TEN

Evenings with Patrick were the times of the day I anticipated most eagerly. Since we'd gotten together (and amazingly stayed that way), I'd looked to this as a sanctuary from the madness of practicing law in Los Angeles.

We were sprawled on the sofa, me reading a novel by Saul Bellow and Patrick just staring off, stroking my leg with his hand and sitting in a rare moment of stillness, so I knew he wasn't in his usual buoyant, if somewhat manic, mood.

'I haven't been paying much attention to you lately, have I?' I asked. 'I've been so caught up in the Trench business that I don't even know how you resolved the problem you had with the script the other day. I'm sorry I haven't been a good girlfriend lately.'

Patrick smiled with a little sadness in it. 'You are always an exemplary girlfriend,' he said. 'I understand that you see the lieutenant as something of a daft mentor or an ally, even when he's not. You care about him and he's in trouble. It's your job. That's where your mind should be.'

It was worse than I thought. Any time an actor thinks of someone else's needs ahead of his own it's a sign that they're not in their usual mind space. I didn't even address his silly idea that I thought Trench was my mentor (it was Holly). I put down the book and turned to look at him. 'What did happen with the script, Patrick?'

He took a deep breath, not because he was reluctant to speak but because he was not pleased with what he had to say. It was a way of cleansing his system. 'I let them keep the dialogue,' he said.

He did not elaborate.

I stared at him. The Patrick I knew and loved would have fought tooth and nail against the kind of third-rate claptrap he'd been reading the night the phone rang from the jail. He'd have pulled every producer string he had, perhaps resorted to refusing to leave his trailer until things were improved, rather than spout that drivel. I searched his face and all I found was embarrassment. 'You did?' If you have a better comeback than that, you have my permission to mentally insert it here. That was the best I could do.

He closed his eyes. Patrick, of all people, worries about disappointing me. I know. 'I decided it wasn't worth the fight,' he said. 'You know I like to be a hands-off kind of producer.'

'Yeah, but you want to put out a good show and you think that scene especially is going to hurt your reputation. Isn't there something you can do?' I already had an idea, but this wasn't the right way to spring it on him.

'We only have two more days of shooting; reshooting that scene after tomorrow would cost us far too much money,' Patrick said. 'The rewrite would have to be done tonight.'

That was it; I had to put another impetuous plan into action. 'I can help,' I said. 'Or, more to the point, I know someone who can.'

It took five minutes of persuasion to get Patrick to see my point and about a minute and a half on the phone to get Angie working on the problem. She showed up at our house thirty-five minutes later, still talking into her mobile and looking like a woman who would not, under any circumstances, be denied.

'No,' she was saying, shrugging off her jacket on to her favorite chair in our living room and heading for the kitchen, where a bottle of spring water would be waiting for her in the fridge. 'It's not an option, Bobby. Patrick is an executive producer on the show and he's the star. If there aren't new pages in my email within two hours, neither of those people will be on set tomorrow. *Capisce?* Yeah. Two hours. I'll be watching the clock.' She disconnected the call, pulled the water out of the fridge and took a very healthy swig. Then she looked at a somewhat astonished-looking Patrick. 'You'll have the new pages in an hour and a half, tops,' she told him.

'Angie!' Patrick took the hand not holding the water bottle in his own. 'I've seen veteran producers, men who fire their assistants for wearing the wrong shoes, throw up their hands and surrender when Bobby says something can't be done. How did you do it?'

The thing about Angie is that she's not afraid of anyone. She adores Patrick and would defend him against Godzilla if necessary. 'I just did the Jersey thing,' she said with an innocent tone. 'I threatened him.'

Patrick didn't let go of her hand, so Angie led him (and, by extension, me) back into the living room. He dropped it when she sat in her favorite chair, dumping her jacket on the rug. 'You're brilliant,' Patrick said. There was a time that word was taboo when discussing me, but it had passed and I knew it was the highest compliment he could have paid her. 'Absolutely brilliant.'

She waved a hand at him in an exaggerated gesture of what for Angie could pass as humility. 'Aw, go on,' she said. Then after a moment: 'No. Really. Go on.'

They laughed but my phone was ringing and the Caller ID suggested Lt Trench was on the other end of the line. It was beyond unusual for him to be calling me, particularly on my cell phone and not my office line, where he'd get my voicemail. 'Lieutenant,' I said as soon as I accepted the call. Patrick and Angie both looked up in surprise.

'I apologize for intruding on your personal time, Ms Moss.' Trench sounded like Trench, but more. This must have been what stress sounded like on him. 'But I feel there are a few issues we should discuss before we proceed with my defense. Would it be a terrible imposition for me to meet with you in your home?'

I'd been visited by Trench at home exactly once, when I was sharing the apartment in Burbank with Angie. It had been, um, a little awkward because he's Trench. And Angie had offered him some leftover chocolate cake, which the lieutenant had refused. Politely.

'Feel free, Lieutenant,' I said. Patrick and Angie continued to look at me quizzically, which was at the very least understandable. 'Do you need the address?'

'No,' Trench said. 'I am idling my car at your security gate as we speak. Would you let me in, please?'

Someday, I resolved, I'd find out what planet the man had left to come stop crime in Los Angeles. But tonight, the only thing left to do was to push the button that opened our driveway gate and let him drive through. I could see his car on the security camera. It was nondescript.

I updated Patrick and Angie on the contents of the phone call, which they had probably heard clearly from across the room, and as soon as I had completed the epic tale, which took about thirty seconds, Trench was, according to closed-circuit TV, about to ring our doorbell. Angie got there first and opened the door for him.

If Trench was surprised to see Angie, and not Patrick or me, in the doorway, no one except maybe his mother would have been able to tell from his reaction. He nodded in Angie's direction and said hello. By then I had made it into the front room and relieved him of the hat and coat he was not wearing. But he *was* in a blue business suit because it was the closest he could get to an LAPD uniform right now.

'Ms Moss,' he said to me as I ushered him in. 'Thank you for seeing me on such short notice.' Then he saw Patrick and did his quarter-bow thing again. 'Mr McNabb.'

'Come in, Lieutenant,' Patrick said, despite the fact that Trench was already in. 'May I offer you anything?' Patrick is always the host. That's absolutely fine with me. This is LA. The TV star *should* be the host. I was not his arm candy; I was more like arm kale, but Trench had, by his own admission, come on a business call and that made it my business and not Patrick's. Or Angie's, even though she was still staring at him with her mouth slightly open – out of concern, I thought. Only Angie would see anything to be concerned about in Trench's complete lack of outward nervousness.

'No, thank you,' he told Patrick, then turned his attention to me. 'Is there somewhere we can talk privately? I fear this will be all about my current situation.' I'd never employed a butler, but if I ever do, I want him to talk like Trench.

I figured it was best to be just as right-to-the-point as my client. 'Certainly,' I said. 'There's a room that's supposed to be a library, but we haven't got it completely set up yet.'

Patrick and Angie retreated to the living room while I showed Trench the way to the supposed library, which was now housing some of Patrick's movie memorabilia, a vast collection that he was having curated in order to donate much of it to the Academy Museum of Motion Pictures, something that had been recommended to him by his financial manager for the tax benefits and by me because I didn't actually want to live in the Academy Museum of Motion Pictures.

I closed the door to the room and tried to ignore the severed leg from *Jaws*, the tambourine used in *A Hard Day's Night* and of course the tap shoes James Cagney had worn in *Yankee Doodle Dandy*, about which I have said much elsewhere. I turned on a lamp and gestured toward a chair we luckily had placed in the room to better view the collection, while I sat behind a table upon which all the books cataloguing the items were resting.

'Is it something specific, Lieutenant, or are you just here to get a general overview of your case at the moment?' It's always best to get the client's expectations up front so you can dash them right off the bat and dispense with any possible tension between the two of you.

Trench sat straight up in the high-backed chair, feet firmly on the floor in front of him. Right now, he was the very model of posture in the state of California. 'As I mentioned, there are a few isolated issues I think we should discuss just as we are getting started,' he said.

I didn't have anything on which to take notes but the ledger books and pens in front of me were certainly going to be put to use. I picked up one of each and turned to an empty page. 'Like what?' I asked Trench.

He took a moment, but I couldn't figure out why; this meeting had been his idea. Then he made a point of looking me in the face and said, 'I did not kill Detective Schaeffer.'

I waited, but that was it. 'I never really thought you did,' I told Trench.

'But the detectives who investigated and continue to investigate the crime have many reasons to believe I am responsible, and when you see the discovery information for the trial, you might very well decide you'd prefer to resign from the case. I am here to tell you I will understand if you do so.'

I felt my face screw up into a mask of Jersey attitude. 'Believe me, Lieutenant, I have no intention of withdrawing from your case, no matter how much evidence the prosecution has at its disposal,' I said. 'Now, if you're here to tell me you prefer to be represented by another attorney . . .'

He cut me off with a quick gesture, raising his right hand like he was stopping traffic, which perhaps he did early in his career. It looked very professional.

'I asked you to defend my case because I believe you to be the best attorney for the job,' he said. 'That has not changed.'

'So, what are you referring to?' I asked. There was something he wanted to say, and I wanted him to say it so I could get back to my boyfriend and my bestie in the next-ish room.

'Ms Moss, I did once threaten to kill Detective Schaeffer, and I did so in public.'

ELEVEN

'The story is this,' I told Patrick after Trench, and then Angie, had left. We were getting ready for bed in a room not terribly large but a bed on which a game of touch football could comfortably be held. 'Apparently it was not long after his wife's funeral, at an LAPD holiday party. As you might expect, a large number of police officers were in attendance. But when Trench saw that Schaeffer had chosen to show up, he wanted to leave but felt he couldn't. Then he thought Schaeffer was making light of Susan's death, and that did it.'

'Understandable, wouldn't you say?' Patrick asked. 'He was grieving, and I get the impression it was no secret he blamed Detective Schaeffer for his wife's death.' Because he was a man, he had finished preparing for bed and was pulling back the blanket on his side. I was still removing traces of makeup and moisturizing because that's what you do in Southern California. I stood on the other side of the bed and estimated that if I were given a compass and a bag of trail mix, I might make it to Patrick to kiss him good-night once I managed to situate myself.

It's a big bed, is what I'm saying.

'I understand that, and probably so did most of the cops who were there, but when he thought Schaeffer was laughing, he said Schaeffer should essentially shut up or Trench would kill him. That's not a direct quote.' I got myself into bed and made sure I had a book on the bedstand. There was no reason to think I wouldn't, since I'd left it there the night before, but I like to double . . . OK, quintuple check.

'And Schaeffer was killed, and Lt Trench is considered the most likely person to have killed him,' Patrick said from an area somewhere to my left. 'That's all they have on the lieutenant, yeah?'

I sighed a little. It felt good to lie down but the subject matter was not comforting at all. 'Well, I don't have the complete ME's report yet, but he was shot in the head and that would seem to be a really strong contender for cause of death.' I didn't even know if I wanted to sleep right now. I just wanted to lie there and wait until

Trench's case was resolved. Since that would take months, it didn't seem the most practical solution.

'I imagine the district attorney will troop in a number of the officers who heard him say that,' Patrick said. Patrick, uncharacteristically, wasn't helping. It reminded me of when he was my client and he *thought* he was helping.

'If I were the prosecutor, that's what I'd do,' I admitted.

'But it was years ago,' Patrick said. That was a little more useful. 'Surely no one will think the lieutenant took all this time to make good on his threat.'

I had thought of this, of course, because I was Trench's lawyer. 'They'll try to make the point that Schaeffer *had* stayed away from Trench until they were assigned this case together just before Schaeffer was shot. They'll say Trench, because he's so organized, waited until then because Schaeffer, or the people assigning cases to detectives, had been careful to adhere to the rules Trench had laid down.'

'So how will you defend against that?' he asked.

I closed my eyes. It felt good to close my eyes. Maybe I'd keep them closed and apply for a service dog. 'The minute I figure that out, I'll let you know,' I told him. I still wasn't sleepy, but the whole eyes-closed thing was working for me.

'I wish I could help.' Patrick wants to help me with everything, and he wants to help everyone else with some things. The Dunwoody Foundation (his real name at birth) did some of that for him, but it couldn't help me clear Trench. I was hoping Nate Garrigan would do that, at least to some extent. Because right now I had a whole lot of nothing other than to remind everyone that my client was a really good detective.

'Thank you, Patrick.' I opened my eyes and crawled over to the county he was in. I gave him a kiss and he responded exactly as I was hoping he would. We kept that up for a few minutes and then I remembered I was covered in moisturizer and got embarrassed. I crawled back to my place of origin.

I turned off the light on my side because the book wasn't going to make me feel better. I needed to find more cheerful books for nights like this one. But Patrick wasn't quite finished helping everyone for the night.

'Now, about that loan we were discussing, which I'd prefer to be a gift . . .' he began.

My partnership. 'You have an interesting view of pillow talk, Mr McNabb,' I said.

'We hardly ever get to see each other when we're not working or Angie isn't here,' he protested. 'This is the time I can make my pitch. Take the money, Sandy. Be a partner. It's what people . . . like us do.'

I almost turned the light back on. What did he mean by that? 'People like us?'

Patrick grunted, indicating he hadn't intended to use those words. 'People who are together but are not legally a couple,' he said. 'People who love each other and care about each other and want to . . .'

'Help?' I said.

'Yes.' He sounded a little defeated.

'I'll take the loan, Patrick,' I said.

He sat up against the three pillows he sleeps on. 'Now we're talking! But I think you should accept the money and not have to pay it back. I don't need the money and you do. That's enough for me.'

I sat up, too. What the hell, I wasn't sleeping yet anyway and here we were making major life decisions. 'Patrick, you need to understand. I really do appreciate what you want to do for me. But I can't go through life being the woman who owes everything to Patrick McNabb. You already own much more of this house than I do. I have to be able to look myself in the mirror after a partners meeting and say, "You did that." If I just take your money, it would be like you bought me the partnership. I have to earn this myself.'

Patrick is a good listener, which is one of the things that makes him a good actor. He doesn't listen defensively; he's not always looking for the counter argument before you finish speaking. With me especially he is trying to hear the other character's (if you will) point of view. He took all that in and did not respond immediately because he was actually thinking about what I'd said and not about how he could convince me of his position.

'I didn't know you felt like that,' he said after a while. 'I just wanted to make a loving gesture.'

'And you did,' I told him. 'But I think you know why I can't accept it.'

He considered that. 'One question, Sandy. Would you hesitate to take the money if we were married?'

I hadn't seen that one coming. On the one hand, as an attorney I understand that marriage is, more than anything else, a contract between two people, and Patrick knew that. On the other, I was dealing with a living, breathing man I loved and not a collection of possessions to be claimed and divided. I'd never been married or divorced, although I'd represented many of Seaton, Taylor's clients in such proceedings for prenuptial agreements and negotiations over settlements. Patrick knew that, too.

And yet he was offering to pay a lot of money just so I could be who I wanted to be. 'I think I would,' I said. 'I know you're doing what you're doing to help me achieve something I've always wanted. But the fact that I've always wanted it means I have to do it myself.'

'But you will take the money?' Now he was confused, and I certainly didn't blame him.

I reached over and touched his face; he was such a dear, if exasperating, man. 'Yes, I will, gratefully, because I trust you more than any bank that ever existed. But I'm going to have a lawyer from my firm draw up a contract and we're going to stick to it. I'd advise you to get an attorney to do the same.'

Patrick let out a small laugh. 'The problem is your firm handles my legal issues,' he said.

Now I was sleepy. I lay back on my pillows and shut my eyes. 'We'll work it out,' I said.

TWELVE

'I think you need to meet with Schaeffer's wife,' Nate Garrigan said.

'Ex-wife,' I corrected.

I was driving to work the next morning with a lot on my agenda. In addition to two divorces and a custody negotiation, I had updates on Trench's case, research on motions that I hoped Emma would have done by now, and arranging a meeting with Holly so I could tell her about the agreement I'd made – and which she would not understand – with Patrick. And now Nate had called me while I drove to work in my 'classic' Hyundai Sonata, which Patrick had, when he was my client, brought back from the dead and refurbished with such amazing upgrades as Bluetooth, so I could talk to Nate without using my hands. Although a Jersey girl almost always uses her hands when talking. But they didn't have to be touching the phone.

'Whatever,' Nate went on. 'Her name now is Marcia Kendall and she's living in Encino with her fourth husband. I talked to her briefly and she's got a story or two to tell about the late Wallace Schaeffer.'

I sort of grunt-sighed. 'I'm sure they're interesting but they're probably not relevant to the case,' I told Nate. 'The trial isn't about what a lousy person Schaeffer was, and we're not suggesting he had it coming so it's OK the lieutenant shot him. The lieutenant *didn't* shoot him, so we need evidence that other people probably wanted him dead. Be great if we could narrow it down to whoever actually did kill the guy.'

There was an LAPD cruiser coming up behind me so I checked my speedometer and was going only three miles over the speed limit, which in New Jersey would be seven miles under the speed limit because we have more room on our roads than the ones in LA, which is weird. There are parts in the greater Los Angeles area where you're lucky if you're moving at all. Satisfied that I was not violating any traffic laws, I turned my attention away from my rearview mirror and back toward the road.

'Thanks for schooling me on that,' Nate said, 'because as you know I just started investigating criminal cases a week ago Tuesday and don't know anything about how any of this works. I'm saying our pal Marcia has stories about people the late detective annoyed to the point of distraction, and she can give us a list that's probably much longer than you'd like of people who would have wanted him dead.'

That was more like it. 'Cool. Set up an appointment. Let me know when she's available.'

'I'm also hoping for a better autopsy report by the end of business today,' Nate said.

The cruiser behind me turned on his lights, indicating that I should pull over, as there were no vehicles between us. Maybe he was in a hurry and just wanted me out of the way. I pulled on to the shoulder. 'Gotta go, Nate. I'll talk to you later.'

Fully on the shoulder of the road, I watched for the cruiser to pass me and go about his business, but he pulled up right behind me and the cop got out of his car. That's not good, but I couldn't think of anything I'd done wrong. I turned on my hazard lights but did not get out. They hate when you get out of your car without being asked – sorry, *directed* – to.

While the cop was walking from the cruiser to my window, I reached into the glove compartment for my insurance card and registration. I had my driver's license in my purse. I like being ready.

I also opened the window. It wasn't an especially hot day, but I'd been keeping the windows closed to hear Nate more clearly. What blew into the car was mostly exhaust fumes. The wonders of the LA highway system.

The cop took his time getting to me, which seems to be something of a tradition among the men in blue. Maybe he wanted me to think about how I'd been misbehaving, like mothers who tell children to just wait until their father gets home, or vice versa. But I seriously couldn't identify my traffic infraction, so I'd stopped thinking about that pretty much as soon as I'd pulled the car over.

After checking my license plate for what I figured had to be the third time, the cop ambled over to my window. Now I was getting annoyed with the guy. If you want to give me a ticket, give it to me. If you don't, why are you wasting my time? I started crafting arguments I'd use in traffic court. The first would be that I hadn't been doing anything wrong.

'License and registration, please,' he said. It's the universal police officer greeting. I wondered if they said it to each other at parties: 'License and registration, Bob. How are the wife and kids?' (In New Jersey, they ask you for your insurance card, too.)

I produced the documents in question. 'Can I know why you pulled me over, Officer?' I asked. I thought it was a logical question.

Apparently there was a difference of opinion on that point. 'Just let me do my job, Miss Moss,' he said.

Hang on! He seemed to know my name before he checked any of my documentation. 'Have we met?' I asked.

The cop turned and walked back to his cruiser, carrying my documents with him. I knew that was standard practice, but now I was worried about whether I'd have a driver's license when we were done with this little psychodrama.

Quietly I told Siri to call Holly on her cell so I wouldn't be seen dialing my phone. She knew if I was calling at this time of the day something was at least different. 'What's up?' she asked. I immediately turned down the volume, still watching the cop in my rearview mirror, checking up on me.

'I've been pulled over by a cop on the 405.' (Yeah, I say that now. I still feel weird whenever I do. At home in New Jersey it's 'Route 1' or 'The Parkway.') 'And I can't figure out why. He knew my name before he checked my license. Am I being paranoid?'

Holly took a moment to reply, which indicated I wasn't sounding terribly crazy after all. 'He could have gotten your name and information from your license plate. But you weren't speeding? Nothing?'

'Nothing,' I confirmed. 'Look, if you don't hear from me again, tell Patrick I love him.'

'Now you *do* sound paranoid,' Holly told me.

The cop was getting out of his car. 'He's coming back,' I said.

'Turn your phone off speaker,' Holly said. 'I want to hear this.'

Officer Krupke got to my window in considerably less time this trip, but I did manage to turn off the speaker on my phone. He leaned his elbows on the door. He was getting way too much into my personal space for my taste. 'Is this registration up to date?' he asked.

Enough. 'It is and you know it by looking at the card,' I told him. 'Why did you stop me, Officer?'

'Your brake light is out,' he said.

I had driven after dark last night. 'No, it isn't,' I said.

'Would you exit the vehicle, please?'

He made it sound like I had a choice. 'I'd prefer not to, thanks.'

The cop, who I noticed was not wearing a badge with his name on it, a clear violation, clenched his jaw. 'Exit. The vehicle.'

That seemed like a stupid thing to do. 'Why?' I asked.

'Because I'm a police officer and I just told you to.' He opened the door from his side. 'Get out.'

Now I figured I had no choice because, as helpful as it would be to have passing strangers take video of a cop forcing me out of my car, I didn't care as much about making the evening news as I did about getting to my office uninjured. I grabbed my phone from my lap and stood up outside my dear old Hyundai. I closed the door behind me because the one thing I am paranoid about is leaving the car door open while other cars are whizzing by at speeds approaching the limit. 'What's this about?' I tried to sound like I was demanding.

'I want to show you why I pulled your vehicle over.' Now he was using a voice that I'm sure he thought sounded soothing and reasonable. 'Come with me.' Those were three words I'd have preferred not to hear at this moment.

But all he did was walk to the back of my car and point at the red lens over my brake light. 'See?' the cop said. 'The brake light is not functioning.'

Maybe he was just crazy. 'Nobody's foot is on the brake,' I pointed out. 'There's no reason for it to be on now.'

'It's broken.' His voice was harsher and in my opinion menacing. He reached for the baton on his left hip and I felt my breath catch.

'Holly,' I said.

Maybe the cop didn't hear me. He pulled out the baton and swung very specifically at the red lens, smashing the brake light into pieces that fell to the gravel. I gasped. I don't gasp often, but I felt that was an appropriate time.

'The brake light is broken.'

I stood there with my mouth wide open, looking I'm certain like a complete fool. My hands gestured at the shards of plastic and glass (there had been a bulb in there) as if he hadn't seen what he'd done himself. I felt my anger rising and my mouth closed. I bit my lower lip and was certain I'd drawn blood. 'Why?' I managed.

The cop, who had very blue eyes, looked me directly in my

brown ones. 'Some of us really liked Wally Schaeffer,' he said. 'You're trying to get his killer off. That's a real bad idea.' He pivoted on his heel and said, 'I'm letting you off with a warning.' Then he walked back to his cruiser. I just stood there and looked at my broken taillight and the possible dent in my bumper. My poor Hyundai had not been doing well since I'd arrived in Los Angeles.

I put my phone to my ear as the cop drove past me back into the flowing traffic. He didn't even wave.

'Did you hear that?' I asked Holly. She didn't answer until I remembered to turn the volume back up.

She was already in mid-sentence: '. . . that you got his badge number so we can sue the LAPD for what will hopefully buy you a partnership in this firm.'

'He wasn't wearing a badge.'

Holly was probably considering retracting her offer of a partnership. But she tried to sound optimistic. 'You got the license number of the cruiser?'

'Um . . .' I hadn't known the guy was going to beat up my car.

'Come into the office,' Holly said, sounding very much like my boss. 'We'll figure this out.'

This was going to be a fun trial.

THIRTEEN

'It's never a good idea to base a defense on finding the real killer,' Jon Irvin said, and of course he was right.

We were walking to lunch after I'd had an eventful morning. My first stop after making it to the office's parking garage (and being convinced the whole way that another cop would stop me because now I really did have a broken taillight) was Holly's office, where I found my boss even more incensed than I was, suggesting her recording of our phone call should be sent to a sound mixer to isolate out the traffic noise and then we could 'sue the LAPD for all they're worth, which is a bundle.' We decided to table that suggestion until after Trench's trial just in case, as Holly put it, 'more cops decide to get in on the fun.'

Fun.

Then I'd told her about the agreement Patrick and I had sort of made regarding the partnership and Holly brightened up considerably. She said I was a fool for insisting on paying Patrick back and that she agreed with him that I shouldn't pay him interest if he wasn't asking for it, but that was something else that would be tabled for later. She would inform the rest of the partners – my partners, potentially – of my decision and the wheels to get me in place would begin turning.

I wondered what that meant. I knew what it would mean to be a partner, and that was no small undertaking, but the process of becoming one was something I'd obviously never undergone before. If it was like anything else I'd ever done in my life, I'd find it stressful. Go ahead, judge me.

Then I'd conferred with Emma over motions to request a speedy trial because my client had insisted on it, losing his usual limitless control because he couldn't go out and investigate crimes, still vaguely threatening to investigate his own case, and another motion to gather all the discovery material the prosecution had so far accumulated, which is standard. For one thing, I wanted that detailed autopsy report on Schaeffer no matter how obvious it was going to be. For another, I wanted to know who the DA was expecting to put on the witness stand, because surprises are not only bad in any court case, they're not allowed. Forget what you saw on TV, including Patrick's own *Legality*. Maybe that one more than any other.

So now Jon and I were walking to the local pizza place, where I would get anything but pizza because I was born in New Jersey and this isn't pizza. My apologies to my Southern California neighbors, but true is true.

'Of course I'm not pinning all my hopes on finding the person who really shot Schaeffer,' I told Jon. 'But you have to admit it would be a boost to a case that so far hinges on the jury believing Trench when Barnett is going to have a mountain of circumstantial evidence *and* Trench's own gun to prove his side.'

We got to the door and Jon opened it for me because he's delightfully old-fashioned. I walked in and we joined the line to order at the counter. We only go to the classiest places. 'I admit it would be great for our case, but we can't count on it,' he said. Then he walked to the counter and, with a completely straight face, ordered a salad at a pizza place. Jon is a dear but he's sensible to a fault. I got the baked ziti and promised myself I'd take at least half home. 'What, in your opinion, do we have right now to convince a jury that the lieutenant didn't take his revenge on the man he thinks is responsible for his wife's death?'

We sat down at a table and placed down the number 12 on a stand that the counter guy had given us. Of course, first we had filled our own cups from the soda machine just past the counter. Classy.

I took a sip from my diet ginger ale. 'Maybe that's not what we need to do,' I suggested. 'Maybe what we need to do is convince the jury that Schaeffer really *was* responsible for Susan's death.'

Jon put down his cup of tap water – no, really – and his eyebrows met in the middle. 'Why? We don't want to concede that Trench actually shot the guy. Making the jury angry at Schaeffer and understanding why Trench was angry himself isn't going to help us get him acquitted.'

'No, that's true,' I said. 'It's only one tactic I think we should employ. We're not putting Schaeffer on trial, largely because he's dead, but we can illuminate to the jury that he was the kind of guy a *lot* of people might have been happy to see shuffle off this mortal coil. Then we hit them with all the solid evidence we've amassed.'

Jon studied my face for a few seconds. 'So you're conceding that we don't have any solid evidence, aren't you?'

I didn't have to answer him, thankfully (I had nothing) because I noticed Jon's gaze first drifting away from my face and more to a space over my left shoulder, and then become mystified. 'Lieutenant,' he said.

I was in the midst of saying, 'What?' as I turned to look at what Jon was seeing and sure enough, Lieutenant K.C. Trench, usually of the Los Angeles Police Department, was standing next to our table.

'Ms Moss,' he said, then to Jon, 'Mr Irvin.'

Since I was the designated Trench Whisperer for our team, I looked up at him and said, 'Lieutenant. Did our office tell you where we were having lunch?' Because if someone did, I would have them fired. I could do that. I was a partner now. Or would be after the partners voted. Probably.

'Of course not,' Trench said. 'I followed you from your office building. May I sit down?'

'Um, sure.' That was Jon. I was trying to figure out what I'd done wrong and whether Trench was going to fire me.

'Thank you.' Trench took the chair facing the entrance, like he was Jesse James and didn't want his back to the door. He sat straight and at attention, of course. Just assume from now on that if I say Trench was standing or sitting, he was doing so straight and at attention. I'll let you know if it was anything else. You can also assume that I'm breathing at any moment. So far.

'How can we help you, Lieutenant?' I had regained the power of speech and remembered that Trench had already said he wasn't going to fire me, so I figured I could kick things off before my ziti showed up.

Yeah, I was going to ignore that he followed us. He was a detective. Detectives follow people. If he followed me home, I'd have a problem – but wait. Wasn't that just him at my house the night before?

'It strikes me that you will be trying to mount a defense of me in court based strictly on my years of service to the Los Angeles Police Department and little else,' Trench began. This was starting to feel like a job evaluation. 'I believe we should concentrate on proving that I was not capable of having shot Detective Schaeffer on the night in question.'

Well yeah, that'd be nice. What was Trench getting at? He had a long track record of proving that people *had* committed crimes and no doubt had proved in the course of many investigations that certain suspects had not. He might have some ideas. 'Can you prove that you didn't shoot him?' I asked.

'No,' Trench said.

Well, that was a huge help. 'You're not giving us a lot to work with,' Jon told him. I wouldn't have put it that way, but he wasn't wrong.

'I am aware of that,' Trench told him. 'But I believe that I can analyze the situation and give your defense some ammunition. I have studied the incident report on Detective Schaeffer's murder and there are some discrepancies.'

Suddenly there was a plate of baked ziti in front of me and a very nutritious-looking salad by Jon. I found myself wondering if Lt Trench would think that I was a bad eater. Then wondering why I would possibly care about such a thing.

We thanked the server, and I turned my attention back to my client. 'What sort of discrepancies?' I asked.

Trench raised an index finger in the air – not as a sign of triumph, but of interest. 'For example, there might be some question as to the time the murder took place. The preliminary medical examiner's report estimated death to have taken place between nine p.m. and midnight. But I was in my apartment a few minutes after eight p.m.'

Two men took a table right next to ours, but they didn't have a number flag to signal a server. I didn't think much of it, but it registered in my head.

'Does that one-hour difference matter?' I asked Trench. 'Were you somewhere that people might have seen you at eight in the evening?'

'It is possible but not likely,' he answered. 'I was on my way home after having arrested and booked Darren Wharton, the man who strangled his ex-lover, Joanna Barnes. I did stop at a super-market for some supplies. If there is video security of that night, it might show me in the store. I wasn't there very long.'

'You worked on the Darren Wharton case with Schaeffer,' Jon pointed out, as if Trench had forgotten. 'Why wasn't he there with you for the arrest and booking?'

'Detective Schaeffer called in sick that morning and was not heard from all day,' Trench answered. 'It wasn't until the next night that his body was found.' Then without so much as a blink, and without turning his head, he said, 'Is this your day off, Officer, or did you take off your uniform because you were afraid you'd spill marinara sauce on it?'

The two men at the table next to us shuddered as if they'd been tasered. The one with a shaved head opened and closed his mouth twice and then said, 'Um, just here for lunch, Lieutenant.'

'Really? And somehow you neglected to order any food. Would you like to tell me why you're here?'

Then I noticed the other man at the table, hard to recognize out of uniform. He'd spent the morning causing damage to my Hyundai.

'Lieutenant, the other man at that table pulled me over on the way to work this morning to warn me that defending you would not be a popular choice among himself and his fellow officers,' I told Trench. 'He also smashed my driver's side brake light.'

The cop from this morning stiffened and looked at me with fury in his eyes. You've probably never seen anyone with real fury in their eyes. It's not pleasant.

'That's a lie!' he shouted much too loudly to suit the surroundings or the circumstances. People who had never seen him before and had no idea he was even in the room ten seconds ago were aware he wasn't telling the truth.

'Ms Moss is not in the habit of lying, in particular to police officers,' Trench said, still not looking at the two cops. 'But you have a history of using the truth in a flexible way. So if I have to weigh her word against yours, I'll take hers.'

The two men stood up, and so did Trench. People were looking in our direction now. I was hoping there wouldn't be a shootout before we left. I hadn't seen enough westerns to know how the lawyer should act. (Memo to Patrick: Maybe you should be in a western. Hey – Errol Flynn did it.)

'You're not even a cop now,' 'my' officer said.

I saw the muscles in Trench's jaw clench. If I hadn't been sitting right next to him it would have been imperceptible.

'You two are out of uniform, and since you stopped and cited Ms Moss here for a taillight that you broke, you are violating the code of the department,' he told the two cops. I didn't mention that I'd been let off with a warning. 'I might not be an active member of the force at this moment, but I can certainly report misconduct on the part of those who are, as can any member of the community.'

'How do you come off telling us what the code of the department is?' the first officer sneered. 'You killed a cop.'

Trench's eyes never showed anger; they stayed as dispassionate and calm as they had been throughout this toxic exchange. 'If you had been eavesdropping more effectively, you would have heard the three of us discussing how to prove without a doubt that I did not do such a thing,' Trench said. From the sound of his voice, he might have been giving tourists directions to the Le Brea Tar Pits. 'But you don't seem to have sufficient powers of observation to make such a determination, which is why both of you will be giving out speeding tickets until the day you retire.'

That really got the first cop, with whom I'd had no official inter-action yet. His face reddened and his voice sounded like he'd swallowed a little shard of glass with the soda he had not ordered from the counter. No doubt he'd grown up hearing about the free things people gave to the friendly cop on the beat, which might have been true in 1944.

'At least we'll still be on the force,' he hissed. 'You'll be in a cell for the rest of your life, you traitor.'

Trench put his hand into his jacket pocket and made a quarter turn to face the two uniform cops who were not currently in uniform. 'That will not happen,' he said. 'But when I get back to active duty, I will make it my mission to see the two of you dismissed from the Los Angeles Police Department as soon as is possible. Enjoy your day, gentlemen. I'm sure you have some commuters to harass.'

The veins in the cop's neck bulged and the one who had broken my car pulled back his right arm, obviously about to throw a punch at the lieutenant. But he didn't know who he was dealing with, and that's always vital information. I made a mental note to have Emma research Barnett and determine his predictable patterns in court.

Before the guy could snap his elbow to hit Trench, the lieutenant had drawn a handgun from his pocket and leveled it directly at his assailant. 'You don't want to do that,' he said. Calm. Almost too quiet.

'You're not going to shoot me,' the cop said.

'I imagine not,' Trench told him. 'But if you really believe I killed Detective Schaeffer, can you take the chance?'

The cop had taken that in, and his fist stopped before it was even a fist. 'Are you crazy?' he said.

'Quite possibly,' Trench said, and I cringed. These two guys just made it to the top of the DA's witness list. 'Now leave this restaurant and go about your day. I have a lot of time on my hands these days, so I'll be watching.'

My cop almost tensed his arm up again, but his partner had the sense to put a hand on his bicep and say, 'Let's go, Cliff.' They exchanged a look, then a glare at Trench, and walked out of the pizza shop. Errol Flynn had won the day after all.

Trench, face never changing expression, sat down. 'Now. We were discussing how to prove that I could not have shot Detective Schaeffer.'

'Yeah, but that was before this little playlet,' I said. 'Congratulations, Lieutenant. I didn't think it was possible, but you just made your position a lot worse.'

FOURTEEN

After that I didn't really want the baked ziti. We took our lunches to go and let Trench tail us back to my office, where I stashed my leftovers with my name written on the box in the break-room fridge. Then I called Nate and put him on speaker in a small conference room that wasn't being used. If we were going to have a meeting about Trench's case and Trench was present, Nate might as well know what was being said. I had a flicker of hope that he might be able to contribute some new information himself.

We keep a stash of bottles of spring water for conferences, so I gave one each to Trench, Emma and Jon. Nate, whatever he was drinking, would have to fend for himself. I took a bottle for me and mentally berated myself for destroying the environment. It's a hobby.

Once Nate answered the phone, I told him everyone who was present so he would refrain from any less-than-complimentary terms he might have employed when discussing Trench. 'Where are we right now?' I asked the assemblage. 'Let's start with you, Nate.' Because I couldn't point at Nate. It wasn't a video call.

'I've got a lead on the idea that Schaeffer was making illegal loans from his job at the LAPD,' Nate said. He doesn't like to be caught without some new information to share. 'There's a woman called Phoebe Tennyson who used to work for the fraud division and says Schaeffer used to stop by at least once a week. She never saw her boss give him any money, but Schaeffer always seemed to be happier when he left than when he arrived.'

It wasn't much. 'That could be a number of things, and I don't want to think about most of them,' I said.

'Granted,' Nate agreed. 'But if I press Phoebe a little harder and talk to her ex-boss, I think I might be able to get more. I haven't been on this case that long.' Nate gets a little defensive when he thinks I'm pressing him to do things faster. Which I wasn't in this case.

'What about the lieutenant's former in-laws?' Jon asked, because he doesn't see the need for delicacy when there are legal matters to attend. 'Have you gotten in touch with them, Nate?'

'I've left messages, but they haven't gotten back yet,' he answered. 'Give me a few days. The trial's not starting anytime soon.' See? Defensive.

There was no point in pushing Nate any further, so I turned toward Emma. I had to call her by name because otherwise Nate would think I was still talking to him. 'Emma, have you written up a petition to the court for me about the trial date, since Nate brought it up?'

'It's in your email,' she said. She avoided looking at Trench. I'd have to find out what her beef with the police might be, because I had no reason to think that Emma and Trench had ever crossed paths before, so this was more a general thing.

'Good. Now—'

Trench, by turning his head slightly toward me, indicated he wanted to contribute so I nodded to him. I admired his willingness to let me be the authority figure in this meeting; Trench knew the value of a clear line of command.

'I think there should be some attention being paid to the weapon that killed Detective Schaeffer,' he said. 'It is registered to me and kept in my home, but somehow it seems the killer managed to get it into his possession and kill the detective, then return it to where I store the weapon so the investigating officers might find it. That is a very complicated operation and must have taken a good deal of preparation. I have examined the locked box in question twice myself, since it was confiscated as evidence, and found no sign of tampering. It's quite a challenge indeed to determine how it was done.'

He was right. The gun was going to be a major part of Barnett's case and we had not yet begun our investigations into its theft and return. 'Nate, that's more for you. Can you handle it?' I asked.

'Of course I can handle it.' I wasn't sure if Nate was being snarky or if he was sincerely offended at the question. 'Lieutenant, can I come by your house and see where you keep the gun?'

'Yes, you may.' Trench didn't emphasize the grammatical correction, but it was there. 'I will send you an email so we can set up a convenient time for both of us.'

So it was agreed, and after a few details about Nate's billing process should he have to fly to Michigan, and Emma's work on some minor motions to submit to the court, the meeting, such as it was, had been concluded. Emma couldn't wait to get away from

Trench, so she was the first one out of my office door. Jon said something about a drug possession case he needed to work on, and then he left as well. Nate just hung up.

That left me and Trench.

The lieutenant stood and his suit looked like it was still hanging in the store where he bought it, unwrinkled and in perfect condition. I looked at this strange, dignified, confusing man who was usually trying *not* to give me the information I needed and wondered if he was doing the same now for personal reasons.

'Lieutenant, I don't understand you,' I said.

Trench turned to face me and, if his face was capable of expression, the one he'd have given me would have been puzzlement. 'What do you not understand?' he asked.

'That stunt you pulled in the pizza place. You knew that the two cops there were hostile and you goaded them. Then when they threatened to get physical, you pulled a gun out of your pocket and pointed it at them.'

'That was pure self-defense,' Trench said. 'I had no desire to enter into an altercation with other members of the Los Angeles Police Department, no matter how inappropriate an example they were making of themselves.'

He was being evasive and I could tell, but I couldn't figure why. 'But you already had your hand in the pocket of your jacket so you could be ready with the gun very quickly,' I said. 'Our friend, whose name I still don't know because he'd never been wearing a badge when I saw him, hadn't started to clench a fist yet.'

Trench raised one eyebrow perhaps half an inch. It was the equivalent of a full-blown tantrum in anyone else. 'It was quite clear that the conversation was headed in the direction of a confrontation,' he said.

'Yeah, because you were steering it there. It was like you *wanted* them to get violent so you could draw the gun and end the scene. But that's the part I don't get. You had to know that pulling a weapon in a crowded public place like that, with two LAPD cops who would be on the DA's witness list, would be a devastating blow to your defense. But you pushed them into a fight and then you ended it with the service weapon. You're much smarter than that, Lieutenant. Why did you do it?'

Trench never broke eye contact. That didn't mean he was lying and it didn't mean he wasn't, because he's Trench and he has more self-control than 58 of your closest friends combined (which made the whole gun thing even less characteristic of him). 'Haven't you ever done something just because it felt like the right thing to do, Ms Moss?' he said.

'Sure. But I have never, in the time I've known you, seen you do anything for that reason. Everything you do seems to be intended to help close an investigation or improve the image of the LAPD. So, which one were you doing at the pizza place?'

Trench smiled a tiny smile, his only kind, and turned toward the door. 'If I may offer some advice, Counselor, I think you need to start treating your client less like a paragon and more like a man. It will help your case.' And he left the office.

I stood there motionless for three full minutes.

FIFTEEN

'I don't feel like we're getting anywhere,' I told Patrick.

We – Patrick, Angie and I – were sitting on a soundstage between shots of Patrick's TV series *Torn*. This was hardly my first visit, but I was still struck by how long filming, particularly lighting, takes to get right on a TV or film set. I understand that it's necessary, but I also understand why so many actors retreat to their trailers, which are like little apartments (sometimes not so little), nearby to wait for everything to be prepared. The waiting can drive you to distraction. And the last thing I needed today (a Saturday, but they shoot when they need to shoot) was a distraction. I felt like I hadn't been focusing hard enough.

'It's still very early in the process,' Patrick said. 'I'll be in front of the cameras in twenty minutes.' He was in costume, a black business suit, and wearing a paper bib around the collar because of his makeup, which always made him look a little odd, like himself but more. He was sitting in what they call a director's chair, but they give one to any number of people, including the star/executive producer. I marveled that he didn't get two chairs. Angie and I were borrowing ours from other cast members who had chosen the trailer route or weren't needed in this scene at all.

'I meant that we're not getting anywhere with Lt Trench's case,' I said.

Patrick looked a little embarrassed, as he does when he acts like the world revolves solely around him. To be fair, he does that a lot less than most of the other actors I've met. 'Oh,' he said.

'What did you expect to get done so soon?' Angie gets right to the point. 'You're just getting started. Are you thrown because of what the lieutenant said?'

The technicians, each of whom had a job title I didn't understand (best boy? That's not a title for a cocker spaniel?), were setting up lights based on the instructions of the director of photography, who had consulted with the director, who was in constant communication with the showrunner, who was a producer, who had probably not talked to the writer, who lived in the house that Jack built. A man who was pretending to be Patrick but wasn't stood in his place (his 'mark') on the set so they could light him accurately. Patrick's stand-in (not to be confused with his stunt double) was a very nice guy named Steve whose job was exactly that: to be the same height and general build as Patrick so he could be lit and give Patrick time to sit in a director's chair while the director stood telling the director of photography what he wanted.

I don't know anything about the movie business and I still find it exhausting.

'I don't think so,' I told Angie. 'I don't really understand what he said. I'm treating him the way I've always treated him. And the court date won't even be set for another week, probably, and then it'll be months before we actually go in there and try the case. But I feel like there are things I'm missing, things I'm not doing, that I should be. And if I make a mistake anywhere along the line, the lieutenant could be spending decades in jail.'

'That's it,' Angie said. 'Don't put pressure on yourself.'

'I'm putting pressure on Nate to come up with something, but he keeps acting like I'm being unreasonable.' There was no point in addressing Angie's comment. I speak Jersey and I got the message, even if I disagreed with it. 'Nobody seems to be as committed to this case as I am.'

'That's because you're emotionally involved; you consider the lieutenant a friend.' Patrick, the peacemaker, wanted me to take things easier because it makes me a more reasonable person and girlfriend. Wasn't anyone seeing what I was seeing in this case?

Before I could answer, one of the production assistants, a young (early 20s) woman with her hair back in a ponytail, approached Patrick, which I thought was a signal he was needed on the set. As with everything else in this conversation, it turned out I was wrong. 'Mr McNabb, there are two police officers here to see you.'

I looked up and, even before I could see their faces, I knew who the two cops were going to be. Sure enough, my opponents from the road and the pizza place were standing ten feet away, doing their best to look intimidating. 'To see me?' Patrick said. 'Did they say why?'

The PA, probably out of college for at least a week, looked terrified. She was giving the boss bad news and no doubt expected to be blamed for it. I was mentally preparing a lawsuit about harassment aimed at the LAPD. The poor girl just shook her head. The ponytail wagged fetchingly.

'All right,' Patrick said. He stood and waved toward the cops to approach. 'Be careful about the cables on the floor,' he told them. 'The crew get awfully testy when someone shakes one of those loose.'

The cops showed no effort to keep the cables in place, not even looking at the floor as they walked. They were too macho for all that.

My highway nemesis got to Patrick first. The two were in uniform and this time he was wearing his badge, which didn't sport a name but did have a number, 7316, which I saved to my phone. I was willing to bet Nate or even Trench would be able to get a name from that. Or I could look it up online as a matter of public record. There was that.

'Yeah, Mr McNabb,' he said. His voice didn't have the tough New York accent he undoubtedly wished it did, and he sounded like his next sentence would be to ask for directions to the nearest surf shop. His 'yeah' sounded more like 'ja.' 'I have a warrant for your arrest.'

Well, that served as a jolt of caffeine to the morning. I shot up out of my director's chair, which wasn't nearly as comfortable as you'd like to believe they are. 'On what charge?' I demanded before Patrick could find the words. Angie was already balling her hands into fists. You don't want to get on Angie's bad side.

'This is about Mr McNabb, not you,' Badge 7316 said. 'It's not about his girlfriend.'

Don't reduce a Jersey girl to that role and expect to be welcomed with open arms. 'I'm his attorney,' I said. 'What's the charge?'

His partner, Badge 2869, was not looking as cocky. 'We have a warrant,' he said, as if that answered the question.

'OK,' I told him. 'Let me see it.'

Good old 7316 scowled like he wanted to hit me, largely because he probably did. 'I don't have to let you.'

'Actually, you do,' Angie told him. Angie didn't go to law school, but she's been hanging out with me a long time. 'If you have a warrant, you're obligated to produce it for his scrutiny, and that of his attorney. So where's your warrant, big guy?'

I saw 2869 sort of shrink at 'big guy.' He had clearly thought this would go much easier for the two of them.

One thing you need to know about the company of *Torn*: They all loved Patrick McNabb. So I wasn't terribly surprised when I saw a few of the Teamsters watching with interest at the little scene, and picking up wrenches and other metal objects just in case they were needed. They didn't close in yet, but they knew they could quickly if necessary.

'The charge is obstruction of justice,' said 7316. 'You're going to have to come with us, Mr *McNabb*.'

'I believe my attorney said it best,' Patrick told him. 'Let her see the warrant, if you have one.'

'We, um, left it in the car,' 2869 piped up. He was watching the Teamsters and sweating. 'Come to the car and we'll show it to you.'

'No,' I said. 'You go to the car and bring it here. We'll wait.' If there really were a warrant, he could probably call it up on his phone, but there wasn't, and who were we kidding?

Both of them stood there and stared at me. I don't usually get that kind of attention, especially when Patrick is present; he sucks all the excitement up for himself without trying. Which is how I prefer things. But the two cops weren't there for him. They were there for me and everyone in the building knew it.

'Your life is mine now,' 7316 snarled at me. 'You can watch your back all you want, but you're not gonna let that cop killer walk the streets and get away with it. If we have to arrest your boyfriend and see how he likes jail,' (and that's where he grinned an evil grin) 'then that's what we'll do. Warrant or no warrant.'

He took a step toward me and the Teamsters, at least six of them, closed in around us in a circle. Bob Watkins, whom I knew from repeated trips to the set, stroked his beard a bit and assessed the situation. 'Any problem, Sandy?' he asked.

'Not yet, Bob, but I'm glad you're watching.'

Bob nodded. 'We're always watching,' he said. The Teamsters moved back a bit and the two cops clearly relaxed. I saw that 7316 had his hand on his gun, but he didn't draw it because he wasn't as stupid as he looked. No one was.

At that moment Bob noticed a nod from the PA. 'They need you on the set, Patrick,' he said. 'Want an escort?'

Patrick stood up and took off the protective collar. A makeup artist appeared out of nowhere and started applying small touches to his face as he walked. 'I don't think so, Bob, but thanks for asking.'

They walked toward the set where the director and other cast members were waiting. I looked 7316 in the eye. 'If you're gonna be a cop, learn the law,' I said. 'And if you're really gonna be a cop, stop violating other people's rights. I can call the LAPD and have you suspended right now. There were at least thirty people who heard you harassing Patrick and me.'

'This isn't over,' he said. He'd seen too many bad movies.

'It really is,' Angie told him. 'Now get back in the car without a warrant and go resign from the police force. Save us the trouble of having you thrown off.'

'You'll see us again.' The cop hadn't run out of bad exit lines yet. 'Or maybe you won't see us coming at all. Come on, Cliff.'

I'd like to say they slunk away but they were just as cocky and stupid leaving as they had been walking in. Some people are beyond help.

Once they were safely out of sight, I exhaled and sat back down in the director's chair. Angie did the same a few feet to my right.

'What do you think?' I asked.

'I think it's time to call Judy.'

SIXTEEN

I knew her only as Judy. A few times since I'd arrived in Los Angeles, I had employed her, through an agency, as a personal security operative, or bodyguard, if you must. If Trench is unemotional, Judy might very well be a walking instrument of AI. She had never eaten, tapped her foot to music, or smiled since I'd met her. Judy was the perfect security machine.

Angie had the contact information for the agency that employed Judy and used it even before Patrick had uttered a line of dialogue in the scene he was filming. Judy appeared less than twenty minutes later, already cleared by studio security, dressed as efficiently and blandly as she always had been. In a movie, Judy would be an extra from Central Casting. Until you needed her.

I wanted to welcome her with a hug based on all the times she had, you know, saved my life, but I thought Judy would find that embarrassing, so we exchanged nods and she silently took up her position behind me (for a better vantage point). I didn't have much to do because Patrick was the one filming the scene, but even so, Judy and I weren't really at the chatting stage. She was at work and I respected that, since I was the work.

The two cops did not resurface. I watched while Patrick did his job, then sat with Angie and him between shots. Finally the scene – the only one on the schedule for the day – was completed to the satisfaction of the director and Patrick, and the crew started to shut down the set, which would not be needed again for this episode. Patrick, Angie, Judy and I collected our belongings (Judy had none) and left the soundstage.

She requested that Angie drive her car back to our house because Judy wanted to ride with Patrick and me (basically me), but would need her vehicle to go home after her shift was completed, so Angie had the pleasure of driving Judy's dark gray Chevy Traverse through the streets of Los Angeles and intimidating the people who were alert enough to take notice. She must have loved every minute of it.

We had barely set up camp in the living room, waiting for a takeout delivery because enough with the cooking this week, when

Nate Garrigan called and asked for directions to the house. He didn't ask for permission to come by, of course, because Nate always assumes he's welcome. Since he was working for me, and a suggestion that he come by had to mean there was something to report, I gave him the address and told him how to get around the GPS misinformation that would be fed into the system because we were trying to keep Patrick's address confidential, and Nate showed up before the guy from DoorDash.

He was rumpled, of course. I think Nate considers it to be a sign of his professionalism that he never looks like he should be reporting to an office. He had on a denim shirt and jeans, but the shirt was bleached so he didn't look like he was wearing a matching suit. Never let it be said that Nate Garrigan was sartorially coordinated.

'I've got a few pieces to the Ikea bookcase, but I can't put them all together yet,' he said after saying hello to all of us and noting that Judy was back, but not asking why. If Judy was there it was to do a job and it wasn't Nate's place to interfere with that. He stood despite being offered a spot on the loveseat next to Angie. When Nate spoke, he wanted the floor and all the attention to which it entitled him. 'They're all little pieces and I don't know what the puzzle looks like so far.'

'What areas are we talking about?' I asked so that he would stop making painful metaphors about the case I was preparing.

'Mostly it's about the gun that Trench says was stolen from his apartment and then carefully replaced so it would look like he shot this Schaeffer guy,' Nate said. Nate knows everyone's name and their situation in the case, but he likes people to underestimate him because he thinks he's Columbo. I don't know how many people he's fooled that way over the years, but the act has never worked on me, and Angie, who apprentices with Nate a half-day a week, insists that he's actually a genius.

'Are you saying that you believe the lieutenant is lying about the gun being removed and returned?' Patrick asked. 'You think he killed Detective Schaeffer?'

I felt some goosebumps on my arms. I decided it was too cool in the room but I didn't get up to adjust the thermostat.

'Let's not get all ahead of ourselves here,' Nate said. 'I told you I can't put it together yet. But I can say I went over to the lieutenant's place today and checked out the lockbox where he says he keeps the gun. Of course it's not there now, because the cops confiscated it for evidence, but I examined the room where he keeps it and the lockbox, and I'm here to tell you if that gun took a trip like that and came back, it must have escaped under its own power because there's no sign at all that the box was tampered with or that the room had been entered without permission. The lieutenant's front door and all other entrances also had no indications of forced entry. If someone stole that gun and brought it back, the over-whelming odds are Lt Trench knew about it and probably gave them permission.'

I was sucking air in through my mouth and letting it out slowly. 'That's not good,' I said.

'How does the lieutenant explain it?' Angie asked. She knew Nate would have asked.

'He doesn't,' was the answer. 'He can't come up with a scenario where that happened without his knowledge and left no mark.'

'And I'm guessing he didn't give anyone permission to do it,' I said. I wanted to close my eyes and escape again, but I'm a profes-sional attorney and I only do that when it's just me and my boyfriend in the room. Can't show weakness.

'Absolutely not,' Nate said. 'He's at a loss to explain how the bullet that killed Schaeffer could have matched the test one they fired from his gun. He insists he never took it out of the box that day. It's not the gun he uses on duty most days and he didn't have it with him on the night in question.'

'But he says he spent the night at home alone.' Angie would never doubt Trench's word and neither, for that matter, would I. 'How can we prove he didn't use it to kill Schaeffer?'

'At the moment, we can't,' I told her. 'But it's something to start. Nate, is it possible someone stole the lieutenant's gun earlier and replaced it with the same model?'

Nate grimaced a little, possibly at my use of the word *model*, because he knows my knowledge of firearms could be described as nonexistent. 'Anything is possible, but Trench says the cops checked the ID number on the gun and it's his.'

'I need to get all the items in discovery from Barnett.' I was thinking out loud. 'I'm tired of going on their good word. Let them show me what they can prove.'

Nate, who had bristled a bit at losing the spotlight, cleared his throat and for some reason that was enough for the rest of us to look in his direction. 'There's more,' he said, keeping the irritation out of his voice almost successfully. 'About the victim here having run a loan shark scam while being a police officer who was supposed to look out for bad guys who run loan shark scams.'

'I get so easily confused,' Patrick lamented.

Nate chose not to explain it all because Patrick was probably just being dramatic – and, anyway, I could tell him all about the scheme later. 'If Schaeffer was leaning on his fellow officers with crazy interest rates on money he must have gotten . . . somewhere, there's damn little proof of it aside from a couple of cops saying they heard it was true.'

'So there's no evidence Schaeffer was crooked?' I wasn't that concerned about it, because the victim wouldn't be on trial, but if he had been illegally soaking down other cops, it would add to the list of people (that seemed to be shrinking every time we spoke) who might have had a reason to kill him and frame Trench.

Nate looked amused. 'Oh, no. There's plenty of evidence he was a bad cop. But he was apparently fleecing other cops. He made loans and then upped the interest about once a week so they couldn't pay him back.'

That confused me more than Patrick had been a moment before. 'How does *that* work?'

'I haven't worked out where Schaeffer got his initial stake yet, but I'm guessing it was from someone he was shaking down through his job,' Nate explained. 'He didn't just go out and buy a new Tesla. He started offering loans to his fellow cops and then squeezing them for more money to keep them on the hook as long as he could. That's why he couldn't keep a partner. Word had gotten around and nobody wanted to work with him.'

We all took a moment to absorb what he'd said. 'That's crazy.' Angie can always be counted on to revive first, and to offer an opinion that is clear and concise.

'It sure is,' Nate said. 'There's no way to prove it unless other cops will testify, and nobody I talked to would agree to that. It'd be interesting to hear what the commanding officers in the homicide division might have to say as well.'

'Figure out which ones and I'll put them on the witness list,' I said. 'Do you think any of the cops who got injured as Schaeffer's partner, maybe someone who's no longer in the department, might be persuaded to speak up in court?'

'I'm working on it,' he said.

'Well, while you're at it, I need the ballistics report on the bullet that killed Schaeffer. It's not public information yet and I want to see it.'

'The police are already saying it matched the lieutenant's gun,' Patrick pointed out. 'Will the written report tell you anything other than that?'

I stretched my legs out in front of me because I needed to awaken from the daze I'd been in since Trench called me to tell me he'd been arrested. 'That's what I want to find out,' I said.

Nate looked skeptical. 'OK.'

'Now. The really important stuff,' I said. Nate, intrigued, leaned forward just a bit. 'What does Trench's house look like?'

He didn't get to answer because the DoorDash guy buzzed in from the security gate. Patrick let him through with the button on the wall.

'So. What did you guys order for dinner?' Nate asked.

SEVENTEEN

One last thing Nate told us (before he managed to make two portions of pad thai disappear all by himself) was that his police contacts had identified our two antagonists, Badges 7316 and 2869.

'Their names are Clifton Armstrong and James Clanton,' he said. 'Armstrong you should have gotten from the summons he issued for you, Sandy.'

From the corner of the dining room where she had situated herself, Judy lightly cleared her throat. She is an ex-cop who knew Trench before I met him and has a history with the department that I gather is not especially friendly.

'He didn't issue a summons,' I said. 'He broke my taillight and then told me he was letting me off with a warning for having a broken taillight.'

Nate made a slightly nauseated face and grunted a bit. I assumed it was Armstrong and not the pad thai making him feel that way. 'Clanton is an old rookie. He didn't apply to the department until he was in his thirties and just made it on to the job this year. They assigned him to Armstrong, maybe out of a sense of sadism, and he follows his partner around like a puppy, learning all the wrong ways to be a cop. Bureaucracy at its best.'

Nate left after dealing with his free dinner and I considered calling Trench with an update, but discussing the failings of the Los Angeles Police Department was only going to make him grumpier than usual so I figured it could wait until Monday morning. Instead, I started making up a list of potential expert witnesses I could contact to testify in opposition to the ones the DA would already have on salary. When they say 'the state versus' the defendant, they're not kidding.

Patrick and I were getting ready for bed when Judy texted me. *Please come into the living room. Both of you.*

That's Judy telling me something urgent was going on. She never disturbs me unless it's necessary and will not enter our bedroom if there are no guns pointed directly at my heart in that moment. So something was up. 'Get dressed,' I told Patrick. 'Judy wants us in the living room.' He looked appropriately concerned and started taking the same clothes he'd been wearing out of the closet.

We got ourselves together quickly and headed into the living room, where sure enough, Judy was standing in clear view of the front door. The lights were out. She had a gun in her right hand. Judy was not running a fire drill.

'My company contacted me a few minutes ago,' she said. 'I'm sorry to bother you both, but there is someone on the grounds, clearly looking for a way to enter the house.'

'Is this person armed?' Patrick asked, nodding at the weapon in Judy's hand.

'Unknown at this time, sir.' Judy hates not controlling a situation and I could tell this was worrying her.

'On what part of the grounds was the intruder first spotted?' he asked.

'They had parked a 2009 Impreza just outside the security gate and walked through, indicating this is not someone used to doing such things. Walking through the gate set off the sensors and alerted your security company. They put out an alarm which reached my employer and that is how I found out. What I'd like you both to do right now is walk to the center of the room, away from any windows or doors, and sit on the floor. Don't turn on any lights, please.'

Like obedient children, we followed her instructions to the letter and looked scared doing so. There was a large square coffee table in the center of the room. Patrick sat on one side and I sat next to him around the corner of the table. I reached for his hand and it was already there.

'What do we do now, Judy?' I asked.

'Just stay quiet.' The one thing on the planet I am worst at doing. Now this unknown intruder was really starting to piss me off. I would have folded my arms in frustration, but I was still holding Patrick's hand and in no hurry to let it go. 'I'll let you know when it's safe,' Judy added.

She was wearing an earbud in her right ear and had it plugged into her phone, which was in the hand not holding the gun. Every few seconds she would nod as if someone who had told her something could see her. 'Do we have a location?' she said in a low tone to her mobile. 'Copy that.'

I looked at Patrick, whose whole being was pointed toward me.

He was more concerned about me than he was about himself, and don't forget, Patrick is an actor. Being self-centered and egocentric is just part of the makeup. 'You still want to marry me?' I asked him in a whisper, kidding.

Patrick was not laughing. 'Are you saying yes after all this time?'

I looked at Judy, who had a very severe expression on her face, then back at Patrick, and shook my head. 'Bad joke,' I said.

Patrick squeezed my hand. 'You know the offer stands,' he said quietly.

'When you're ready,' I told him.

'When *I'm* ready?'

'Ma'am.' Judy always calls me 'ma'am' and I can't begin to tell you how that disturbs me. 'It would appear the intruder is headed to your front door and should be there in a matter of seconds. Whoever it is seems to be unarmed, but it's dark outside and we can't be certain.'

I felt my stomach clench. 'What should we do?' I asked Judy.

'We should let them in,' Patrick said. 'You can handle the situation from there, can't you, Judy?'

Judy seemed to be weighing options. Her lips were pursed like she was tasting something and deciding if she liked it or not. 'Another possibility is to call in some people from your security firm and have them approach this person before they enter the building, but we'd have to do that now.'

'I'm all for someone else handling it,' I said. Never let it be said I was killed trying to be a hero. In fact, I'd prefer it if it was never said I was killed at all.

Patrick, who has played the action hero a couple of times, appeared to be less than thrilled with my suggestion, but he didn't raise an objection. Judy, on the other hand, knew who was paying her freight (it was Seaton, Taylor but why bring that up?) and nodded. She spoke quietly in the direction of her phone. 'Take them peacefully if you can and report back,' she said. 'That's a go.'

And that was the moment when I was more afraid than I had been up to this point. When you know something is going on that can endanger your life or that of someone you love, but you *can't see what's happening*, your mind goes to dark places. I trusted Judy with my life, literally, but I couldn't stop thinking about what might be happening just beyond the front door of our house.

Thankfully, it didn't take very long (but tell that to my nervous system). I heard a few seconds of scuffling outside the door, then Judy put her hand to her ear to listen to the report. 'The intruder says she's just here to talk to you,' she said to Patrick and me. 'She was not armed.'

'She?' Patrick was surprised that a woman was advancing on his house? Frankly, it didn't happen as often as I'd expected it to when we moved in together. The address had not yet made it on to social media.

'Yes, sir.' Judy is ex-military in addition to being an ex-cop, and chain of command is her religion.

'Is this a fan thing?' I asked. People get awfully attached to the characters they see on television or in the movies, and they often mistake the actor for the role he plays. In addition, Patrick is really handsome. And no, that's not bias.

'No, ma'am,' Judy said. 'Apparently it has something to do with the case against Lt Trench.'

Not that the thought hadn't crossed my mind, but I was more expecting a couple of burly cops with a grudge than a woman. Maybe she had a grudge. Maybe she was burly. 'Do you think there's any danger in letting her in and hearing what she has to say?' Patrick asked Judy.

That wasn't going to be my first choice, but I remembered that the intruder was unarmed and Judy was decidedly not. Still, I put my hand on to the coffee table and stood, hefting a porcelain vase we had that I didn't especially like.

'I always think there is the potential for danger in such a situation,' Judy answered. 'But in this case the risk seems to be pretty low.'

Patrick looked at me. 'So we let her in?'

The best way to defend a client in a criminal case (or any case, for that matter) is to have all the facts you can gather. Apparently some facts were standing outside on our inordinately expensive welcome mat. I nodded.

Judy said, 'We are opening the door,' into her phone, and then put the phone into her pocket so she could reach for the doorknob and hold her gun at the same time. I thought the weapon must have gotten heavy in her hand by now, but Judy showed no sign of arm fatigue. She opened the door.

Standing there were three people: a man and a woman in the 'uniform' of our security company, which essentially amounted to a polo shirt and khakis plus a Kevlar vest, and a small, thin young woman (in her twenties, I guessed) dressed all in black, as one does when trying to avoid security cameras or when going to a party in Brooklyn. She looked, to be charitable, badly shaken up, but not at all physically damaged. I guessed the apprehension of our intruder had not been completely without incident.

'You're the guard?' the man asked Judy.

'I am here for security, yes,' she answered.

The security guy, who probably thought he could have handled this particular threat on his own, grunted. The woman he was working with said, 'I think you can handle it from here,' to Judy and gestured for the young woman in black to enter the house, which she did, very slowly, like there might be crocodiles in our living room, which was silly. We'd had the moat filled in months before. (I'm kidding. Geez.)

Judy, having assessed our intruder, had most likely surmised that she presented a very small threat indeed. She thanked the two members of the security force and closed the door so they could go back and fill out the requisite tons of paperwork that in these days would require no paper at all. But 'PDF work' doesn't have the same ring to it.

'All right,' Judy said to our new guest, who was so thin I thought about offering her some Thai leftovers, but held back just in case this girl was evil and didn't show it. 'Why did you sneak past the gate and make all those security people leave their base to come here?' Judy always has her fellow bodyguards' interests at heart. It's a tight bond. I guess.

'I needed to see her,' the young woman said. She pointed at me. 'She's defending Trench in the Wally Schaeffer case.'

It wasn't the first time I'd heard Schaeffer referred to as 'Wally,' but the only other person to get that familiar had been my old blue-eyed pal Clifton Armstrong, who had not given me a summons for a broken taillight. 'Do you know something I need to know?' I asked her.

'Maybe.' The young woman was starting to shake off the panic she'd had when she was caught and swaggered a bit. 'Maybe not.'

'Who are you?' Patrick asked. It was a sensible question.

'I'm Francine Schaeffer,' she said. 'Wally Schaeffer was my father.'

EIGHTEEN

When a dead detective's daughter comes commando raiding at your house, the thing you do is, you offer her a mug of cocoa. So after a few solid moments of blank stares, that's exactly what Patrick did. Minutes later, Francie (as she asked to be called), Patrick and I were seated around our manageable kitchen table waiting for the hot chocolate to become, you know, hot, while Judy stood facing the door just in case Schaeffer's golf caddie decided to drop by unexpectedly and deliver an opinion on Lt Trench's case.

'I couldn't just call up your office,' Francie said. 'I mean, I think the police are watching me and I didn't want to be seen.' The fact that a security company, multiple closed-circuit cameras and Judy had all caught her just trying to knock on our door didn't seem to have really penetrated into Francie's mind yet.

'Of course.' Patrick is at his best when he's dealing with people who are in some sort of distress. It's his desire to fix every problem for every person he's ever met that makes me love him and simultaneously drives me nuts. 'But you had something you wanted to tell Sandy, didn't you?' The milk on the stove was getting warmer, so he stood to stir in the cocoa and get the process started. It was also a way to get Francie to concentrate on me. Patrick is a famous actor. I'm some lawyer from New Jersey. It's natural.

'Yeah.' Francie seemed to have been reminded of the reason she'd gotten into her car, driven to an address that I'd like to know how she'd discovered, dressed in black from head to toe, snuck through a security gate and dashed to the front door. Oh yeah, her father's murder. 'I want you to know I don't blame Lt Trench for my dad's death.'

Call me callous, but that didn't seem like much. I mean, she could have emailed me that and the cops watching her, if there were any, wouldn't have cared a whole lot. So I figured there was more and waited for what it might be.

Turned out I was right. As Patrick was bringing three mugs (matching, which never would have happened in my apartment with

Angie) of hot chocolate to the table, Francie seemed to prepare herself for an ordeal; she straightened her spine in her chair and rearranged her face into a more determined expression.

'My father was a difficult man,' she began. 'As a detective, he was out at crazy hours when I was growing up, and he tried to be a good dad but he didn't know how to do it. After a while he sort of left me to my mother and just saw me before school. He was out a lot of nights, and my mother never said anything, but I am willing to bet he wasn't working all that time.'

'You think he had affairs,' I said. I mean, that's what she'd meant but I needed for Francie to face it head-on if she could. 'Do you think one of the women he was involved with might have killed him?' OK, so it was blunt, but I will insist until the day I die that it was not cruel.

You may count as evidence of that the fact that Francie didn't break down in tears or even flinch. 'I thought Lt Trench killed my father,' she said. 'Didn't he get arrested?'

Not what I was expecting. 'But you just said you didn't think the lieutenant shot your dad,' I said.

Francie shook her head a little. 'No. I said I didn't blame the lieutenant. If I were him, I probably would have shot my father, too.'

Patrick was watching the way an actor watches, noting behaviors in each of the people in the room in case he ever had to recreate or draw upon the emotions he was seeing. It's a little cold but it's part of the business and I'd grown used to it. Everything is material.

'I'm a little confused,' I told Francie. 'You came all the way here just to say you thought Lt Trench killed your father but you're OK with it?'

She took a sip and seemed pleased with the hot chocolate, if not so much with me. 'Those aren't the words I would use,' Francie said. 'Obviously I didn't want my father to die. But he'd grown more distant and meaner these past few years, and I can certainly understand why the lieutenant might have blamed Dad for what happened to his wife. I mean, that was awful.'

'It was also five years ago,' I said. 'Look, Francie. I'm Lt Trench's attorney and I'm defending him against homicide charges. But aside from my professional responsibility, I truly believe that he was not the person who killed your father. It doesn't fit his personality and it doesn't make a lot of sense. There is circumstantial evidence against him, but I think we'll prove in court that the lieutenant didn't shoot your dad.'

Francie stopped with the mug halfway to her mouth and looked stunned. 'Really,' she said.

I'd show her; *I* took a sip of the hot chocolate. Patrick had done an admirable job. It was delicious. I was used to Swiss Miss packets and boiling water. This was not that. 'Really,' I said to Francie. 'Lt Trench didn't do it.'

'Wow.' She seemed genuinely surprised, as if she'd never actually considered the possibility before, because she probably hadn't. She drank a little more. 'This would be good with some Baileys in it.'

'Francie,' I said, trying as hard as I could to sound like a sympathetic friend. 'Do you know anything about your dad's murder that might help me prove the lieutenant is the wrong man to be blamed?'

She thought about that. 'I wasn't there that night. You know, I don't live at home anymore and my parents are divorced. I never lived just with my dad.' Not to get too technical, but wherever you live is home. 'I was living with my mom in Encino for a while but now I have a place in Burbank with three roommates. But my father was jumpy the last few months, like afraid of something, or somebody.'

Now we were getting somewhere! 'Who was he afraid of?' I asked. I actually forgot about the hot chocolate for a minute.

'Oh, I don't know,' Francie said. 'He never mentioned a name. I got the feeling he didn't want anyone else to know, or that he thought he was keeping Mom and me safe by not being specific. But it was never Trench. Dad hated him enough to say it out loud if he'd wanted to.'

I took a long swig. Patrick saw that as a gap to be filled and he hated unfilled gaps. He sat down with his own mug in front of him. 'Francie,' he said. Immediately her attention shifted to him; it's just something that happens when he's in the room. 'Why did your father hate Lt Trench?'

Francie didn't look away, but her eyes weren't focusing on Patrick anymore. She looked like she didn't want to answer the question, but after a moment and a glance at Judy, who looked exactly like Judy, she said, 'I don't want to say. I know you guys are friends of Trench, and until a minute ago I thought everyone agreed he had shot Dad, so it just feels weird.'

Patrick didn't get to be a famous and, in some places, acclaimed actor by failing at getting people to trust him. He gave Francie his acting eyes, which I've come to recognize but you wouldn't. He said, 'Anything you can tell us will be helpful, even if it doesn't strike you as being complimentary. Sandy isn't just Lt Trench's friend; she's also his attorney. If you can answer her question, you can count on her to use it or not depending on the lieutenant's defense.'

'And if you think it's something that proves the lieutenant really did kill your father, you should bring it to Assistant District Attorney Barnett on Monday morning,' I told her. I would have crossed my fingers behind my back, but after the age of six that never works. I did lightly bite my tongue.

'I don't think it has anything to do with what happened to my father,' Francie said after a moment of thought. She was looking at me now, and not Patrick. 'But you asked why Dad hated Trench. I think it was because he knew Trench was better than him. Trench kept getting promoted ahead of my father. He was, technically, one of his superiors in the department, but they knew not to put Trench directly in charge of Dad. There was bad blood because of all those things, and then once Officer Wright was killed in the line, Trench blamed Dad and Dad knew it. So it was a mutual hate.'

It was now especially late at night and the adrenaline rush of being under attack had long since faded. I was, if you really need to know, longing to go to bed. Patrick can stay up all night and look like he just had a sound sleep, but I tend to resemble an unmade bed if I haven't spent enough time in one. 'Francie, if you're afraid to come to my office, can we meet somewhere else to follow up?' I asked.

'Give me your cell number,' she said. 'I'll call you if I think of anything.'

Judy walked Francie back to her car, but she didn't like it. She doesn't feel comfortable when there's no one watching over me. It's kind of like being with my mother, except less judgy. I dragged my weary butt back to the bedroom while Patrick put all our used mugs and such in the dishwasher. He found me climbing into bed a few minutes later.

'Did you believe what she said?' he asked.

I might have groaned a little because all I wanted to do was turn the light off. 'Oddly, I did,' I said. 'I think she really believed Trench killed her father and now she's confused.'

'Is she?' Patrick said, getting in on the other side of this stupidly large bed. 'She just seemed to decide that the lieutenant didn't kill Detective Schaeffer just because we said so. For someone who was so convinced when she arrived, dodging almost all our security devices, that seemed like an awfully quick turnaround.'

I hated him being right. 'Are you just giving me something to worry about when I'm trying to get to sleep?' I asked.

Patrick laughed lightly. 'No,' he said. He traversed the miles between us to give me a kiss. 'You stop thinking about that immediately and sleep well, love.' Then he traversed himself all the way back to whatever zip code the other side of the bed was in. He turned off his bedside light.

I didn't sleep more than a half-hour that night. Eventually over the next six months until the trial started, I worked my sleep time all the way up to four hours a night. But not in a row.

NINETEEN

I met with Trench again to give him an update on his case two days later, after Holly had informed me that she would 'put you in for a partnership as soon as the Trench case is done,' but was softening the ground among the partners now. That was good news because, frankly, once that process begins, if you don't end up a partner you generally leave the firm and try to start climbing the corporate ladder somewhere else. But, oh yeah, Trench.

Jon, Emma and I met him at a small Greek restaurant in Venice. The one in California. Calm down. It has maintained its reputation for a hippie haven and counterculture atmosphere, but a lot of that now is façade and Venice is another beach community. Even so, Trench's immaculate blue suit, white shirt and navy-blue tie were a little out of place among the surfers, flip-flops and bathing suits. When you have an image you have to keep it up. Both Venice and Trench were doing that.

The stated purpose of the meeting, when I'd called the lieutenant to arrange it, was to give him an update on our progress. But in my mind, it was meant to gauge Trench's state of mind. I wasn't concerned that he was wasting away in worry about his trial, because worry isn't a Trench thing. But I had never heard him say he hated anyone until Wallace Schaeffer's name had come up and, frankly, I didn't need a seething client next to me in a courtroom sometime soon.

This morning I had gotten to see the slightly updated medical examiner's report on the homicide and, I'm sure you'll be shocked, but Schaeffer had died of a gunshot wound to the back of his head that had lodged in his brain. That was the kind of shot an expert marksman like Trench could have lined up. The bullet had been fired from roughly twenty feet away, no small feat for Schaeffer's apartment, where the rooms weren't exactly enormous. The detective who had filed the report, Anthony Basilico, had concluded that the shot had been fired into the living room from a hallway just at the entrance to the apartment. Whoever had killed Schaeffer had walked in, fired and then presumably left because there were no bloody

footprints and no marks on the living-room rug other than where
the body had been found. The neatest of possible executions.

The kind of killing Trench would commit if he decided to do
such a thing.

So far, the lieutenant was going to be my star witness because I
had so few other people to testify (that would change, obviously,
over the months between now and the trial). So knowing what he
would say under pressure was important. It had shaken me to hear
him say the word 'hate.' He had never said that before.

I'd tell you what everyone ordered for lunch but, to be honest, I
don't actually remember. I was intent on questioning my client like
the DA would do when the time came.

'Lieutenant, have you ever been inside Detective Schaeffer's
apartment?' To my right I saw Emma start a bit, probably because
she had expected me to ease into things a little bit more amiably.
But my inner prosecutor, the one I'd used when I worked for
Middlesex County in New Jersey, was reviving herself and, I'm
sorry to say, enjoying it.

'Yes, once.' Trench might or might not have known how my mind
was working, but his answer would be the same if he knew I was
picturing him on the stand or not. 'About six years ago I went there
after one shift because we were discussing a case that had us stumped
and I thought another detective's views would be helpful. Instead I
got Detective Schaeffer's.'

Sarcasm? From Trench? It was like hearing drunken sea shanties
from Sherlock Holmes. This was going to be an interesting meeting.

'I take it you didn't socialize.' I was role-playing Barnett and
nothing was going to stop me. Almost nothing. I make no
promises.

'You are correct.' Trench's demeanor was no different from usual.
He was impassive, alert but logical. He was the Mr Spock of Los
Angeles detectives. 'No. We were not friendly.'

Jon was watching and no doubt taking notes in his head; I'd
consult with him later. Emma, who had gotten the job by being
downright hostile toward Trench, looked appalled at the crude way
in which I was questioning him. There was still hope for Emma.

'All right, then,' I said. 'You weren't friendly, but you did go to
his apartment once. What can you tell me about it?' Trench had a
detective's mind, he noticed everything and he forgot nothing. He
undoubtedly could have told me not just what every case left on

his desk when he was arrested was about, but also its file number.

'The apartment was on the seventh floor of the building,' he began. 'It had one bedroom and one bath. There was a kitchen, which appeared to have been used very infrequently. No dishes were in the dish drainer. No food was visible on the counters. Schaeffer wasn't that neat in any other aspect of his life, so it was safe to assume that he did not cook very often.'

This, and he had been in the apartment once, years before. 'How was it decorated?' I asked.

'Not very lavishly,' Trent said. 'There was a rug on the floor in the living area. There were no prints or art works on the walls, which were painted beige, no doubt by the corporation that owned the building. The kitchen's vinyl floor had a floral pattern that repeated throughout. I did not see the bedroom, as we never walked in that direction.'

'How far from the living room was the junction in the hallway that led inside?' I asked.

'Roughly eighteen to twenty feet,' the detective answered. 'If you're asking about a gunshot from that spot into the living room, it would be a pivot to the left and not an easy shot, but hardly an impossible one. Whoever killed Detective Schaeffer knew how to use a firearm.'

'Like a police officer?' I asked.

Again, not so much as a twitch on Trench's face. 'Some would be able to make the shot. Others wouldn't. It would be enlightening, if there were an officer one suspected, to review the officer's scores at the department's shooting range. All members of the Los Angeles Police Department are required to stand for evaluations at the range periodically.'

I paused for dramatic effect, as one might in a courtroom. 'What are your marksmanship scores like, Lieutenant?'

'Given the standards set by the department, they are excellent.'

'So you would have had very little difficulty shooting Detective Schaeffer in the back of the head from that distance?' It was sort of a question.

'I believe I could have. If I had been there.'

Time to shift the conversation. 'Give me an evaluation of Anthony Basilico, the lead detective investigating your case,' I said.

I knew Trench didn't like to criticize other detectives in his division especially, and he didn't really enjoy praising anyone because he thought cops should just do their job. But he clearly understood the importance of the question.

'Detective Basilico is an efficient investigator, but not an inspired one,' he said. 'He won't overlook glaring details, but he probably will ignore some points that occasionally become crucial to the case.'

'OK. How would you expect that he would investigate this case?' Jon asked.

'He will do the typical things, like talk to people who know me because I have already been charged with the crime, and he will take the proper statistics and measurements of the crime scene.' Trench was discussing a case that could send him to jail for decades with the detachment of a man ordering at an Olive Garden. Maybe less engaged even than that. 'He has already been told that I am the guilty party based on the weapon used in the shooting. He likely will not vary from that theory unless something obvious comes to light.' We needed to provide the 'something obvious,' I guessed.

Something had been bothering me since the first conversation I'd had with Trench in the attorney conference room at the jail. 'Lieutenant, after all that time, why do you think you were assigned a case with Detective Schaeffer the week he was killed? Surely the captain knew about the history between you.'

K.C. Trench wouldn't ever suggest that the LAPD could be a corrupt or unworthy government body. He took a moment to compose his thoughts and said, 'I am not familiar with the captain's thought process in this case.'

'Speculate,' I suggested. 'There was a gap of some years between the time you and another member of your own section had worked together. It's not unreasonable to think that was a result of planning. Why after all that time would the policy change? You know the department, and particularly the homicide division, better than anyone. What caused you to be assigned to Schaeffer after all that time?'

Trench never betrayed much in the way of emotion, but this line of questioning was clearly making him uncomfortable. That was fine with me because we were not yet at trial and he wasn't testifying under oath, but I wanted him to be prepared if such questions came up once those things actually happened. He pulled in his lips very slightly and didn't so much bite down on them as he positioned them between his teeth, and then let go.

'I would have to assume Captain Moran had his reasons.' That was his way of telling me to back off, but I had no intention of doing so.

'All right, I'll get right to the point,' I said. 'Do you think the captain knew Schaeffer was going to get shot and wanted to set you up for the crime?'

Lt Trench did not flinch or even widen his eyes. He just stood up, walked out the door of the restaurant, and did his very best to blend into the Speedo-clad populace around him.

'You think we should take that for a no?' Jon said.

'Let's get Nate looking into Captain Moran,' I told Emma.

TWENTY

Marcia Kendall, who had been Marcia Sweeney, Marcia Schaeffer and Marcia Liebowitz before taking on this name, was an attractive woman in her fifties who had spent a good deal of time in the California sunshine and tried to disguise that fact with the help of some plastic surgeons. But she still had a welcoming smile and sat on the back porch of her Encino home offering iced tea from a pitcher on a table with an umbrella that was not opened. Marcia hadn't learned that much about the sun yet.

'Thank you,' I said, accepting the glass without actually intending to drink any of the iced tea inside. I shouldn't tell Patrick, but I'm not a fan of tea. He is from England. I'll say no more. 'I spoke to Nate Garrigan after he talked to you, and he said you might have had some ideas about people who could have held a grudge against your ex-husband.'

To her credit, Marcia did not ask which ex-husband I might have had in mind. 'I can only think of two or three people who *didn't* have a grudge against Wally, and they're all bad cops,' she said.

Judy, as always present and trying not to appear like she was, stood at one end of the porch and scanned the area continuously. Encino is an upscale area of Los Angeles, and while Marcia and her husband Dick (a film producer) were clearly not in need of a GoFundMe collection, they were hardly the most affluent people on the block. The house was lovely but not a mansion.

'When you say "bad cops," do you mean they were not good at their jobs, or corrupt in some way?' I asked. I probably already knew the answer, but you have to get the other person to say it out loud.

Marcia seemed amused by the whole scenario, or had spiked the iced tea, which I had not yet sampled. 'Both,' she said. 'I knew a few of the people he worked with, and they became cops for all the wrong reasons. They wanted to boss other people around and show off how macho they were, or how they could think of ways to make the job pay for them. Or both. Mostly both.'

I would ask for names later, but that probably wouldn't bring me any closer to getting Lt Trench exonerated. 'Of the others, the people who didn't like Detective Schaeffer, was there anyone in particular you thought might have been angry enough to shoot him?' I asked.

'Well, he got K.C. Trench's wife killed,' she answered, looking to see if I'd react. I used my best Trench impression and did not. 'But that was years ago. Trench could have offed Wally twenty times over since then, and he probably would have done it smarter than to use his own gun and just blast away.' She'd been reading the news reports about the case, or she knew someone who was investigating it.

'You think your ex really meant for Officer Wright to die that day?' That would have been an enormous lapse of judgment and would surely have put him before a conduct hearing and almost certainly under arrest.

Marcia had clearly been drinking something more than iced tea. Her eyes were at half-mast and, while her speech was not at all slurred, she was taking time to think about each word before she said it. I didn't mind, because people with a little alcohol – not a lot – in them might be more apt to tell you something you could actually use. Not in court, necessarily, but to chart a path.

'Oh, I dunno,' she said. 'If I know Wally, he'd probably hit on her and she turned him down so he was mad. Figured he'd show her the price of doing business with the great Wally Schaeffer.' She took another long sip. 'The sick part is, I'm actually a little sorry he's dead.'

When you're dealing with a person who's a little impaired, you have to work quickly because you won't get good information for long. 'Your ex called in sick before he was shot and wasn't heard from for two days. Did you hear from him on those days?'

She sat there and stared into the middle distance for what seemed like a full minute. I tried the iced tea. It was full of sugar and might very well have had some vodka in it. To each her own.

'We didn't talk much after the divorce,' Marcia said finally. 'I don't remember talking to Wally right before I heard he'd been shot. But if he took two days off, he was probably with the latest bimbo.'

I ignored the word and plowed straight ahead. 'Do you know who that might have been?'

She waved a hand like I was an annoying gnat. 'Nah. What difference does it make? Look for a blonde who can fill up a t-shirt and you'll find her sooner or later.'

The window of Marcia's coherence was closing so I threw in a Hail Mary question while I still had time. 'Marcia, the police report indicates there was no sign of forced entry at Detective Schaeffer's apartment. That means he let in the person who shot him. Who would he let into his apartment?'

'Besides the bimbo?'

What the hell. 'Yeah, besides the bimbo, Marcia.'

'Francie, maybe. He liked Francie. Or one of his cop buddies. Or his mom. Or somebody he knew from the academy. Or the bimbo.'

She was still adding possibilities when Judy and I left the porch and walked to my car.

While I was driving back to my office, Judy asked me if this kind of interview is often helpful in a case. 'One where someone is progressively drunk?' I said. 'Early on, but not once they cross the line. I hope Marcia's current husband, or one of her friends, or Francie, notices she has a problem and encourages her to get help.'

'This is an ongoing situation,' Judy said. 'You see the signs in my line of work. Her hands were shaking from the time we arrived. She didn't slur her speech, but she had to work not to do it. She knows she has a problem. Whether or not she understands how large a problem it is might not be answerable yet.'

'I tend to believe much of what she said,' I told her. The GPS was guiding me because I have given up my futile attempt to learn Los Angeles streets. They make no sense and there are too many of them. 'Am I wrong to do that?'

Judy is not comfortable with such talk. She knows we are client and bodyguard, not close friends. Any attempt to be more personal would probably interfere with her efficiency, which is Judy's worst nightmare. So she didn't answer me right away. 'I don't think it's my place to offer advice, ma'am.'

'I'm drawing on your experience,' I told her. 'I'm asking for your professional opinion. Normally I ask Lt Trench this kind of thing but we're in a weird place right now.'

She nodded; that made sense. Judy doesn't judge. Or if she does, she keeps quiet about it. 'I think she was being accurate when she said her ex-husband was probably with a woman on the days he called in sick,' she said. 'That's the kind of thing a bitter ex-wife might often say, but the incident report did note that the bed was unmade in the evening and that there was the lingering smell of either perfume or cologne in the air. Several long blond hairs were found in the apartment. If Detective Schaeffer was ill, it seems unlikely he would have called his mistress to his apartment.'

'So which parts do you disbelieve?' Because Judy had left the door wide open for that question.

'I think it unlikely the detective would have deliberately set up Lt Trench's wife to die,' she said. 'It would be far too easy to track it to him and he would have ended up in jail, or at the very least discharged from the department.'

'I think you're right, Judy,' I said.

'Thank you, ma'am.'

It was dodgy but I figured I might as well ask. 'Judy, do *you* think Lt Trench killed Wallace Schaeffer?'

'Not my place to offer an opinion.' Classic Judy.

'Maybe not, but you used to be a police officer. Would you have arrested him for the crime based on the evidence you have clearly researched?' The details about Schaeffer's apartment had given her away; Judy had been doing some studying.

She made a noise in the back of her throat because she didn't like to break protocol, but I'd asked her about her time on the LAPD and she was proud of that. 'No, ma'am. I don't think there was sufficient evidence for an arrest, even with the murder weapon in the lieutenant's possession.'

That was interesting. 'The gun wouldn't have been enough? Why not?'

Judy was watching the road. 'There is evidence that the weapon belongs to Lt Trench,' she said. 'There is also evidence the weapon was used to kill Detective Schaeffer. But from what I have read, there is no physical evidence that Lt Trench shot Detective Schaeffer, or even that he was present in the victim's apartment on the day he was killed.'

The analysis was so clear and logical that it left me stunned for a moment. It was even designed to help me in court.

'You're more than just a pretty face, Judy,' I said with something approaching awe.

'Thank you, ma'am.'

TWENTY-ONE

'We've been working on this case for three months and I don't like cops any better,' Emma told me.

We were walking around the block on which our office building stands because I had decided that we needed to be outdoors for a bit, even if outdoors consisted of other office buildings, some relatively greasy restaurants and cars, cars, cars. It helps me to clear my head sometimes. I'd brought Emma with me so I wouldn't look like someone having a conversation despite having no ear buds or mobile phone visible. Appearances matter in Los Angeles.

I felt like I'd hit a wall: For every opening I could see for Lt Trench's defense, the discovery materials given up by the DA's office had four ready rebuttals. We had never found the witness who could identify another possible killer. We had no lead on someone having stolen Trench's gun and then put it back, nor on how such a thing could have been accomplished under the vigilant lieutenant's very nose.

In short, what I had on my hands, with only some weeks before trial, was a losing case. At a time when my partnership was in process to be voted on by the firm (at some point), I was getting conscious of the cost of Trench's case, even though he didn't seem to worry about the expense. I'd even sent Judy home because there had been no further threats and she was an expense on the case budget.

'The idea was not to recruit you for the police academy,' I said to Emma. 'What I was hoping was that working with Lt Trench might just convince you that the people who take that job are human beings like us.'

Emma, who clearly thought the idea of walking without having a destination in mind was a sign of mental illness, gave me a side glance worthy of a Jersey girl. Emma had grown up in Colorado. 'He hasn't exactly been making me feel especially sympathetic,' she said.

Well, she had me there. The months of not being a working detective had worn on Trench. At first it was impossible to notice because the lieutenant expressed emotion at roughly the same level as the average houseplant. But as the weeks wore on and he had to refrain from investigating his own case, let alone anyone else's, the fraying around Trench's edges was starting to show. Once he'd walked out on us in Venice it had become obvious, on a Trench scale, that he was not handling his new life terribly well.

This past week he had shown up at a progress meeting without wearing a tie. I'd almost called 911. And he'd told Emma privately (she'd said) that it didn't matter if he was found not guilty because the people he worked with would never hold him in the same level of respect he had spent years trying to earn. If Trench had gone on a drunken binge, it wouldn't have been more surprising.

'It's because he's a good cop that he's suffering,' I said. 'He's being kept from following what he sees as his calling and it's making him act in ways I've never seen him act before.'

We turned the corner at exactly our halfway point (because I'd promised Emma we wouldn't 'circle the building like vultures over and over again') and she slowed down a little. Maybe Emma didn't want this conversation to end too quickly. Was there something she needed to get off her chest?

'Hang on a second,' she said, moving toward the building on our left. Then she bent down and retied her Nike. She straightened up. 'OK.' Perhaps her chest would remain as burdened as it had been before. 'Anyway, if you thought I was going to discover that K.C. Trench is anything but a tool of the patriarchy and an authoritarian, telling me he's suffering because he can't put people in jail isn't the best tactic.' Emma had no qualms about speaking truth to power. Her truth.

I probably sighed. It's mostly an involuntary impulse that I don't always notice but Emma looked at me with an expression that indicated she was concerned she'd gone too far. In my view she hadn't, so I said, 'Look. Some people do things that make it right for them to be imprisoned, and Lt Trench is one of the best at imprisoning them, it's true. But I've never once seen or heard from anyone else that he had arrested someone because of how they looked, their gender, their socioeconomic status or their political beliefs. He follows the law because the rules make sense to him. And now those rules are coming after him, and I'm not sure Trench knows how to handle that. I didn't expect you to become his best friend; I just wanted you to see him as a man.'

'I have some thoughts about men,' Emma said.

'Let's get back to the office.'

We were about fifty yards from the entrance to our building when I heard the first siren. That's not unusual in LA, so neither Emma nor I turned in the direction of the sound to take a look. But the next thing we saw consisted of three firetrucks converging on the building entrance and several very intense-looking firefighters heading inside very quickly.

'Omigod, look up,' I heard Emma say.

There was black smoke coming out of an upper-floor window. It wasn't exactly pouring out – there wasn't enough for that – but after some quick counting of windows from the ground floor up, I gasped.

'That's our office,' I said to no one in particular.

Almost before I could get the words out of my mouth, people from Seaton, Taylor began rushing out of the front entrance. I heard fire alarms from inside the building. No doubt the whole structure was being evacuated.

Holly Wentworth came striding through the door (Holly does not run if it will show fear) and walked directly to Emma and me. 'Thank goodness you two are here,' she said.

Two more firefighters from the third truck went inside. I was wondering why they were carrying axes into an office building, but hey, I didn't go to firefighter school. 'I take it there was a fire in the office,' I said to Holly.

'Not just in *the* office,' she answered. 'In *your* office.'

That took a moment to sink in. 'What?' That was the best I could do.

'Even before the smoke alarms went off, Janine noticed something in your office,' Holly said. Janine McKenzie is our receptionist and sits at a desk central to the floor. The walls of our offices are largely glass (although thankfully we have shades or blinds inside so we're not always on display), so Janine can see everything. Most things. She'd see a fire. 'She was calling 911 before anyone else even smelled smoke.'

I texted Angie to get Judy back on the job in a hurry and was confident she'd be back before I had a chance to think about what could have happened.

The crowd outside the main entrance was getting very large and very dense. Holly, Emma and I moved across the street, which was a little less crowded, while police officers cordoned off the area and the traffic stopped on our street. In LA, that's equivalent to there being no people. It was eerie.

The only activity around the entrance now (aside from the crowd, which was dispersing to every coffeeshop, smoothie store and salad vendor in the area) consisted of cops and firefighters entering and leaving the building. Some of the crowd had decided this was like a snow day and headed for their cars to go home. The smoke not-quite-billowing out of what clearly had been my office window had pretty much stopped by now. Mostly there was a lot of standing around.

One of the uniformed police officers was talking to people in the horde, and it became clear he was focusing on Seaton, Taylor employees, many of whom I recognized. A few of them spotted us across the street and started pointing in our direction. Snitchers. The cop walked in our direction just as Jon Irvin joined us on the corner, watching what had been a tense situation turn into an opportunity to wait for . . . something.

When the officer reached us, he looked at Jon, then Emma, then me, and focused on Holly. 'Are you Holiday Wentworth?' he asked. He must have gotten descriptions from the witnesses he'd talked to, or just decided that I didn't look like I should be in charge, an opinion I was starting to adopt myself.

Holly admitted to being herself and the cop, whose badge read *Rodriguez*, nodded in the direction of our office building. 'The fire's out,' he said. 'There really wasn't that much to it. You caught it pretty quickly.'

'Our receptionist did,' Holly corrected. She wanted Janine to get the credit.

'Sure,' Rodriguez said. I'm not sure he cared about handing out medals at that point. 'The thing is, we've been inside the office long enough to take a preliminary look, and there's reason to believe that this fire was not an accident.'

Whoa. 'That was my office,' I said to the cop. 'I wasn't there when the fire broke out. Are you saying someone set it on purpose?'

Rodriguez studied my face for a moment. 'It appears that way. They weren't even very concerned with covering their tracks. If you weren't there when it started, it would be really interesting to find out who was in your office *before* that fire started.'

My first thought was: It was probably a cop who didn't like what

I was doing for Lt Trench. But if that were the case, that meant they thought the defense team was getting too close to a surefire acquittal for the lieutenant.

What was I doing right?

Then I noticed that one of the cops walking out of the building, looking less intensely concerned than the others, was Clifton Armstrong. The guy who broke my taillight.

I started to look around for Judy.

TWENTY-TWO

Our offices were going to be undergoing repairs for a couple of days – mostly to get the smell of smoke out, and also to put my little office back together (which apparently was going to take longer) – but luckily our technological society has made the law less paper-reliant and almost everybody could work from home. I had convened a meeting of the Trench defense team in my home while Patrick was off shooting the last episode of *Torn* for the season. Emma was sitting on the floor with an iPad taking notes and accessing files while Jon and I used the easy chair and the loveseat, respectively, to spread out laptops and get to the case.

'The fire has to mean that somebody thinks we're doing something that could help get the lieutenant acquitted and spoil whatever plans they had,' I suggested. 'But I don't see that we're even going into court with a decent amount of confidence. What am I missing?'

Jon had heard me ask this before and had clearly been thinking about it since yesterday. 'It's got to be the gun,' he said. 'The prosecution is centering their whole case around the weapon that was used to kill Schaeffer and using the fact that it was Lt Trench's gun to make it seem that there's no other conclusion to be drawn. We can show that to be circumstantial and force them to find any other evidence that Trench shot Schaeffer.'

'That's all true,' I answered. 'But you and I both know that the thing about circumstantial evidence, no matter how clearly we point out that it proves nothing . . .'

'It works,' Jon and I said together.

'Exactly. Judges can tell juries to disregard things all day long, but they heard it and it's going to get into their minds,' I said. 'Tell them it's circumstantial evidence and their heads will tell them, "Yeah, but those are the circumstances." It's hard to combat.'

'Besides,' Emma said from the floor, 'that doesn't give us any tools we don't already have, and you think we don't have enough. So, what else is there to look for?'

I'd been wracking my brain on that one for so long now that I couldn't find any new trains of thought to buy a ticket on. I decided, as I do when I'm feeling inadequate, to make someone else do the work. 'Well, let me ask you this, Emma,' I said. 'You don't like the police and you don't like Lt Trench. So tell me, if you were on the jury, what would convince you that he didn't kill Detective Schaeffer?'

There had been a little stuffed bear on the bookshelf in my office. It was wearing a t-shirt whose legend read 'LAWYER.' My father had bought it for me and sent it on the occasion of my law school graduation. I hoped it hadn't burned up.

Emma, meanwhile, was thinking hard about the question I'd asked her. She was a very intelligent young woman and wanted to make a good impression, despite already having done so months earlier. She also wanted me to agree with her about Trench, and that wasn't going to happen.

'I think I'd need to know more about the lieutenant's wife,' she said finally. 'Maybe knowing someone who loved him would make me think about him differently.'

It wasn't a bad idea, but it was one I couldn't use. 'We run into the same old problem,' I said. 'If we concentrate on reasons the lieutenant *could* have shot Schaeffer, we give up the idea that he *didn't*. And he didn't.'

Out of the corner of my eye I saw Judy fiddling with something on her phone. She didn't look alarmed, but then Judy wouldn't look alarmed if this building too was suddenly on fire. She just did what she did and then put the phone back on her belt.

'Are we certain of that?' Jon asked.

What? 'You're asking if we're sure that our client didn't randomly kill another detective one night?' I looked at Jon for some reassurance. 'Whose side are you on?'

'I'm on the lieutenant's legal team,' he answered. 'Since everyone is entitled to a rigorous defense, I am rigorously defending him. And if you asked me directly whether I think that he shot Detective Schaeffer, my answer would be no. But do I know for a fact that he didn't? No, I don't. I'm not seeing conclusive evidence either way.' Jon is a lawyer much in the same way that Bugs Bunny is a cartoon. Like, all the time.

I shook my head in something approaching disbelief. Jon was a very good lawyer and, if I were to ask his wife, I'm sure she'd say he had many other facets to his personality, but he didn't let emotions get in the way of his interpretation of the law. 'Jon, I honestly believe that if Lt Trench had really shot Schaeffer that night, he would have a level of integrity so high he would look us in the eye and tell us he did it.'

I heard the front door close and turned to look, but before I could swivel that far round, I heard Lt Trench say, 'Oh, I'm not certain I would do that.'

At that point I realized I should have noticed the nod exchanged between Trench and Judy as he walked in. She'd opened the security gate for him remotely because he was Lt Trench. I stood up and headed toward him. 'Lieutenant,' I said. 'What brings you here today?'

Another man might have said, 'My car,' but Trench was Trench. 'I received a text message from you saying there were things to discuss. Was that sent in error?'

I could feel my eyes narrow. 'It must have been, because I didn't send it,' I said. 'But we are plotting strategy for your case, so why don't you take a seat?'

Trench didn't move. 'I think it's significant that I received a message you didn't send, Ms Moss. How is that possible?'

He knew perfectly well how such a thing was possible, certainly better than I would have known. My best bet was he had gotten no such text. 'May I see it?' I asked.

'The text message?' Was Trench being coy? Was that even possible?

'Yes, please.'

Unlike most humans, Trench did not then reach into his pocket to produce his mobile phone. 'I deleted it,' he said. 'I delete all text messages as soon as I read them. It saves space on my phone and leaves less to be discovered if something happens to me.' Now that was a side of our good lieutenant I hadn't seen before: The morbid cop.

'Why wouldn't you want there to be as much as possible for people to follow if something were to happen to you?' Jon, having found someone who spoke his language, was intrigued.

'I always assume the wrong person will find my phone first,' Trench said. Wow, that *was* morbid.

I decided to set an example and go back to my perch on the loveseat. Trench walked deeper into the room but remained on his feet. It seemed to be a point of honor for him not to relax in any way possible.

'Lieutenant,' I began.

'That is still technically my title, although I am not an active member of the Los Angeles Police Department.' Yeah, no kidding.

'We've looked over the video records of the supermarket you said you stopped at on the way home the night Detective Schaeffer was shot,' I told him. 'It would take much better technology than we have at our disposal to be certain, but we did not see anyone who resembled you at the time in question.'

'That is unfortunate,' Trench allowed.

'It's more than that,' Jon told him. 'If we can't establish that you weren't in the area when Schaeffer – sorry, Detective Schaeffer – was shot, we have to somehow prove that someone stole your gun and then replaced it without a trace of physical evidence that such a story is plausible.'

Trench's eyes lit up for a nanosecond, and it wasn't because he was angry at what Jon had said.

'What?' I asked the lieutenant.

'I'm sorry?' He was going to play it coy.

'You just flashed on something. I'd like to know what it is, if it pertains to our case.'

Trench is a difficult man to read. His face shows virtually nothing and his manner is as consistent as any AI chatbot you've ever met. 'You have been very clear that you do not want me to act as an investigator on the case, and as an attorney, I understand why you have said that. I have no intention of betraying that trust,' he said. I have a mother who majored in passive-aggressive at college, and she couldn't have done better than that.

I let myself breathe a moment. 'Lieutenant,' I said. 'You are probably the best investigator I have ever met. It's not that I don't want your expertise. It's that I don't want you interviewing witnesses or showing up at the crime scene to evaluate. If you have observations on the case that can be helpful, or analysis that will point us in a good direction, I'd very much like to hear them from you. Please.'

Trench, who clearly had expected a response very much like that one, nodded. 'Physical evidence,' he said. 'That was the key.'

Jon, Emma and I traded puzzled glances. I knew Trench would make it coherent, but I didn't see how. 'The key to what?' I asked.

'Your defense,' the cop said, as if that explained it. He waited a moment, saw his 'analysis' had not landed, and went on. 'The physical evidence all points to the idea that I shot Detective Schaeffer. Since I know that I did nothing of the sort, the motivation for the killer or killers to create that evidence has to be something other than Detective Schaeffer's death.'

Sometimes I need a Trench-to-English dictionary because Duolingo doesn't offer Trench in its list of languages to learn. But then what he said clicked in; sometimes it just takes a moment of analysis, something I would need plenty of when this case was over. 'So the real goal in this killing was getting you arrested for Schaeffer's murder,' I said, ostensibly to Trench but really to myself.

'That's right. Someone hated Detective Schaeffer enough to shoot him, but they hated the lieutenant even more,' Jon said, his voice betraying a certain amount of admiration for the people who killed Schaeffer.

Trench didn't flinch. 'So it would seem,' he said.

'So, what would your advice be, as an investigator?' I asked the lieutenant.

'I think the first thing you need to do is ask me who hates me that much,' he said. 'And the short answer is, I don't know.'

'That's not very encouraging.'

Trench got a certain gleam in his eye that I'd seen before when a case was coming together in his mind. 'So I understand there is an arson to investigate,' he said. 'That might be a place to begin.'

TWENTY-THREE

'I'm not going to be partnering with Trench on this case, or any other case,' Nate Garrigan said. 'But especially not this one.'

I had to go to my office to pick up some files (OK, really to check on the stuffed bear) and was talking to Nate via Bluetooth in my car. As I had very much expected, he was not tickled to death about Lt Trench making a few 'very subtle' inquiries into the fire in my office. Trench, of course, was not doing *anything* in an official capacity, but was monitoring all the incident reports on the fire and making a few phone calls to the few cops he felt he could still trust.

'Nobody's making you partner with *anybody*,' I told Nate, who could be as jealous as an eighth-grade boy whose best friend just asked the girl he had his eye on to the dance. 'The lieutenant will make a few inquiries and then report anything he finds out to me. You're my first phone call when that happens. He's not going anywhere or talking to anyone that could get in your way.'

I pulled up to the building and was a little surprised at how normal it looked only a day after we'd been forced to evacuate. (OK, *they'd* been forced to evacuate and I wasn't able to get back inside for my extra shoes or my stuffed bear.) There was no sign of a police presence or yellow incident tape anywhere at the entrance to the building. People were coming and going as if nothing had ever happened because, in truth, for most of them that was exactly the case.

'I don't like it,' Nate grumbled.

'Yeah, I think you've made that clear. Listen, I'm going into the garage so I'm going to lose you. I'll call you later.'

'That's what they all say.'

I (wisely, I think) chose not to reply and disconnected the call as I drove into the parking garage underneath our building. Judy, who had been sitting in the passenger seat and remaining silent the whole time, was watching for anyone in the garage who might feel it necessary to kill me. Luckily, she did not appear to be finding anyone of the sort right now.

The car got parked in a reasonably convenient space, not terribly far from the elevator. I made a mental note to ask Holly if a partnership would get me a better parking spot.

Judy got out first, as she had instructed, because she wanted to have a vantage point in all directions around the car before the target (that was me) was in clear view. It wasn't a terribly comforting thought, except that she was Judy. She did her scan of the area and gestured to me that I could exit my own Hyundai. Somehow it felt like a victory.

'Let's get you up to your office, ma'am,' she said. That's as loquacious as Judy gets.

We took the freight elevator on Judy's suggestion and were up on my floor in very little time and with absolutely no other people in the car. This was the way to travel.

The office was down a corridor from the freight elevator and I found myself feeling anxious as we walked. I knew the fire had not done a large amount of damage, but it was the sense of having my privacy violated, that whoever had set this fire had been in my office and had access to everything there, that made my stomach queasy.

Sure enough, when we turned the corner and saw the entrance to Seaton, Taylor, I felt a little nauseated. There was still a slight smell of smoke in the air. The front doors to the office bore traces of police tape. No one was inside, which surprised me in a way. I knew the damage was confined to my office. I figured some of my colleagues would have snuck in when no one was watching. But they had not. Everyone was playing by the rules, or enjoying working from a remote location.

I clenched my jaw a bit and walked to the door, Judy immediately behind me. I reached for the door handle. It was locked.

My only reaction was to stand there and pull again and again, but the door wasn't going to open. Maybe when I became a partner, I'd have a key to the office. But this was just making me want to cry.

'Excuse me, ma'am.' Judy gestured for me to step aside, so I did. She reached into her belt, where she found a ring of key cards. She sorted through them, selected one, and then reached over and tapped it on the sensor between the two doors. There was a click. We were in.

'How did you do that?' I was stunned. Judy could do anything.

'You just have to tap it on the sensor,' she said. She opened the door for me and we walked into the office.

'No. Why do you have a key card to my office when I don't even have one?'

'Your firm is paying my employer,' Judy said. 'They provide access so I can do my job.' Now I had to decide whether I wanted a partnership in a prestigious Los Angeles law firm or to become a bodyguard. The perks seemed about the same. Especially if I didn't get a parking space.

'You're amazing, Judy,' I said.

'Um . . . thank you, ma'am.' Judy clearly didn't think she was all that amazing.

I turned the lights on in the office – I could do *that* at least – and we walked down the hall and to the left to get to the hub of my division, and the home of the criminal justice division, which was basically my office and Jon's. Each step felt a little scarier.

The first glimpse of my office didn't make me feel any better. The glass door had been smashed to bits, probably because I'd locked it before Emma and I went out for a stroll and the firefighters had needed to get in fast. Made me wonder how the arsonist(s) had managed access. It was among the many things I was wondering.

But even with the light in the office turned off, I could still see there had been a lot of disruption in my private space. Shelves had been emptied or knocked over. My coatrack, which luckily did not have my good jacket on it because I'd worn it to go outside, was lying across the small sofa for clients. My Rutgers University Law School sweatshirt, which had been hanging on the coatrack, was not visible. I didn't want to walk closer because that meant I would be able to see more.

'Do you want to go inside, ma'am?' Judy asked.

Even though she probably already knew, I couldn't let Judy think I was an emotional wreck and a coward. 'Yeah,' I said, with a little bit more vibrato than I'd been planning on. I walked over to the door.

The glass had been cleared, although there were still a few shards on the carpet. The maintenance crew and contractors we'd been told were hard at work restoring our place of work were nowhere to be seen. Maybe eleven in the morning was their lunch break.

Even with the door essentially missing, I still pulled on the handle and opened it to walk in. That, too, was locked, and I used my own key card to open it. Judy did not point out that we could have just walked through the empty opening.

My breath caught when I hit the light switch and saw what had been done. The fire had obviously been started in one of my filing cabinets, which had been left open so it would spread. There was still a whiff of some oil-based accelerant (gasoline?) in the room. Trench had been right; these people weren't subtle about it being an arson. They wanted me to know they'd done it to me.

Clearly I was the target, but the files they'd used to start the fire (slowly so no one would notice right away?) had not been related to Trench or his case, which was just as well. All that stuff was in the firm's computers and would be retrievable no matter what had happened in my tiny office. So, this fire had strictly been a statement: Mess with us and this is a taste of what we'll do.

But my immediate destination was the far bookshelf, from which my LAWYER stuffed bear had been dangling. The fact was that I barely looked at the bear (which I had not named because I was an adult) very often at all. It had become one of those objects that's simply there all the time, so it requires no direct attention. Now it had become the center of my focus.

And the result was heartbreaking for reasons I couldn't begin to understand: The bear was on the soot-stained rug in front of the bookshelf. At least, what was left of it was there. The head was completely gone and singed; stuffing was erupting from the neck. The shirt with the LAWYER legend was there, but only the W and the Y were intact; everything else had been burned off or blackened to the point of illegibility.

The feet were gone and the legs, which had been dangly and adorable, were irreparably torn and burned.

I sat down on the filthy floor because my desk chair was only partially there. And because I completely didn't care. I started, against my own resolve, to sob. It took a long time before I even considered the fact that Judy, standing inside the doorway, was watching me dissolve into tears and soot over a burned teddy bear. But I knew I would call my father tonight and cry.

'I'm sorry,' I said to Judy when I could speak.

'No need, ma'am.' I could have taken off my clothes, rolled in the soot, swung from the ceiling light fixture, licked my desk chair and then done the splits on my desk and Judy would not have found a reason to feel offended. Or, at the very least, she would never have let me know she felt offended.

She reached a hand down and helped me up off the floor, which

was the closest to a friendly moment the two of us had ever had. I
was trying my best to get back into a professional demeanor, so I
asked Judy, 'From a security standpoint, what does this room tell
you right now?'

'Someone wanted to send you a warning,' she said.

'I figured that part out on my own.'

Judy looked around the room in a slow pan. 'My training is to
prevent scenes like this,' she said. 'Lt Trench is more qualified to
assess the crime scene.'

'I'm sure he's doing that online as we speak,' I assured her. 'But
you were also a police officer and you were in the military. You
have a great deal of training and experience and I think you're just
holding back on me because you just saw me cry. Don't let that
prejudice you.'

Judy stopped her scanning around the room to make eye contact
with me. 'I would never do that, ma'am.' Good. I'd snapped her
back to normal, too.

'So what do you see in this room? And please tell me now, so
we can leave it as soon as possible.' I reached over and picked up
the remains of the stuffed bear. I put it into the tote bag I carry with
me when I've decided to go without a purse. The tote bag, after all,
was canvas and therefore washable.

'The indication is that the person or people – and I think it was
one person based on the size of the room and its proximity to the
receptionist area, which means the arsonist would be more likely
to elude notice if there were just one – were concentrating mostly
on being out of the room when the fire started. There is some
evidence that the police removed an electronic ignition that they
had likely placed in the file cabinet, possibly on a timer or activated
from a remote location.'

'So they didn't want to get burned up. That's not a huge surprise,'
I said. 'Sorry. I didn't mean to make it sound like you were disappointing me, because you're not, Judy.'

Judy's eyes, which were looking at the file cabinet and not me,
indicated that she had not interpreted my comment that way. 'I think
you're missing the point, ma'am. The person who started this fire
was not very concerned with being injured when it started. The key
was not to be detected. They knew it was never going to be a big
fire. Your building includes a fire alarm and sprinkler system, so it
would not burn long. Not enough accelerant was used to spread the

flames outside your contained office. This was a very carefully set fire whose purpose was to frighten you specifically and not to do major damage.'

I looked over the remains of the place that was my business home. 'Well, if they wanted to scare me, they did a very professional job,' I said.

'Yes, they did,' Judy agreed.

I picked up the tote bag with the charred remains of my stuffed graduation bear. 'Let's get out of here, Judy,' I said. 'I think I need to go home, shower, change clothes, maybe shower again, and then begin to wage war on the person who burned up my bear.'

'Yes, ma'am,' Judy said.

TWENTY-FOUR

'I like to begin with a list of suspects,' Lt Trench said.

My office was the only one in the Seaton, Taylor building that was still under renovation, since it had been the only one seriously damaged. There were a few water problems elsewhere because the sprinkler system had indeed activated three weeks earlier when the fire started. So, with Holly's approval, I had commandeered an office on the fifteenth floor that had previously been occupied by people in our human resources department. They had been relocated two months ago to another building entirely, which seemed to go against the function of human resources. When I became a partner, I'd ask about that.

I had been careful not to personalize this room, which was big enough for a desk and three chairs and that was about it, at all. I didn't want to form attachments. And I wanted to be back in my real office ASAP.

As it was, Trench, Emma, Nate and I (Jon had to work on another case) were squeezed into this broom closet with a desk about two-thirds the size of my actual desk and a coatrack, which we didn't need because we were in Los Angeles and it wasn't raining. Judy had agreed to stand guard outside the door because it just wasn't possible anyone else could get inside to threaten me. Once Nate had closed the door behind him, we could more or less breathe comfortably. More or less.

Trench had walked in apparently believing he had been asked to present a seminar in crime detection. It was a wonder he hadn't brought a PowerPoint presentation and a laser pointer. But he did have a large piece of legal paper from a pad I'd given him, and he'd written on it – in perfect characters, legible from San Francisco, a place I had yet to visit – the names of the people he considered suspects in Wallace Schaeffer's murder.

Yes, it had come to this. Lawyers should *never* rely on finding the real killers. Here we were trying to find the real killers. I'd barely been able to eat this week. But I had managed.

'How did you compile this list, Lieutenant?' Nate asked. He was, being Nate (and somewhat understandably), a little rankled at me allowing another party, even Trench, to steal his thunder in a case that we had contracted him to investigate. But he was a professional and he knew that Trench could be seen as a colleague. I'm sure Nate would have preferred the word 'asset.'

'This is a preliminary list, Mr Garrigan.' Trench was probably more engaged today than he'd been since the night he was arrested. I'm sure he felt that he was back in the game, doing what he did best and helping us achieve the common goal. The fact that the goal was to keep him out of jail for many years probably was a motivator as well. 'The idea is to include every possible name and then we as a group can discuss them, you can help with the information you have compiled, and we can decide who the best possible candidates might be.' He might as well have been discussing a group of college graduates competing for a summer internship.

I felt we needed to push this along. There was a window in the room, but it was small and offered an unparalleled view of a parking lot across the street. 'What names are on the list?' I asked Trench.

'First, I have included Detective Schaeffer's ex-wife, Marcia Kendall. She undoubtedly had some anger with her ex-husband and could have killed him as an act of revenge for the numerous extramarital affairs he had while they were married.'

Nate and I were both shaking our heads. 'They've been divorced for years,' Nate said. 'She's been married twice since then. Why kill him suddenly after all that? Besides, there is no evidence at all that she was even in town the night Schaeffer was shot.'

Trench showed us his palms as a way to calm the masses. 'I am not suggesting that all of these people are equally likely suspects. I believe we should consider all the possibilities and then narrow our focus.'

Properly chastised, Nate folded his arms across his chest and I leaned my elbows on the 'desk' I'd been given. Immediately after this conference I was going upstairs to stare at the men renovating my office and look impatient. It's a motivator.

'Another possibility is the detective's daughter, Francine,' Trench went on. We didn't protest that she was an unlikely suspect because we knew we'd get the same speech. 'Her relationship with her father was strained, certainly, and recently she had discovered that he had stopped paying child support years before she reached the age of majority.'

'What about one of the cops he was giving bad loans?' Nate asked.

Trench didn't like being asked to change his presentation, but he let it go. 'I know there were three who owed him more than twenty thousand dollars,' he said. 'I spoke to an attorney who is representing one of them in another matter.'

For the first time I felt it was necessary to admonish my client. 'You shouldn't be talking to anyone involved in this case,' I told Trench.

'I spoke to the attorney before the shooting,' he said. 'It wasn't the most professional action I've ever taken, but I was asked by a task force of the Los Angeles Police Department to look into officers they believed had unauthorized and possibly illegal streams of income. Detective Schaeffer was one of them, which was probably the reason I was assigned with him on the Joanna Barnes case, a crime even he could easily have solved himself. They wanted me to observe him and a few other officers. He was the only one I was able to see before the shooting.'

My jaw must have been scraping the surface of the desk. 'Why didn't you mention this before?' I sort of demanded.

'It was part of a confidential operation.' Trench seemed surprised I would ask the question. 'It has been reassigned to other detectives and I am no longer a factor in that investigation, even to the point that I do not receive emails or text messages on the subject.' He would never let the regret inherent in that sentence find its way into his voice.

'You think that Schaeffer got your wife killed.' Emma was being her usual tactful self, but Trench didn't so much as blink. His people don't do that. I'm not sure they have eyelids. 'Did you mention that when you were asked to spy on him?' Emma hated cops so much that she resented it even when they were investigating other cops.

'That would have been unprofessional,' Trench said. 'I did not have verifiable evidence I could present, or I would have put in the paperwork to arrest Detective Schaeffer long ago.' He gestured with the legal pad. 'There are other names on the list. For example, there is Louisa Lombardo.'

That was a new name to me, but apparently not to Nate. 'The woman who was with Schaeffer the day he died,' he said.

'Correct, Mr Garrigan. Very good work.' Trench thought he was holding a training session for new detectives. Nate didn't scowl. Point for Nate.

'How did either one of you get her name, and why haven't we spoken to her yet?' I asked. It was getting a little close in here and I was approaching testy at a rapid pace.

Nate cleared his throat to claim the floor. 'Schaeffer didn't exactly live in the most exclusive building in Beverly Hills, but the place he had in town required a sign-in for guests, and Louisa didn't mind signing her real name. It wasn't that hard.'

Trench nodded, but he was not to be denied. 'She was also fairly well known in the detective division. I had heard her name more than once, but had not connected her to Detective Schaeffer until another officer mentioned it.'

'Lieutenant,' I said.

'I am not conducting an outside investigation, Ms Moss. I do talk to some of my former, and hopefully future, colleagues on occasion. And no, I will not divulge the name of my source as I have promised not to do so. It was a private conversation.' Well, that was convenient. I was glad Nate had verified Trench's discovery.

But now getting these people to leave before I dissolved into a pool of sweat was my top priority. 'Are there any other notable suspects on your list, Lieutenant?' I was sure he had dozens more, but I was asking for the TikTok version. Quick and hopefully with dance moves.

Trench looked like I'd asked if he could condense his mother down to just a head and a chicken soup recipe. 'I believe we should definitely look into possible gambling debts and other women the detective might have snubbed,' he said in that emotionless teacher voice.

'Is that what we're calling it now?' Emma muttered.

'How about the cops who have been following you and Sandy?' Nate asked. 'What about the superiors who put you on to him and set you in a position to be arrested for his murder?'

Trench actually blinked. Twice. 'Those are members of the Los Angeles Police Department,' he said.

'All right, we'll leave those to you, Nate.' I looked at the door in case anyone needed a hint.

But Nate was staring at Trench. 'Maybe you and I can have a separate conversation, Lieutenant.'

'If we must.'

'We must.'

Nate stood and opened the door, which allowed some welcome,

if not fresh, air into the room. But he didn't walk out. Emma did, no doubt happy to get back to the paralegal office downstairs, where they had perks like ventilation and windows. Trench packed his legal pad into a briefcase, said his goodbyes and left. For some reason Nate was hanging back, so I waited until the others were out of earshot.

'OK, what?' I said.

'You need to requisition a couple of airline tickets and hotel rooms,' Nate said. I always love it when he tells me what I need to do.

'No kidding. Where are you and your guest going?'

'You mean where are *we* going, and the answer is Ann Arbor, Michigan. We need to go visit with Lt Trench's in-laws.'

TWENTY-FIVE

'Where is Ann Arbor, Michigan?' Patrick asked. 'For that matter, where is Michigan? Is that a state?'

I would like it understood at this point that if I were to go to England with Patrick, which I sincerely hope to do, I would not know the difference between a township, a county, a district and a province. I'm not even sure if those are the right words. So I did not consider his question an especially uninformed one. For Patrick I have a much more forgiving attitude.

'Yes, Michigan is a state. It's in the middle of the country toward the Canadian border,' I said. 'It gets cold there. I'll be flying into Detroit.' Patrick didn't react; he probably wasn't aware of Detroit, either. Most of his time in the US had been concentrated in California and New York.

I wasn't quite at the point of packing a bag yet, but I would be in the morning. Holly had once again been generous with the budget for the trial, which I guessed she had cleared with our client. Where Trench was getting the money for all this – because Seaton, Taylor is not cheap – was a mystery to me, but luckily one I did not have to solve. 'Why can't this be done on the phone or on Zoom?' Patrick asked.

It was at least one very good question. 'It's taken Nate three months to convince the family to talk to us,' I said. 'He doesn't know if they're protecting Trench or if they can't stand him. He says the only way to find out is to talk to them face to face.'

'So why are you going?' Patrick doesn't like it when we're not together. We had a period where he was working in New York and I was here in LA, and neither of us had enjoyed the experience much.

'Nate thinks they'll respond better to a woman than a guy who talks like a 1940s noir movie,' I said.

Patrick has an actual vinyl-record stereo console in our den. I think the cabinet is one of his movie souvenirs, perhaps from a 1960s sex comedy or something. It didn't have the actual workings in it when he bought the item, so he had an up-to-the-minute record player built in with state-of-the-art speakers. He walked over and put on an album of Harry Nilsson singing standards from what they call the Great American Songbook, which no one has ever seen in print. The music seemed appropriate to the moment and the instrument on which it was being played. Judy, who after all had to sleep sometimes, was at her home, and her relief, a somewhat less vigilant version named Dolores, was in the spare bedroom nearby but out of sight and earshot.

Patrick walked back over and sat next to me in a separate comfortable chair that did not recline. This was, I thought, what we would look like watching television when we reached our seventies. 'It's just a couple of days,' I told him.

'I know. It's not unreasonable.' Patrick would go off on movie shoots during his television hiatuses (virtually every spring and part of summer) and he didn't like it, but he understood that it was necessary. He knew my work mattered too, but it was more troubling to him when I went away because that's how humans are. 'I will miss you, of course. But there's one thing I need to tell you before you leave.'

Uh-oh. This was taking an unexpected turn. Had he finally tired of me, like I'd anticipated? Had I been right to turn down all those marriage proposals because I knew he preferred the pursuit to the capture? In short, was this it for us?

I leaned forward involuntarily. 'What's wrong?' I asked.

Patrick put up his hands and shook his head negatively. 'Nothing. Nothing at all. But now that we've finished shooting, I wanted you to know that this was the last season of *Torn*. We're not coming back in the fall.'

Well, that was the opposite of anything I might have expected. 'Oh, Patrick!' I said. I knew how he'd invested his time and money into that show, and how lately it had been disappointing him. 'I'm so sorry.'

He grinned. 'I'm not,' he said. 'The show hasn't been good for at least a year and my name is on it as an executive producer. It's not what I want to be doing. I think we're leaving it in a good place. But it does mean that I won't have a steady job for a while.'

I looked around, probably involuntarily, at the house we'd just bought. And when I say 'we,' I mean that I threw in a little money as a token and Patrick paid the rest. Not to mention the huge loan he was giving me to pay for my partnership in the firm. 'I hate to be crass, but . . .'

Patrick laced his fingers behind his head. 'We can afford it, love,' he said. 'Don't you worry.' If he'd told me not to worry my 'pretty little head,' I would have had to reconsider my relationship with him. 'You know Josh the Agent will have something else for me soon. I won't be idle for very long. And besides, my new producing partner already has a number of projects in the works that should bring in a considerable amount of income for Dunwoody Productions.'

His new producing . . . 'Angie?' I said in a small voice.

Patrick's grin was almost at the limit of smug acceptability, but not quite. 'She's on her way here now to celebrate,' he said.

I had to get ready for an early flight and Angie was coming? Not the best combination ever, but I couldn't step on Patrick's happiness for . . . being out of work? 'I might not sleep at all tonight,' I said before I realized I was talking.

Immediately he looked concerned and reached for his phone. 'You're right. I should cancel.'

I put my hand on his hand holding the phone. 'It's OK. She's Angie.'

She arrived perhaps fifteen minutes later. I gathered this was one of Patrick's surprises that I should have seen coming, but I didn't know he was thinking of ending his own TV show. Angie burst into the house the way she bursts into everywhere, this time carrying two bottles of champagne (for three people?). 'Sand! Ain't it great?' Other people say, 'Hello.' My best friend is not other people.

'If you and Patrick say it is,' I said. I reached into a cabinet for our ice bucket, which as it turned out was in an armoire in the living room. The place was big, compared to everywhere I'd ever lived before. We managed to get ice into the bucket and the bottles of wine into the ice. 'What are you planning for Patrick to star in?' I asked Angie.

She was uncorking the first bottle, something Angie can do expertly but prefers to do with a satisfying gush of foam from the neck of the bottle. Patrick stood back because it always looks like Angie is going to shake the bottle up and spray us all with champagne as if we'd just won the World Series, something she also probably thinks we can do.

'It's not that simple,' Angie said. 'I don't just look for projects for Patrick to act in. I look for projects that Dunwoody Productions might want to produce, then make truckloads of money and win Academy Awards.'

She was pouring the champagne into flutes that she knew were in a kitchen cabinet (and I didn't) when Patrick, with a self-conscious chuckle, said, 'Let's not get too far ahead of ourselves, Angie. I'll take something we can produce that will make its investment back.'

Angie, pouring me a glass, shook her head. 'Don't think small, Patrick. We are gonna do both.'

The champagne was very good, as far as I could tell (I am an ignorant wine consumer) and I had eaten well enough this evening that I wasn't afraid one or two glasses would be a problem. 'What's your favorite that you haven't told Patrick about yet?' I asked Angie, because I knew there would be one.

'A western comedy.' She would never pretend she hadn't been holding something back. She wanted to add that level of mystery to it. 'It's about a posse after a bank robber but the sheriff, who's leading the posse, knows the bank robber is his ex-wife.'

'Sounds hilarious,' I told her. She heard my tone.

'You haven't read the script. *Blazing Saddles* doesn't sound funny if you just give the tagline.' Tagline. That's what my best pal from high school was saying now. Tagline. Luckily she still dressed like she was going out to a dive bar later to see who'd have the nerve to try and pick her up.

'I'll read it,' Patrick said. 'But I make no promises, Angela.'

Angie smiled. She knew he was already sold. So she turned to me. 'I hear you're going away.'

Wow. Had Patrick been that melodramatic? 'Just for a couple of days,' I said. 'I'm going to Michigan to work on the case.'

'Yeah, that's what I heard,' Angie said. Like she might have heard it from anyone besides Patrick. 'What's in Michigan?'

'Lt Trench's in-laws.'

Angie, who had been kept pretty much up to date on the case because she's always around and I like to get her perspective, looked like I'd told her I was going to interview a family of walruses. 'The lieutenant's married?' she said. She was being a wiseass. Sometimes it's hard to tell in print.

'All right. His *former* in-laws. You happy? The parents of his late wife.'

Angie nodded. 'That's going to be a scene and a half,' she said. 'Can you imagine the parents of someone Trench might marry?'

I looked around the room in the house I was starting to feel was home. The cushions on my chair were soft and inviting. My boyfriend and my best friend were sitting here having a glass of champagne with me. There was music playing on the stereo. If there had been a raging fire in a fireplace, it would have been perfect, but it was seventy-five degrees outside and that would have been, at best, superfluous. Why was I getting up early to fly to Detroit, again?

'When I meet them, I'll be able to imagine it,' I told Angie.

TWENTY-SIX

'It's not Casey's fault.'

Bob Wright, the late Susan Wright's father, was a large man without being extremely anything physically. He was not obese, and he was not thin. He was not immensely tall, and he was not short. He was not muscular like a bodybuilder nor flabby like someone who hadn't exercised since he was forty. He was a man in his late sixties or early seventies, cleanshaven, with clear blue eyes and most of the hair he'd had in his youth. His tone wasn't rueful or angry; he had become used to the idea that his daughter was dead, and while the sadness was present in the room, Bob did not wear it around his neck to weigh him down.

And he insisted on calling Lt Trench 'Casey.' I guessed the idea of initials as a name had never really appealed to him much. He had made an adjustment.

Nate and I were sitting at a dining-room table, not made up for a meal, with Bob and his wife Kathryn, a woman around the same age as Bob, who appeared uncomfortable with the conversation, which was understandable. Bob wasn't so much comfortable with it as he was resigned to it and determined to be straightforward and honest.

'Why would you blame your son-in-law?' Nate asked. 'He wasn't involved in the incident when your daughter was killed.' Nate is the very model of tact, but even Kathryn didn't flinch at the word 'killed.'

'I just said I *don't* blame Casey,' Bob corrected. 'He wasn't even there. But I do think he could have kept Suzy away from that Schaeffer guy, and that was the problem, wasn't it?'

'I'm sure you heard that Detective Schaeffer was shot and killed a little while back,' Nate said.

Bob's face showed not an iota of emotion. 'What a pity,' he said.

'Did you ever meet Detective Schaeffer?' Nate asked. It seemed to me he was going into painful territory without softening the ground first, and I wondered why he was doing that. Did he think Bob would break down and confess to murdering Schaeffer, thus saving us a great deal of time? Judy, ex-cop that she was, stood as inconspicuously as someone who looks like Judy can, but her face indicated only slightly that she would have handled the questioning differently than Nate.

Bob looked impassive, which seemed to be his default expression. 'Nope. Never wanted to. I heard what happened. A hostage situation in a supermarket and that coward sent my daughter in to get shot. How he didn't get kicked off the force for that kind of behavior is beyond me.'

'Mr Wright, do you own a firearm?' What was Nate going for? Did he want to see if he could get Bob so angry he'd drop his guard? Because so far, I'd felt his answers had been pretty honest, so dropping his guard wasn't really a high priority for me.

Bob's eyes got cold and he stared directly into Nate's. 'What are you suggesting, sir?' he asked. His voice had picked up a little gravel along the way.

'Bob.' That was Kathryn, who seemed aghast at the idea that her husband was being rude to the man who was being rude to him.

'No, Katey. This man is doing his best to accuse me of . . . what? Getting on a plane to LA, with a gun in my suitcase, driving over to the apartment of a man I'd never met in – I guess a rental car – shooting the man *years* after he got Suzy killed, and then hopping on the flight back here? You want me to be polite to him after that?'

Not once in the course of that speech did Bob's voice rise a decibel. Not one time did his lips curl into a sneer. His eyebrows didn't drop to the bridge of his nose. If you'd been watching through the dining-room window from outside, you would never have had an inkling that Bob was discussing anything but the best place in the area to find a decent steak.

'Mr Garrigan is a guest in our house,' Kathryn reminded her husband.

'That's not the way a guest acts.'

I had to admit he had a point.

Since Nate had been doing all the questioning, and not getting terribly far, I decided the best thing to do here was divide and conquer. And since I knew Bob wouldn't leave his wife alone with the villain he thought Nate was, I said, 'Mrs Wright, is there some-where you and I can talk privately?'

Kathryn looked at me, then at her husband, whose expression

was constant, then at Nate and finally back at me. 'There's my sewing room,' she said.

'You mean Suzy's room,' Bob growled.

'Yes.' Kathryn wasn't going to have the argument, but it was on her own terms. She led me to the door and then up a flight of stairs to a very bright and comfortable-looking room on the second floor. 'Bob's right. This *was* Suzy's room, fifteen years ago.' Since then it had been turned into a very efficient but welcoming sewing room/ office, with a desktop computer on a white desk in one corner and a rocking chair, probably best used for sewing and hand crafts, in another. There were two generous windows and they were letting in plenty of light. Judy stopped in the doorway after checking the room, knowing that she might have intimidated Kathryn just a bit and I surely would not.

'For the record,' Kathryn said, 'we did the room over years before what happened.'

Since she had opened the door, I figured I might as well walk on through. 'I imagine that time must have been so awful for you,' I said. 'I can't even think of how you must have felt.'

Kathryn Wright was not a woman to showcase her grief. She showed the pain in her eyes but that was as far as it got. Time had strengthened her a bit. She did not shed a tear. 'I felt like the best person I'd ever known in my life was gone forever,' she said. 'I was absolutely devastated and barely left the house for six months. I was wounded and gasping for breath. But Bob was angry. I was just sad. Bob was *angry*.'

'Angry at the man who shot your daughter?' I knew that wasn't the answer, but I didn't want to be the one to say it.

'No.' Kathryn was going to oblige me. 'He was livid with Wallace Schaeffer. He blamed that man for sending Suzy into a room with dangerous people and no backup. He knew it was wrong, and Schaeffer knew it was wrong. I thought it was just a mistake, but Bob was convinced that Schaeffer did it on purpose.'

This was leading to a possible theory, but I didn't want to lead the witness. Better to let her take me where *she* wanted to go. 'Why would he want to do that to your daughter?' I asked.

Kathryn's face looked like she had eaten something very sour. 'He was a womanizer and he wanted Suzy, probably because she was married to Casey,' she said. 'She refused him and he was taking his revenge.'

I could see the prosecutor vaulting out of his chair at warp speed. Had to head that off quickly. 'How do you know that happened?' I asked. 'Did Susan tell you that?'

Kathryn was hearing me and I had no sense that she was mentally elsewhere, but she did not look at me; she was gazing out the window into the lovely, well-kept backyard. It took a while for her to speak. 'She said it like it was a joke,' she said, shaking her head. 'Like she thought it was funny this unappealing man would approach her, a happily married woman, about something like that and then refuse to take "no" as an answer.'

'Did she file a complaint with the department?' That would be far too good to expect.

'No.' Kathryn was still watching the grass grow outside. Someone – either Bob, Kathryn or a gardening service – had done a lovely job in their yard. 'She said it would make her more unpopular in the department and inhibit her chances to advance. She said she could handle it just fine on her own.' She shook her head again but didn't say anything more.

Maybe time to switch gears just a little. 'What do you mean, "more unpopular"? Was Susan having problems in the LAPD? What made her unpopular?'

That was when Kathryn turned away from the window and looked me in the face. 'Being the wife of Detective Lieutenant K.C. Trench,' she said.

Well, Trench had said that he wasn't well-liked in the department, and I could tell why, to be honest. He was better than most, if not all, of the other detectives at the job, and his anti-charming personality wasn't likely to have won him many friends. 'But she loved the lieutenant, didn't she?' I asked. I didn't think that was an open question.

'Oh, of course she did,' Susan's mother said. 'She said there was something about him that was almost like a little boy, the way he'd tell her about his cases to try to impress her. Once she found a flaw in one of the cases he was working and when he saw she was right and he was wrong, he asked her to marry him on the spot.' And I'd thought Patrick's marriage proposals were weird.

She gestured toward the rocking chair. 'I've been a bad hostess,' Kathryn said. 'Please sit down. Would you like something to drink?'

I did gratefully accept the very comfortable rocker but turned down the refreshment because Nate and I had stopped for lunch on the way from the airport. Crazy of these people to live three hours later than Los Angeles. I thought it was just past breakfast time and now it would be getting dark in only a couple of hours.

'You said Bob was angry at Detective Schaeffer,' I said, bringing the conversation back to where I needed it. 'Did he get over that as time went on?'

Kathryn was an intelligent woman, and I wasn't exactly being devastatingly subtle in my questioning. 'Are you asking me if Bob could have shot Schaeffer?' she said.

Don't try to fool smart people. 'Yes, I suppose I am.'

'I have asked myself that question a thousand times,' Kathryn said. 'And I haven't wanted to answer myself. But the truth is, I think he was angry enough to do it.'

'But he didn't leave the state for a whole day, not around the time Schaeffer was shot, did he?' I'd thought she'd simply dismiss the suggestion out of hand, so I was a bit thrown.

'To be honest, I'm not sure,' she answered after a moment. 'There was one night he was away, but he said it was in Detroit on business.'

There was something in the way she said it. 'You think he might not have been in Detroit?' I asked.

Kathryn didn't answer me for what felt like a long time. It probably wasn't. 'A wife doesn't like to think too hard when her husband spends a night away,' she said. 'But I know Bob, and if he wasn't here, it was definitely not for another woman.'

I appreciated the obvious and deep trust the Wrights had for each other. But I'm a lawyer and I was there on behalf of my client. I leaned forward and rested my elbows on my legs. 'Do you think he went to Los Angeles?' I asked.

She shuddered, as if awaken. 'You think he went and shot Wallace Schaeffer?' Kathryn's voice was shot through with new alarm. 'Bob?' She stood back and seemed to consider the question. 'I'd never think he would do something like that.'

'You just said he was angry enough to do it,' I reminded her.

'There's a long way between angry enough and booking plane tickets,' she said.

There was going to be more than that, and I knew it. So I didn't respond to her at all. I just watched the thought process travel across her face. Could her husband have murdered the man he blamed for their daughter's death? After years of grief, could he have planned a one-night trip all the way to Southern California, bringing a firearm, finding his target's address and going there, somehow evading the apartment building's video security, to fire a bullet into the back of Wallace Schaeffer's head? Was it possible?

Finally, she shook her head. 'No. He would never have done that.' Then her eyes focused on me in an instant. 'But I'm certain he wanted to.' Then another significant pause. 'Lord knows I wanted to.'

I had any number of additional questions, but wasn't sure I could ask them now. We'd established a rapport here (or at least I had) and I could call Kathryn after I returned home to ask about her relationship with Trench and other character points I might be able to use at trial. I stood up and thanked Kathryn for her help. I'm not sure she heard me.

Once we opened the door to the bedroom, we could hear Nate and Bob downstairs, laughing like a couple of teenagers who'd just seen *Monty Python and the Holy Grail* for the first time. I guessed Nate had established a rapport, too.

Kathryn headed down the stairs and I was about to follow her when my phone buzzed in my pocket, insistently. This was not a text.

Emma was calling from the office and she knew I was out of town. That had to be important. A quick check of the phone indicated she'd been texting me as well and I'd ignored the messages. I picked up the call. 'What's up, Emma?'

'We've gotten a look at some of the security footage from just before the fire started here in the office,' she said, her voice rushed and a little breathless. 'Lt Trench was here.'

I closed my eyes so I wouldn't have to see anything, but that just left me with mental images I didn't want. I opened them again. 'Tell Janine to get me on the next flight back,' I said. Nate could spend the night in a hotel in Detroit if he wanted to. I was going home. Now.

TWENTY-SEVEN

Patrick, for one, was very happy that I'd come home early. He (as has been noted) hates when we're apart, and on top of that he had finished shooting the last season of *Torn* and was now between projects, which is a difficult time for me because it lets his mind wander freely. Patrick is at his best when he has something on which he can focus. When it's not work, it's usually me, and that's nice for a while, but in this case I had a trial beginning in a few weeks and no time to go off on impromptu trips to Monterrey, Mexico or Florence. Patrick is an expert at impromptu.

Never mind how we'd spent the previous evening. I'd flown in as quickly as possible, which (given airline schedules) wasn't all that quickly, and now was fighting the lack of sleep at a war council with Emma, Jon and Trench. Nate had opted to take the hotel room my firm was providing and then was heading home with stops along the way at a few cops he knew who might have some information on Schaeffer that we didn't already possess.

My office was now, once again, a crime scene because the DA had gotten the same security footage my office had and was no doubt gleefully celebrating how easy this case was going to be. For him. Suffice it to say, we were still in my temporary digs, which were just as cramped and uncomfortable as they'd been before. Except now I was tired, too.

'I haven't seen it yet,' I said to Jon. 'How bad is it?'

'It's really bad,' Emma said. 'Trench must have lit the fire.'

Trench, to his credit, did not take the moment to point out to my paralegal that he was in fact present in the room. 'I did not,' he noted in his usual undramatic tone.

Jon almost laughed at Emma's outburst. 'It's bad, but it's not *that* bad,' he said. 'I'd say it's open to interpretation, especially as evidence. Keep in mind that the lieutenant has not been charged with arson and his presence in the building before the fire started is hardly evidence relevant to the murder of Wallace Schaeffer.' Sometimes it's just nice to have another lawyer in the room.

'I have not been charged with arson *yet*,' Trench pointed out. 'I think it is fairly clear that someone in the District Attorney's office would like for that to happen. I have not seen the footage yet either, Counselor, so I can offer no opinion on how *bad* it might be.'

'Then let's see the footage,' I said. 'Can we all watch at once, and if so, how?'

People who are more adept than I at electronics and audio/visual workings (like everyone else in the world) went to work, and within five minutes everyone in the room was sitting in front of a blank screen until Emma, who, let's face it, was the technological genius here, hit a button somewhere and they all blazed to life at the same moment. Technology is grand, when it works.

The camera that had taken the footage was mounted from the ceiling of our offices, pointed in the general direction of Janine the receptionist's station, which is larger than most because she handles all the offices in the section. My office – my late lamented former office – was to her left and a little behind her, and the windows that formed its walls were partially obstructed by the blinds I had insisted be installed when I'd moved in. So the door to my office was visible, as was part of the inside behind my desk, where my LAWYER bear sat resting on the bookshelf (in the security footage; now it was resting in my tote bag and I hadn't looked at it in days for fear of tearing up).

Someone had edited the footage down considerably, it was clear, because the camera was pointing at my office the whole time rather than panning around the floor to get a more complete view. There was considerable traffic around Janine's desk, but the focus was on my office door. Considerable cutting indeed. I asked, 'Who edited this video?'

Emma yelled (although it wasn't necessary because the footage was silent), 'We got it from the DA as part of discovery, but I got a copy from the LAPD arson squad too, so I know they didn't take out or add anything relevant.'

The usual comings and goings went on for about a minute. Then sure enough, Lt Trench himself, wearing a gray suit and gray tie over a white shirt, walked into the frame. He did not consult with Janine but walked directly to my door.

'I think we have to say that's definitely you, Lieutenant,' I said.

Emma must have hit a pause button because everyone's screen froze at the same time and we all looked over at Trench. He was still watching his screen despite the lack of movement. 'It is me,' he said. 'I was there that day.'

All in all, I've been more encouraged by things clients have said to me. 'Why?' I asked in what I hoped was a neutral tone. Sounding like you're going to panic and possibly throttle your client is so unprofessional. Not as unprofessional as doing it, but pretty close.

'I was there to inquire about the ballistics tests on the bullet that killed Detective Schaeffer,' Trench answered. He might very well have been thinking about throttling me at that point, but there was no way you were ever going to know it. 'I have a difficult time accepting the idea that it was my weapon that killed him.'

'And you didn't stay . . . because?'

Trench looked at me with something akin to pity. 'You were not in your office,' he said.

'Lieutenant, the last time I wasn't in my office when you showed up by surprise, you tracked me to a pizza place and threatened to shoot two cops.' It was a cheap shot, but I was looking for some more complete explanation.

Trench showed no sign of irritation, but his voice was perhaps one percent on edge. 'Ms Moss, we have no need to rehash that incident. In this case, I arrived at your office, found you were else-where, and decided to move on. You might find a text message I sent you later that day asking for a conference.'

'Later that day, I was dealing with the evidence that someone had tried to burn down my office,' I said, then nodded in Emma's direc-tion for her to start the security footage up again, which she did.

Before Trench could reply to my impudence, we were watching him approach the door to my office, try to pull it open, then look inside and, without changing expression, walk away. He came back, stuck what looked like a piece of folded paper under the door, and left. Emma's initial review of the footage, that he 'might as well have lit the match,' was a far cry from what I was seeing.

'Emma,' I said.

'Keep watching.' I didn't care for the sound of that.

So I sat back and watched quietly. After Trench left the screen, there was a period of about five minutes where very little crossed the camera lens at all. Three people came to ask Janine about appointments or for directions. Two of them sat in the waiting area. The third nodded and walked off screen again. Janine went about her own work and didn't leave her desk.

Then, gradually, it became obvious that there was smoke rising from somewhere inside my office.

It started from what appeared to be the floor, then rose up through the office until the whole room (which admittedly wasn't very large) was filled with smoke, visible through the glass walls and especially leaking out from under the door. The door through which Trench had just stuck . . . something.

'Lieutenant, what were you putting underneath the office door before you left?' Jon asked. Emma froze the image again, just at the moment when Janine, looking concerned, was gazing toward my office door. She'd look more than concerned shortly after we started the footage up again.

'A note requesting a conference,' Trench said. 'As I told you, I was interested in the ballistics report.'

I could feel my forehead wrinkling. 'You said you sent me a text about that.'

'I did, later, after I received no reply to the note.'

Silence for a short time. 'And why didn't you walk to the receptionist's desk and ask for an appointment?' Jon asked him.

'In all honesty, it never occurred to me,' Trench told him. 'I thought I would hear from Ms Moss later.'

It was Emma who asked the obvious question everyone was thinking about. 'Did the note have something on it that would activate a remote ignition device?'

Trench, no doubt descended directly from the Roman Stoic Marcus Aurelius, simply answered, 'No.'

'Well, this isn't going to play well in court,' Jon sighed.

TWENTY-EIGHT

The rest of the preparation for the trial, over the course of five weeks, consisted mainly of Nate researching the ballistics tests and the fingerprints analyzed by the LAPD, checks on Bob Wright's credit cards for hotels or restaurants in Detroit (there were many restaurants, because he lived quite near there, but only one hotel), the cops whom Schaeffer had 'allegedly' been giving illegal loans, and the locks in both Trench's home and Schaeffer's apartment.

He did manage to locate Louisa Lombardo, the woman who had been in Schaeffer's apartment the day he was shot. She was living in a less-than-ritzy area of the city in a one-bedroom apartment one floor above the bar that Sheryl Crow was probably describing in 'All I Wanna Do'. I didn't have the heart to send Emma after her, so I went myself. It got me out of the broom closet while my real office was still being 'investigated' by the arson squad. They probably didn't like Trench, either.

Louisa was a woman in her forties, dressed well enough if not expensively, in an apartment that could have been a hovel and wasn't because she wouldn't allow it to be. She'd painted the walls herself, recently. She still had some paint spots on the heels of her palms. A subdued green. There was just enough room for Judy, who hadn't had to save my life lately, to watch at a discreet distance. She never pulled out a phone or took notes. Judy recorded everything in her head. If I were to ask her a week later what was in Louisa's dish drainer, Judy would know without hesitation.

I'd called ahead so Louisa didn't need an introduction when she let me in. Louisa also knew why I was visiting. That didn't make her happy about my visit.

'I'm not going to sit here and tell you what a terrible person Wally Schaeffer was,' she said as soon as we sat at her kitchen/dining table, which sported two chairs that matched, probably better than any apartment in which I'd lived before I moved to LA and started making a decent salary. 'He was a sweet guy and I'm not going to run him down.'

I spread the fingers on my left hand and tilted it up from the table toward her. 'I'm not asking you to do anything like that,' I told her. 'I'm not putting Wally on trial.' Using the victim's name in the way the subject of the interview uses it is a standard tactic. It establishes (in theory) a rapport with the person being questioned without being terribly obvious about it.

'Don't call him "Wally,"' Louisa said. 'You didn't know him.' I *said* it was a theory.

'You're right.' Agree to what they think are their rules. You're really playing by *your* rules, or the rules of law when you're in court, but letting the subject think they're in control is usually a decent way to get more information than you would otherwise. 'I didn't know him. That's part of why I'm here. How did you meet Detective Schaeffer?'

Louisa stretched out in her chair and extended her legs out in front of her, no doubt a form of relaxation or stress reduction. She didn't look at her legs, though; she was searching my face for clues: Was I a friend or foe? Could I be trusted?

'I work in catering,' she said. 'A year, year-and-a-half ago, I got called to work a party on a boat – a yacht, I guess – down near Anaheim. So I drove down but I'm worried, because I get seasick, you know. I've never tried to handle food and drinks on a boat, but they told me it was going to stay in the dock so I would be OK.

'Well, it *didn't* stay in the dock, and I was in trouble right from the beginning. Now, this party is for, like, big shots in the city. Government people, like that. And some of them are cops. So, I'm doing my best not to barf while I'm bringing around hors d'oeuvres on trays. I'm not looking at the food at all. I get to this one crowd and the boat tilts hard to the side. I can barely hold the tray and my stomach is right behind it. I reach out with my free hand to balance myself, and I catch Wally Schaeffer right in the chest. I mean *right* in it. Center cut. I figure I'm gonna get fired, especially since some satay goes right off my tray and into his chin.

'But Wally, he's calm. He takes my free hand so I can catch my balance and he doesn't even worry about the satay. The other three people standing around are yelling like I should get fired, but Wally says no, he knows what it's like to be unsteady on his feet when he's working. I found out later he was a cop and a drinker, which ain't a great combination, but I didn't know that then.'

She said she'd taken Schaeffer aside to a quieter area where he

could clean sauce off his shirtfront and they ended up talking for a
while, until her supervisor noticed she wasn't circulating. Schaeffer,
she said, had apologized to the supervisor, said he'd been feeling
seasick and that Louisa had helped him through it. She said he'd
thrown a hundred-dollar tip on to her tray. And once the supervisor
thanked him and walked away, he'd asked her out for a drink once
they were on dry land.

They'd seen each other about once a month after that. She'd
never asked him to her apartment because she said it was a 'pit,'
which it was not. They most often met at bars, where Louisa had
become concerned about Schaeffer's drinking. Occasionally they'd
see each other at Schaeffer's apartment, although Louisa insisted
their 'friendship' had been almost completely platonic, 'but Wally
would get a little kissy when he'd been drinking. He always stopped
when I said no.'

She knew he was seeing other women. 'Of course I did. I mean,
I'm not even sure we had that kind of thing. But he didn't mind
telling me about the other girls. I never knew any names, just Amy
and Janet, I think. But Wally seemed to think I'd be impressed that
he saw a lot of women.'

'Were you?'

'Not really.'

It was time to get down to business now that the back story was
told. 'Tell me about the last time you saw him,' I said.

'It was one of the few times I went up to his place,' Louisa
answered, certainly warming up for another detailed story. 'He said
he'd been sick but now he was better, and I didn't want to go there
because I have this thing about germs, you know. But he said he
was better now and I didn't have to worry. He wasn't contagious.
I bought him a quart of chicken soup at the supermarket and went
up to where he lived.'

The police report after Louisa had been questioned was not
terribly specific, stating just that she'd been there and was
not considered a person of interest in the homicide. So I asked,
'What did you find when you got there?' in the hope that it would
produce more information than that, which wasn't setting the bar
very high at all.

Instead, it seemed my question had the effect of taking Louisa
out of her thoughts of the day and into an area where she was
wondering if the woman she was talking to was an idiot or not.

'Wally,' she said. 'He was in his kitchen making himself a drink. I mean, a real drink, not like orange juice or something you'd have to feel better when you're sick.'

So Schaeffer had been drinking. The blood alcohol level in the medical examiner's report hadn't shown anything especially unusual. Maybe he'd stopped at one drink. Maybe he hadn't had time for more than one. 'Did he seem anxious?' If Schaeffer had known someone was after him, that might (or might not) shift suspicion away from Trench, who would not have been one to announce his intentions to a hypothetical victim.

'He seemed sad,' Louisa said. 'I asked him why, but he said he was just tired from being sick.'

'Did you believe him?' I asked.

'No. But he wasn't going to tell me anything, so I quit asking. We spent an hour or so talking about TV and then I got up and left. He held my hand for a long time when I turned to go. I've wondered about that. Did he know something was coming? I don't know.'

'Louisa, I have one last question. Did Detective Schaeffer ever mention Lt Trench?'

Louisa's mouth puckered up. Maybe she was waiting for a splash of lemon. 'I knew what people thought about Trench's wife and how Wally supposedly got her killed,' she said. 'I don't believe that for a minute.'

'You don't?' I asked. That had seemed to be the general consensus around the LAPD, but Louisa was not connected with the cops except for Schaeffer, so now not at all, I guessed.

'Wally wouldn't do that,' she said. 'He might try to make a little extra money by making some loans for the other cops, but he wouldn't get anybody hurt.'

Yeah, he might . . . wait! Confirmation on the loan shark angle! I decided I'd act like it was news to me. 'Detective Schaeffer was making private loans to other officers?' I asked.

'Yeah, like for friends,' Louisa said. It sounded so innocent the way she said it. 'If somebody was a little behind in the rent or something, Wally would find a way to help them out. He was always looking for ways to help the other cops.'

Yeah. That was what I'd heard. What a gem of a man Schaeffer had been.

'Where did he get the money to loan out?' I asked her.

'I don't know anything about Wally's finances.' Of course not. One can't hope for too much.

I said thank you to Louisa and was texting Nate before Judy and I had made it back down the stairs toward the street-level bar.

TWENTY-NINE

'So, we have Schaeffer on the loan shark thing,' I said to Trench over the phone.

We had sandwiches in front of us that had been ordered from a nearby restaurant. Patrick was mostly looking at his. (Actors don't eat in fear of gaining weight, although they don't concern themselves nearly as much as actresses, who can lose a role if they ever appear to be wearing a size above, you know, zero). Angie was halfway through hers already and I was only nibbling because I hate the way it sounds on the phone when someone is eating. Trench didn't need to hear me crunching down on lettuce.

I did manage a French fry, though, because I was having a nonchalant week. It wasn't especially crunchy and therefore not very audible. Which led to me wondering why I was eating the French fries. 'We have to make certain Louisa and the two cops Nate spoke to will testify at trial,' I said to no one in particular.

'I don't see the relevance,' Trench said, a little too vehemently. 'I am accused of a crime, not Detective Schaeffer.'

'It's part of a larger narrative, Lieutenant,' I told him. 'I'll only call them if I think I can make a point that will help you.'

Trench clearly didn't care for the idea of implicating any LAPD cop in any wrongdoing ever, but this case was looking more and more like that would be necessary. Schaeffer's key area of vulnerability – that is, the reason someone would want him dead – appeared to be scams he was running on other cops, and nobody else. 'Lt Trench, can you outline for me the chain of command above your head?'

'To what end?' Trench wanted to know. It was like he didn't really want me to keep him out of jail if it meant other cops might be in trouble.

'Because I need to understand how things worked, and I need to know who would have known if Detective Schaeffer was in any kind of trouble, and with whom. Now, I know that your immediate superior would have been the captain, is that right?'

You could hear Trench's lips tighten. 'Yes. Captain Bruce Moran is my commanding officer.' Name, rank, and guy who gives you assignments. Nothing more. Trench seemed to think he was being held against his will.

'And above him?' I asked. I'd get nothing more than a name and rank, but that was more than I currently had. To even things out, I already knew who the police commissioner of Los Angeles County was, so that was a plus.

'The commander above Captain Moran is Commander Lenore Carter,' he answered. That was a surprise to me because I wasn't aware a woman was present that high in the ranks. Good for you, Commander Carter. 'The Deputy Chief is Michael Renfroe and the Assistant Chief is Anthony O'Neill. I assume you know who the chief of police is, Ms Moss.' That was as close to New Jersey sarcasm as Trench could get, but I recognized it, and Angie's raised eyebrow indicated she had, too.

'Thanks, I do,' I told him. Well, I could look it up, anyway. I never dealt with the chief, even on murder cases. Someone that high up is generally an administrator and a politician, not an investigator, and has no direct role in specific cases. 'Do you know of any issues any of those people might have had with Detective Schaeffer?'

This, I'm certain, posed quite a conundrum for Trench. On the one hand, he didn't want to open the possibility that anyone – at all – in the LAPD might have had reason to kill Schaeffer. On the other hand, Trench absolutely detests lying and has never done so in my experience with him. If you have a third hand, you could add to the argument that he might (and this was becoming a question) prefer to stay out of prison. But the first two were really the important ones. And you should see a doctor about that third hand.

'Issues?' Trench was going to stall for time before answering. I'd have to make sure he never did this on the witness stand. 'What issues, specifically?'

'If I knew that, I wouldn't have to ask you, Lieutenant. What is it you're trying not to tell me?'

There was silence for a moment. 'I am not conscious of attempting to keep any information from you, Counselor.' More stalling.

'Then I'll ask you directly: Do you know of any reason any of your superior officers might have a grudge against Schaeffer, whether it would be enough to kill him or not?' I knew he didn't like it when I referred to the victim without the honorific 'Detective,' and was prodding him in a sensitive area for a reason. I knew Trench wouldn't break (he wouldn't even bend) but if it was possible to get past that iron-clad veneer of his, I needed to know it.

Trench cleared his throat, the equivalent of a teary confession on his part. 'Because of the conferences I had regarding his activities within the department, I am not at liberty to say.' The ultimate stall.

Angie, who is the embodiment of my id, said, 'Oh, for crying out loud.'

My client had done everything but refuse to cooperate with his own defense. I knew Trench to be a reasonable man, but in this case his loyalty to the LAPD was, in my view, bordering on self-destructive behavior. And as high a level as my respect for him had reached, I had to push back against him for the first time since we'd met. I didn't relish the thought.

I made sure there was an exasperated exhale in my voice. 'Lt Trench,' I said. 'I'm trying my damnedest to keep you out of prison, and you are thwarting me at every turn. If you are not satisfied with the defense I'm building for you, and if you are going to refuse to cooperate from here on in, my best legal advice to you is to find yourself another lawyer. Because I can't defend you adequately like this.'

I pictured Trench staring at his phone in amazement, but because of who he was, the image I had in my mind was of him looking at the phone with no discernible expression at all, which was probably accurate. I counted to seven before he spoke, and almost hung up at five, deciding against it only because he was Trench.

Just as a crutch, I texted Jon as Trench was hesitating. *How would you feel about being first chair on the Trench case? I think he might fire me.*

I can text faster than you might think.

'Ms Moss,' Trench replied finally. 'I do not believe that I have been a hindrance in your work. I have done everything I can to assist in my own defense. If you think you would be better off resigning from my case, I will understand, but I disagree with your assessment.'

This was getting on my nerves now. 'No, Lieutenant. You don't get to dodge this time. Do you want me to stay as your lead attorney or do you not? You're the client and you get to make that determination. This is *my* area of the legal system, and I understand how it works. You tell me: Am I your lawyer, or am I not?'

Jon texted me back: *Are you out of your mind?*

Does anyone ever answer yes to that question?

'If you have no confidence in me as a client,' Trench answered, 'perhaps it would be best if we parted ways.'

Boom.

Someone in this case is out of their mind, I told Jon, *but I swear I don't think it's me.*

THIRTY

'I didn't ask for this,' Jon said.

He pointed to the cup of chicken noodle soup that had been served alongside his tuna sandwich, but the server looked less than sympathetic in the midst of the lunch rush at the little diner we'd snuck into to avoid everyone at our office. 'It comes with,' the server said.

'Can you take it back?' Jon asked. I'd rarely seen him eat more than one item at lunch. This was attacking his sensibility.

'You're paying for it,' the server told him.

'I thought it came with.'

'It's all part of the price on the menu.' But she picked up the cup of soup – which I would have gladly taken off Jon's hands if I could have gotten a word in edgewise – and walked away.

Jon regarded the sandwich, which was on white toast when he'd requested a roll, and sighed lightly. 'This sandwich is the Lt Trench case,' he said.

'Because you didn't ask for it and yet there it is?' I asked.

'Something like that. You know he's not going to be any more cooperative with me than he was with you, but he called your bluff and now you feel like you can't go back on your ultimatum, right? Isn't that how I got stuck with this sandwich?'

My own sandwich, which was a salad because I'd given up not caring again, was just sitting there, not representing any particular legal action. I almost felt guilty eating it. 'You're not stuck with the sandwich,' I told Jon. 'You can send it back to the kitchen.'

'I'm not even sure what this metaphor means anymore,' he said.

I put down my fork because in New Jersey salad is a form of penance. 'OK, forget the metaphor. Trench essentially fired me, but he didn't fire the firm, so as the only other attorney in the criminal justice division, you caught his case. If you want to resign it on behalf of the firm, you can, and I'll make sure that nobody sees that as a bad thing. But we've both invested a lot of time and energy the past few months in setting up a defense for Trench. A new attorney would undoubtedly seek a postponement to start from scratch; that could take up to a year and Trench would probably end up in a psychiatric facility if he can't be a cop again for another year at least. So what do you think you should do?'

Jon took a large bite of the tuna sandwich, which was looking better and better to me as I resumed stuffing plants into my mouth, then he chewed carefully and swallowed before speaking, which I appreciated. 'You know I can't just cut and run on Trench,' he said. 'But you also know, and so do I, that this case is eventually going to end up back in your lap, so why not just call the lieutenant and make your amends so we can go back to normal?'

I could be just as polite. The arugula and tomato in the salad were equally well chewed and out of my mouth before I answered him. 'I don't know for a fact that I'll get the case back.'

'Now who's being evasive? You care about this case more than any I've ever seen you take on, even Patrick's because you didn't know him then. It's killing you that you're not the attorney of record anymore.'

I waved my hands in a ridiculous back-and-forth motion to indicate that I thought his theory was . . . incorrect. 'It's not *killing* me. I just didn't see a way to continue once Trench said he couldn't be more cooperative with me as his lawyer. Anyway, that's not the point. You're the attorney of record now, Jon. How do you want to proceed?' I can bounce the ball into the other guy's court as well as anyone. And I'm pretty sure that's a basketball reference.

Jon is an expert legal tactician. He sees the case differently than I do in almost every instance, and that doesn't mean he sees it better, necessarily, but he gives me perspectives that I wouldn't otherwise have considered, and that's good. But now I was acting as second chair on *his* case, a case I'd been working on myself until yesterday, and we were breaking new ground. Neither of us was comfortable with it. But Jon's expertise would shine through, I was certain.

He didn't disappoint. 'What has bothered me the most is our lack of physical evidence,' he said. 'Even if everything Barnett has is circumstantial, it's all stuff the jury can relate to. They understand that the bullet matches Trench's gun. They'll definitely get that he threatened Schaeffer's life in public. They'll hear the story of his wife and they'll feel bad for him, but they'll just process that as another reason it makes sense he'd kill Schaeffer. What do we have that can counter any of that?'

'Lt Trench's record of stellar service to the city for all these years,' I offered. Yeah, it sounded stupid to me, too.

Jon didn't even answer that; he just gave me a look. 'What we need is something that the jury can hear – or better, see – and say, "That means it couldn't have been Lt Trench." And we don't have that yet.'

'Give me an example of something like that,' I said. Jon thinks best when challenged.

'If there were footprints of someone other than Trench on the floor in Schaeffer's apartment,' he said. 'If there were fingerprints of someone other than Trench on the gun. If there were a threatening note from anyone but Trench in Schaeffer's possession. Anything like that would turn a jury.'

'But none of that exists, at least not according to the incident report.' I'd seen the whole thing now and the cops had painted a picture of an open-and-shut case. I would have arrested Trench myself based on the evidence they'd laid out. 'Wait. Who are the cops who arrested the lieutenant and filed the report, again?'

I'm lousy at remembering names. There are times I let my own name slip from my mind for a moment. But Jon remembers everything he hears and reads. It's a little scary. 'Petrocelli and Andrews,' he said. No checking his phone. No referring to a note-book. Nothing. Scary.

'Do you know anything about them?' I asked.

Jon shook his head. 'Why? You think they doctored the incident report?'

I had no idea about that. 'I don't see any reason to think so. Not yet, anyway. But their allegiances in the department, particularly in the detective division, would be worth knowing, I think. What do you think we should do?' It was Jon's case. I had to keep reminding myself.

'I want to have a long talk with Nate and then I want to have a conference with our client when you're not there, Sandy.' Oof. That one stung, but I got it. Jon had to assert himself as Trench's lawyer and having me in the room would only invite him to talk to me – if we were still talking. Part – a large part – of what was bothering me in our current situation was that I felt it indicated that Trench didn't like me. Call me childish and I won't argue.

'Fair enough, but would you brief me after you have that meeting?'

Jon actually hesitated. 'If something from the client is considered confidential, I'm not going to disclose it,' he said.

Oof again.

I pretended to be fine with that, because I didn't have a choice, and concentrated on my salad for a while. It felt like I needed to do some penance.

It was Jon, who had clearly given up on his sandwich, who broke the slightly uncomfortable silence. 'There are two things you can do for the case, though.'

A chance to feel useful! Yay! 'Name them.'

'Check with the cops for more data on the fire. If we can find out who set it, we might have new suspects for Schaeffer's murder.'

Great. Check with the cops. Something Emma could do. 'What's the other thing?' I asked.

'Do a deep dive on the ME's report,' Jon answered.

'Schaeffer was shot in the back of the head and died,' I reminded him. 'I'm supposed to find nuance in that?'

'All the information we've been given by the city departments has been pretty seriously biased, in my opinion,' Jon said. 'I think we need to start taking what they tell us and verifying it independently.'

'You want us to get our own autopsy? Exhume Schaeffer's body and hire a pathologist to tell us he was shot in the back of the head and died?'

Jon had the class not to look grumpy. 'No. I just want all our bases covered.'

Hey, it was something. 'I'm on it, boss.'

He waved a hand derisively. 'Don't call me "boss." You'll be back in the first chair in no time, and that's fine with me.'

There was something green I hadn't eaten yet and I thought perhaps that was the way I'd leave things for today. 'Not if you won't let me talk to Trench,' I said.

He gave me a look.

'No, I get it, and you're right. I apologize for saying that.'

'You'll be back in a week,' Jon said.

In the end, it took a whole month before I was the first chair on Trench's case again. And it wasn't my amazing legal skill that got me there.

Jon tested positive for Covid with two weeks left before the trial. In all likelihood (since he was vaccinated and his symptoms were mild), he would be back for the first day, but the case needed someone riding herd on it during the crucial late preparation, and I was the only available choice.

In the meantime, we had more or less cleared Petrocelli and Andrews of any deceit involving the incident report, largely thanks to Nate and Angie on the half-day she was working with him. Jon was getting antsy about a full autopsy report, which the ME's office kept insisting was on its way, and he filed motions demanding it immediately, which had been shuffled around to various offices with no results. He had also talked to Trench three times, and had emerged from each meeting (including the last one, which I was allowed to attend) as frustrated with our client and his insistence on protecting everyone who had ever worn an LAPD uniform as I had been. Was.

So it was with some trepidation that I called Lt Trench to tell him the news about my return.

He answered even though he could see my name in the Caller ID, and listened as attentively as ever when I explained the situation. 'So, I will be the lead attorney on the case, at least until Jon can get back,' I concluded.

There was no pause on the line. 'Frankly, Ms Moss, I was somewhat surprised that you ceded that position in the first place. Welcome back.' There wasn't an iota of irony in his voice. But he was Trench and that meant there wasn't an iota of *anything* in his voice.

'You were surprised?' I asked. 'It was your idea.'

'That is not how I remember the conversation.'

I couldn't argue with the client, so I didn't offer my own view of the affair. What would be the point? I was first chair on the case again, and hadn't been for more than a month only because of my own poor communication skills, it seemed. 'Well, I'm glad we've straightened it out,' I said, despite our having done nothing of the sort.

'How should we proceed from here?' Weepy sentimentalist that he was, Trench was on to the next thing.

'First, we're going to set a few new ground rules, Lieutenant. No more evading questions. No more half answers. It's your future on the line here, and you can't ask me to defend it with one hand tied behind my back. OK?'

'I'm not aware of any evasions I have been employing,' he had the nerve to say.

'Fine. Then I'll ask the questions. When you said you wanted to kill Detective Schaeffer, what were the circumstances and how did you mean the statement to be interpreted?'

There was no background noise on Trench's line. I was sitting in my 'office' and I could hear the hum of the air conditioner, the buzz of my laptop and the occasional bump of a person moving or dropping something on the floor above my head. So the silence from Trench's part of the conversation, while not deafening (I've never understood that one), was noticeable. 'Lieutenant?' I said.

'It happened at a holiday party being held by the detective division,' he answered as if no time had elapsed since I'd asked. 'I do not often attend such gatherings, but it was being held directly outside my office and I had no alternative.'

I could definitely see Trench trying to duck out of holiday parties, particularly since the one in question had taken place the first December after his wife had been killed in the line of duty. 'What led to your making that statement?' I asked. 'Had you been drinking?'

'No, Ms Moss.' The slightest hint of irritation. 'I very rarely drink alcoholic beverages, and that night was not an exception. I was absolutely sober.'

We'd had three cops who were present at the time tell us (mostly Nate) the story, but I wanted to hear Trench's version. 'So what led to you saying that?'

'The chief of detectives called for a moment of silence for officers and employees of the department who had died during the year,' Trench said. 'When Susan's name was read from the list, I saw Detective Schaeffer and two of his friends in a corner of the room. They were laughing.'

'Why were they laughing?' I couldn't imagine there was a reasonable rationale.

And I was right. 'I haven't the faintest idea,' Trench said.' But seeing that, and knowing what I knew about the night she was shot, was enraging. Once the list had been read, I stepped into the center of the room and stood facing Detective Schaeffer. I told him that it was his fault she was dead, and that if he ever laughed at her name like that again, I would see to it that he followed in her footsteps.'

Yeah, that was pretty much what we'd gotten from the other cops, but in less formal language.

'Did you ever see him laugh like that again?' I asked.

'No, I did not. And that is one of the many reasons I did not shoot Detective Schaeffer.'

'Lieutenant, I'm going to ask you one more question, and I don't care how loyal you are to the LAPD, you're going to answer me under our new rules. Straight answer. Understand?'

'You were not using unfamiliar words, Ms Moss.' His wit was so dry you could use it as a dehumidifier.

'Do you know of anyone in the upper levels of your division or the LAPD in general who has a grudge against you? Someone who wouldn't mind seeing you go to prison for the rest of your life?'

There was a pause, but I felt it was less Trench deciding how to evade the question and more Trench giving himself time to think of every single person in the LAPD just to be sure he hadn't left out any possibilities. 'I am not aware of such a person, but I will allow that it is possible someone has that level of anger toward me without my knowledge.' That didn't help much at all.

'Do you know of any way a ballistics test could be inaccurate?' I asked.

'Ballistics comparisons are not perfect, as you are surely aware,' Trench said. I was not that aware, but I had not dealt with bullets much since I was a prosecutor. Back then, we always believed in ballistics reports, as long as they showed our suspect was guilty. 'But they are usually quite reliable.'

'One more time, Lieutenant. Is there *anyone* in the upper echelons of your department who you do not trust? And keep in mind, I'm not asking so I can impugn the reputation of the LAPD, but because I want to win your case.'

'Before Detective Schaeffer was shot, there was no one I didn't trust in my division or above,' Trench said. 'Other than Detective Schaeffer, of course. There are always some superior officers with whom one is less open and relaxed than with others, but there was never anyone I believed had bad intentions toward me.'

'And now?' I asked.

'Now there is essentially no one in the Los Angeles Police Department I can trust implicitly,' he said.

'Then there's only one thing left to do,' I said, to Trench and to myself. 'It's time to go to court.'

THIRTY-ONE

There are times when I think Patrick should be more at home in a courtroom than I am. The whole structure, after all, is designed much more like a theater than a place where legal business is prosecuted; there is a stage at the front with at least part of it raised off the floor so the people facing it can get a better view. In California, we attorneys don't dress in costumes as elaborate as those in, for example, the UK, but we don't show up in sweatpants and t-shirts, either. There is a dress code and you'd better follow it.

On the first morning of Lt Trench's trial, I woke up dreading something and couldn't be specific about what it might be. Of course, the case itself was a source of anxiety, but while I was eating a bowl of cereal with banana, I delved a little deeper into my feelings and realized I had been on edge about the level of press coverage the trial would generate.

At Patrick's trial, my first as a criminal defense attorney, the press coverage from every conceivable medium was suffocating. Separate rooms were set up in the courthouse with video screens on which reporters (and 'citizen journalists') could watch the proceedings and offer their invaluable perceptions in real time on social media and traditional media. I'd spent hours after each day in court dealing with interview requests for myself and my client, who had been much more accommodating to the press than I ever would be. Patrick didn't get to be a famous actor by avoiding the spotlight.

This case would not carry that level of interest for the general public, although there had already been internet memes of Trench photoshopped with a gun in his hand and some of the less reputable newspapers (those that still existed) were already claiming there had been bias toward the lieutenant because he was a cop. From my point of view, there had been a pretty substantial level of resistance from the LAPD. It had taken me far too long to get an unredacted autopsy report on Schaeffer and any attempt to contact Trench's superiors for interviews had been unacknowledged.

I got dressed carefully and conservatively. This was a courtroom and I was the last person to whom attention should be drawn. The case was the star attraction at this theater, and I was not even one of the leading players. Trench would top the bill, followed closely by Judge Lawrence J. Huffman.

Huffman, a judge I'd argued before twice previously, was a bland judge, just right for a case like this. No favoritism could be even vaguely implied, and a guy as dull as Huffman would be perfect. He could put a jury to sleep even as they were about to decide a defendant's life or death.

He had a sonorous voice suitable for ASMR videos on YouTube. He never raised or lowered his pitch more than a step or two and he didn't ever raise the volume of his speech. He was to criminal law what a fuzzy teddy bear is to a two-year-old: reliable and absolutely unthreatening.

I tried to sneak out of the house before Patrick could catch sight of me because I knew he'd insist on coming to the trial and he was the last thing I needed in the courtroom. Patrick attracts attention just by being Patrick. That wasn't really an issue here, because I didn't think the jury would be staring at the TV star and not paying attention to the murder trial. But Patrick also attracts attention from *me*, and what I really didn't want was to catch myself wondering if he thought I was defending Trench in an inspiring fashion. I could stand Angie being present, which had been the case sometime in the past when Patrick would send her as a surrogate, because I'd know she would be honest with me – perhaps brutally so – at the end of the day. There was some useful information to find there. Patrick would just keep telling me how wonderful I was, and while that is nice for my ego, it's not very helpful in a practical fashion.

But he was up and padding about as I grabbed my increasingly irrelevant briefcase and headed for the door. 'You on your way already, love?' he said. 'I was going to come with you.'

Yeah, that's what I'd been trying to avoid. 'First day in court, you know how it is, Patrick.' I sounded so chipper, Walt Disney could have made a cartoon about me. 'Don't worry. I'll tell you all about it when I get home.'

He stood and looked at me for a moment. 'Of course,' he said. 'You go and get them, Sandra.'

I kissed him and walked out to the garage. Now I felt bad because I got the impression Patrick thought I'd rejected him. I hadn't in any way, shape or form, but go tell that to a man who spends all day listening to people say how amazing he is. And that is the word:

amazing! You hear it all the time, like an earworm you can't banish from your head.

I drove to the courthouse thinking about things I could do to make it up to Patrick. But then I decided he'd have forgotten all about any perceived snub by the time I got home tonight. Either way, I'd make sure he understood once I was home.

Judy, in the passenger seat because I wouldn't let her drive my still-wounded Hyundai (I was going to get to that taillight, but first I wanted to sue the city for a cop vandalizing my car), was doing her usual statue-of-a-bodyguard impression, but it occurred to me that she had once been a cop in LA. 'Judy, did you know Lt Trench's wife?' I asked.

It was like she'd been awakened from a light nap. Judy shuddered a bit and then shook her head a bit before resuming her usual practice of staring straight ahead, but scanning the area for threats every half-minute or so. 'I didn't know her well, ma'am,' she answered.

'But you did know her.'

'Yes.' That was it. I supposed I should have been grateful the answer hadn't been 'affirmative.'

'Can you tell me what she was like? I have a hard time picturing the lieutenant as a married man. I'm trying to figure out what kind of woman would have broken through to him.'

Yes, there was a legal point to be made. The prosecution was going to use Trench's public threat against Schaeffer as motive. I wanted to know what I could use to counter that argument, and knowing as much as possible about Susan Wright, in addition to what I'd been told by her parents, would only help.

That's my story and I'm sticking to it.

'Officer Wright was a good cop,' Judy said. Wow. Six words in a row.

'What else can you tell me? I get that you saw her as a colleague on the job, but I know you knew the lieutenant back then. What kind of couple were they?'

Judy's upper lip curled a bit. She wasn't angry, but she didn't find this area of conversation comfortable. 'I didn't see them together often, but they appeared to get along well.'

Another tactic was clearly called for. 'I imagine they weren't openly affectionate in public,' I said. It wasn't a question, but it might as well have been.

'Officer Wright was a very dedicated member of the force,' Judy said, which didn't respond to what I had said at all. 'She was very much like Lt Trench, but her sense of humor was much more evident. As far as I could tell, she very much loved her husband and he loved her. But I don't know very much more. We did not socialize.'

'What did the other cops say about them?' This could actually be relevant, if someone in the LAPD was involved in Schaeffer's shooting.

I turned on to the block where I could access the courthouse parking garage, which was underground. There were already news vans outside the building, which wasn't a huge surprise, but no one staking out the entrance to the parking lot, which was encouraging. Maybe I'd be able to get into the courtroom without having to fend off half the media in North America.

'Police officers do not generally gossip about co-workers,' Judy said, which either meant she was lying or mistaken. 'I know the lieutenant isn't the best-liked man in the department, but as far as I know he's never intentionally antagonized anyone there. Officer Wright, when she was alive, was not as prominent a figure and did not have a strong reputation as far as I know, but again, ma'am, we did not socialize.'

I was starting to get the impression that Judy had not socialized with Trench and his wife.

'Did you ever talk to Susan privately?' I asked. Again, anything said out of her husband's earshot could have some bearing on the state of their relationship. If Trench had heard about the alleged advances Schaeffer made toward his wife (which she rebuffed), that could go to motive again.

'Only about work,' Judy said. 'And I left the department a few months before she was killed in the line.'

'Thank you, Judy. I know that wasn't easy.' I saw a parking space and made a beeline for it. They're worth a fortune.

'I don't find it difficult, ma'am. But I have very little to say that can help you.'

Judy chooses her words very carefully when she chooses to use them. 'Does that mean you know some things that might hurt our case?' I asked as I put the car into park.

She didn't answer right away and that made my stomach clench. 'Out with it, Judy,' I said. 'If there's something, I need to know.'

'I know of one time when the lieutenant tried to run over Detective Schaeffer with his car,' she said.

OK, that was bad. When I caught my breath, I asked, 'Does the DA know about this?'

'I can't be sure. I believe no charges were ever filed.'

Wait, though. 'I thought you left the department before Susan Wright died,' I said. 'Why were you there when Trench tried to flatten Schaeffer with his car?'

Judy made a noise in her throat. 'The lieutenant and I had a brief affair about a year later,' she said.

I gave serious thought to putting the car in reverse and driving home to Patrick.

THIRTY-TWO

'I didn't mention it because I did not, and do not, see how it is relevant to our business,' Lt Trench said. 'It was a brief moment when I was dealing with trauma and it had nothing to do with Detective Schaeffer. It has been years since it happened and it has not happened again.'

Under the agreement Trench and I supposedly had, this was him being open and honest. Except that I practically had to tie him to a chair to get him to say that much.

He'd been sitting at the defense table when I arrived, because of course. And he saw Judy walk in behind me, back in her role as the woman who sees to it that I don't get killed. The idea that I might murder Trench when I saw him probably wasn't in her work manifest.

'This is exactly the kind of thing that wasn't supposed to happen under our new rules,' I hissed at him, keeping my voice down and my face passive as I talked. 'You had an affair with Judy and then you tried to run over Detective Schaeffer, the man you're accused of killing, with your car? How is that not the first thing you told me when you hired me?'

'I do not consider my romantic life to be relevant to these proceedings.'

'And now you're obfuscating again,' I said. 'You know for a fact that I meant the part about the attempted vehicular manslaughter.' Why did I take this case, again? Right. Because he was Trench. That didn't seem like a good reason just at this moment.

'There was no such incident,' he said. 'I was stopped at the intersection outside the parking deck for police personnel and Detective Schaeffer happened to be walking into the street at the moment my light turned green. I touched the gas pedal before I saw him. No one was hurt and, frankly, I'm surprised it's even been mentioned. It was never a very close call.'

I didn't have a lucid, pithy response because I was too livid with him, but it was just as well because the bailiff, a guy named Norman I knew from previous cases, let the courtroom know that they should 'rise' because Judge Huffman was entering. With my mind going in seven different directions at the same time, it was the moment when the trial would begin.

I don't like to write out an opening statement or a closing summary. I don't want to stand in front of the jury (once there is a jury) and look like I'm reading something; I want them to feel that I'm talking to them at least somewhat spontaneously. On the other hand, I could be prone to forgetting a particular point or wanting to go back and clarify, and that seems clumsy and unprofessional. So I write up a set of bullet points, no more than one page total (although I save it on an iPad and not a phone because you don't want the jury to think you're checking your Instagram while in court), and I will refer to that on occasion while talking to the jury. Angie says it's me being a genius, Patrick always thinks I'm 'brilliant,' now that I allow him that word again, and I see it as a way not to forget stuff. It's all in your point of view, I suppose.

Selecting a jury was delicate, but not difficult. There were a couple of people who admitted to not trusting the police and they were gone via my challenges very quickly. There were two who were in favor of shooting officers, and the DA got rid of them the same way. And of course there was one person who came dressed as a 1940s mobster because she thought that was a clever way to avoid being empaneled on a jury. We seated her. I let Barnett accept her at the judge's prompting so she wouldn't be especially mad at me, but she was clearly not pleased when she took the eighth chair.

The DA got to present his opening argument first, as is the rule in American courtrooms. And Barnett laid out a doozy of a case: the gun with the defendant's fingerprints on it, check. The fact that the gun was registered to the defendant and was kept under lock and key in his residence, check. The defendant's public threat to kill the victim, albeit a few years ago. Check away.

'In fact,' Barnett went on, 'there was an incident during which the defendant attempted to run down the victim with his car.' I did not swivel my head to stare at Trench only because I'd happened to discuss this with Judy that very morning. I did want to give him an 'I-told-you-so' look, but that could wait until later.

By the time the DA was done, I was ready to vote for a guilty verdict, until I remembered which side I was at least ostensibly on. After he'd gone on for quite some time, Barnett sat down at the prosecution table and Huffman looked at me. 'Ms Moss, perhaps we should break for lunch before you address the jury. Do you have any objection to that?'

In truth, I did have objections. I didn't want Barnett's opening to have time to set in stone in the jury's heads. I preferred to get my opening statement out of the way early so we could start hearing from witnesses. And I didn't really have a good idea for lunch yet. But you don't want to defy the judge on something that stupid, so I told Huffman it was fine with me and he had put us at recess for ninety minutes before anyone could think about it. I guessed he *did* have a good idea for lunch, and I was considering trailing him to find out what it was.

I gathered up my stuff and started up the aisle. Jon was still out, not having tested negative yet although he was feeling fine. The courts have rules and Jon knows every last one of them. So I walked up the aisle with my client striding just ahead of me and wanting, for once in his life, to have a conversation. Nothing like being on trial for murder to loosen the tongue, I supposed.

'I am not well versed in reading a jury,' Trench said to me while I was still deciding if I'd speak to him. 'You are more practiced in this. How do you think they received Mr Barnett's opening statement?'

'Do you have a lunch with you?' I said. Trench was too in control to look surprised and ask, 'What?' so he just walked a bit slower.

'I do not,' he said.

'So we'll order in.' We walked through the doors of the courtroom and into the hallway. '*Then* we can talk.'

Trench did not argue, so I directed us into one of the small conference rooms in the courthouse that lawyers use to talk privately to their clients. Which was exactly what I was intending to do now. We quickly ordered delivery from a nearby deli (Trench got a salad) and sat down to await our meals.

'OK,' I said. 'We know it's going to come up in the prosecution's case. So you tell me how driving through a light into a crosswalk at the man you've admitted to me you hated is not an attempt on his life.'

Trench shook his head slightly, as if wondering why he was

subjecting himself to such impertinent questioning. If he thought I was bad, he was going to be downright appalled when Barnett got hold of him on the stand. If I let Trench take the stand at all; it was still an open question.

'Ms Moss,' he began, 'I have explained this to you. There was no intent. If someone other than Detective Schaeffer had been in the same place, the incident, which was not anything more than a brief moment, would have taken the exact same form, and the outcome would have been the same. No contact, no injury, not even a tire track on the pavement. If your bodyguard is claiming it was a homicide attempt, she is mistaken.'

I folded my arms, less to distance myself from the conversation and more to signal my disappointment in my client. 'Judy has said nothing of the sort, and it's touching to see the level of detachment you can have to someone who used to be a romantic interest of yours. Come on, Lieutenant, let me in so I can help you.'

'That is exactly how it happened. I don't see how I am holding anything back, and my reference to Judith is the easiest way to identify her to you. I would do the same with anyone.'

Maybe the key here was to push through. The car incident was probably not the most damning evidence against Trench, although it certainly wouldn't help our case if the DA raised it again. 'OK. You've said before that you have no idea how the gun used in shooting Schaeffer could have been removed and returned to your home. You're a homicide detective and you've had a great deal of time to examine the crime scene. What have you seen? Because we know for a fact that it'll be a key point in the prosecution's case.'

Trench was considerably more comfortable 'talking shop' – that is, discussing a homicide – than he was referring to his affair (or whatever) with Judy, something I was trying very hard not to picture in my mind. He nodded, accessing the cop part of his brain, and said, 'I have studied the room and the adjoining rooms closely in these months, and I have reached a conclusion.'

OK, so he was waiting for the straight line so he could deliver the dramatic exit line. If it was going to help, I was perfectly willing to supply it. 'What's that?' I asked.

'In my professional opinion, Ms Moss, that weapon was never removed from, nor was it returned to, my home office. There is absolutely no physical evidence it had been anywhere but in my office safe until the officers confiscated it for evidence.'

'So, someone is lying,' I said.

'Someone most assuredly is,' Trench answered. 'And it is not me.'

THIRTY-THREE

'You're going to hear that Lt Trench removed his service weapon from a safe he keeps in his home to ensure its safety,' I told the jury. 'You're going to hear the prosecution try to prove that he did that, then drove to Detective Schaeffer's apartment, despite there being no physical evidence that the lieutenant left his home at all that night. You've already heard the prosecution say he entered the victim's apartment, shot his weapon once and hit the detective in the back of the head, killing him almost instantly. And you'll hear the district attorney say the lieutenant did so because he hated Schaeffer, whom he blamed for the death of his wife, Officer Susan Wright.

'What you will *not* hear about is any physical evidence that any of that actually happened. Are there fingerprints on the weapon? Yes. Are they those of Lt Trench? Well, it's his gun, isn't it? But is there *any* evidence that the weapon even left the lieutenant's home that night? Is there any evidence that ties the lieutenant to the scene, let alone the shooting itself? There is not. There's a reason they refer to some evidence as "circumstantial." It means you, as a juror, are supposed to take the circumstances under which the evidence is being presented and then make the leap to deciding the defendant is guilty because those circumstances *could* explain the crime. But keep in mind, ladies and gentlemen, that the law requires you consider the defendant not guilty unless the evidence presented leaves you with no reasonable doubt. None. Not just a little, not less than the idea that the defendant is guilty. No reasonable doubt at all. And what we in the defense will present will give you many reasons to doubt that Lt Trench is guilty. Because he never went to Schaeffer's apartment; he never shot a gun at Wallace Schaeffer; and he never returned the murder weapon to his safe. Because he didn't kill Detective Schaeffer. Trust me, you'll see.'

You can read a jury sometimes. Not as clearly as Trench seemed to think I could, but if you're paying attention and not just trying to remember what the next thing you're supposed to say might be, you can see inklings in their faces. At the very least, you can see if they're actually listening to what's being said.

And I'm here to tell you that in looking at all fourteen faces (two alternates in case someone has to bow out), I saw a grand total of nothing. They were listening. Beyond that was anybody's guess.

Huffman checked his watch (he would never look at a smartphone while on the bench) for the time and said, 'Is the prosecution ready to call its first witness?'

Barnett stood and thought he was intimidating all of us with his height. Everyone else in the room besides Norman the bailiff was seated, and Norman didn't seem especially concerned. The DA did everything but pull on the suspenders he wasn't wearing and crow like a rooster.

'The county calls Francine Schaeffer,' he said.

Now, don't think I was taken by surprise, because I had known all along that Francie was on the DA's witness list. What I hadn't expected was that he'd call her as his first witness. With your first witness you want to set the tone for your argument and give the jury something they won't forget. Trials can get bogged down in technical testimony and things they hear on the third or fourth day, no matter how significant to the case they might be, can be lost to the jurors' fatigue. So calling Francie first either meant that Barnett thought she'd be a memorable witness because he wanted to humanize Schaeffer, or that Francie had something to say to the jury that she hadn't already said to me.

She stood up from a seat in the rear of the courtroom, like a nominee at an awards show that nobody thinks will win. And that meant her trip to the witness box was elongated and time-consuming. Francie was an attractive young woman, but she wasn't going to stop traffic anywhere. Barnett's tactics were cutting into my confidence because I couldn't figure him out, which might have been the point to begin with.

Francie was sworn in and made herself comfortable in the witness chair. But she mostly looked like she was sitting for an oral exam in a subject she hadn't studied sufficiently. Her mouth twitched a little from time to time and her eyes darted around the room as if she were searching for a friendly face and finding none. She didn't look in my direction at all.

'Ms Schaeffer,' Barnett began. 'Is it OK if I call you Francie?' Oh, brother. He wanted the jury to think they'd never met before, like a magician who just 'happens' to pull a plant out of the audience with the right card waiting in his back pocket.

'It's fine,' Francie said. 'Everybody calls me that.' An older woman on the jury smiled as if thinking of her granddaughter while looking at the witness. If Francie actually had something damaging to say, she might be able to really hurt my case because the jury was already starting to like her.

'Thank you, Francie.' Barnett was going to be so polite to the obviously nervous young woman that he'd be nominated for a humanitarian prize by the time the day was through. 'Now, your father was Detective Wallace Schaeffer, is that right?'

He had been, so Francie acknowledged that and Barnett moved on. 'What kind of relationship did you have with your father, Francie?'

I stood up because my thigh muscles were starting to fall asleep. 'What is the relevance of this questioning, Your Honor?' I asked Huffman. No sense talking to the DA.

'That is a question I would like answered, Mr Barnett,' Huffman said. 'Does this lead us to the matter we're trying in this court?'

'It goes directly to the case,' Barnett answered. 'Just a minute or two.'

'Very well. Proceed, but a minute or two.' Huffman was living up to his reputation. A very boring judge. I hadn't expected more, but a little irritation wouldn't have been an awful thing.

Barnett walked closer to the witness box to better enhance the impression he wanted to make, that he and Francie were a couple of pals just kickin' it around. 'Francie, how would you describe your relationship with your dad?' Now Schaeffer was her 'dad.' When we got to 'daddy' I would have to object again.

'It wasn't the closest,' Francie said. 'My father wasn't around much when I was growing up.'

'Was that because he was busy as a detective for the police department?' Barnett said. What was he going for? I'd already talked to Francie about this, and he'd have to know what kind of answer he was going to get.

'Yeah, but not really,' Francie said. 'My mom divorced him when I was young, and that meant he wouldn't be around as much. And from what she told me, my father was spending a good deal of his time with different women.'

'After your parents were divorced?' Barnett was doing a character assassination on the victim of the murder he was prosecuting. I'd never seen anything like it.

'Yes, but also before,' Francie answered. 'That was one of the reasons my mother filed for divorce, she told me later.'

'Mr Barnett.' Huffman was pointing in the prosecutor's direction, as if we didn't know who Mr Barnett might be. 'I gave you a minute or two. How does this pertain to the murder of Wallace Schaeffer?' That little bit of irritation had shown up, finally.

'Here's how, Your Honor.' Barnett faced Francie again. 'Did your mother say there was someone in the detective division who called your father out because of his cheating on your mom?'

'Objection,' I said, because I didn't know how, but I could see the answer to the question coming. 'The district attorney is asking for hearsay.'

'Withdrawn,' Barnett said before Huffman could rule on my objection. 'Francie, did anyone from your father's work ever talk to *you* about the way your father acted?'

Uh-oh.

'Yes,' Francie said. 'Lt Trench said my father was an immoral man and unfit to be an officer of the Los Angeles Police Department.'

On a pad between us, Trench wrote, 'NO.'

I nodded to my client, assuring him I'd get on that as soon as I could.

'Did the lieutenant say anything else about your dad?' Yes, Barnett, I'm pretty sure he did.

'Yes.' Francie had been coached to answer in as few words as possible.

Barnett didn't even gnash his teeth. 'What else did he say?'

'He said he thought my father had killed his wife and he hoped my father would die.'

Trench simply pointed to the word on the pad again.

I stood. 'Objection. Hearsay again, Your Honor. We don't know the defendant said anything of the sort.'

'The witness is testifying to what the defendant said to her, not what someone else told her he said,' Barnett said.

'The very definition of hearsay,' I pointed out. I managed to do so without waggling my fingers in my ears, sticking out my tongue and saying, 'Nyah, nyah.' Which I thought was very mature of me.

'Ms Moss is correct, Mr Barnett, and I'm relatively sure you know it. I'm going to advise the jury to disregard what was just said, but you and I both know that's very difficult to do. So I'll advise *you* to be more judicious in your questioning from here on.' Probably as animated as Huffman had ever been on the bench in his life, and he didn't raise his tone one decibel. Class act.

'Understood, Your Honor.' Barnett had made his point, been scolded for it, and knew the jury would retain it. My job? Poke holes in it, ASAP.

'Thank you, Francie.' Barnett walked back to his table and sat down trying not to look like the Wikipedia page on smugness. It was a failing attempt.

There was no need for Huffman to call on me; I was already approaching the witness stand. 'Nice to see you again, Francie,' I said, because I didn't want the jury to think Francie had thrown me for a loop. We'd met before. 'So tell me, what were the circumstances when you say Lt Trench made these statements to you?' We'd get to their credibility shortly. I wished Jon were here, but he had said he'd be back within a couple of days. He expected to test negative shortly.

'The circumstances?' Francie asked.

'Yes. Why were you talking to Lt Trench to begin with? Where were you?'

'I went to pick up my father from work one night and he was slow coming out, so I started to talk to the lieutenant.' This story was getting so fishy Herman Melville could have written it, but I looked at Trench and he nodded slightly. That part was true, I guessed.

'Did you speak to Lt Trench often?' I asked. They always tell you never to ask a witness a question when you don't know the answer, but based on my observations of Trench, I would have bet my Hyundai itself that I knew what Francie would say.

And I was right. 'No, that was the only time we actually had a conversation.' If you weren't involved in one of his cases, Trench would be less than enthusiastic about striking up a convo, especially if you were the daughter of a man he despised.

'And he just started to talk about how much he hated your father?' Again, something the lieutenant wouldn't do even if he was facing physical torture.

'Yes.' No, he didn't, and you know it, Francie. What's your game here?

'Did it strike you as odd that a colleague of your father with whom you'd never spoken before would suddenly volunteer the opinion that your father should die?' Of course she'd say yes, but it would lead me into better territory.

'Well, yeah,' Francie said while I tried to get into her head and figure out what her motivation to commit perjury on the stand might be, and how I could prove she was doing so. 'I mean, what was that supposed to do, right?'

I did not volunteer an opinion on whether she was right. 'Why were you picking up your father at work?' I asked.

Francie looked startled at the change of topic. 'What?'

'I said, why were you picking up your father at his work? Why wasn't he driving himself home that evening?'

Francie took a moment, probably to think of a plausible answer. 'I had just gotten my license and I was showing off.'

'How old are you, Francie?' I asked.

'I'm twenty-one.' So I could take her out for a beer after court. I wouldn't, but I could. Legally.

'And you had just gotten your license, so you were sixteen at the time.'

'Yes, that's right,' Francie said.

'Francie, Lt Trench's wife, Officer Wright, was killed in the line of duty almost exactly six years ago, when you were fifteen. So it's unlikely he made those statements to you that night. Do you know the penalty for perjury in California?'

Barnett stood up. 'Objection. No one is bringing perjury charges. The witness has clearly misstated the timeline.'

'I don't think that's clear at all, but please proceed, Ms Moss.'

'Thank you, Your Honor. Francie, since you obviously were not celebrating your brand-new driver's license that night, please answer the question: Why were you meeting your father at the end of his shift?'

The wheels were almost visibly turning in Francie's head, and I thought the mention of perjury might have spooked her, because she was definitely committing it. She blew out a breath. 'OK,' she said. 'I was picking him up because he'd been drinking.'

'On the job?' I tried not to sound too shocked, largely because I wasn't.

She nodded, and a tear fell from her left eye. An actor colleague of Patrick's once told me that if a person cries out of one eye, they're faking. People cry from both eyes, he said. I'd never had the occasion to test that theory before. 'He was drinking pretty heavily at that time,' Francie said.

'Objection.' Guess who. 'Detective Schaeffer's character is not the issue here. We're concerned with the man who shot him.' And he looked at Trench for emphasis. I had to admire his technique, if nothing else.

'Ms Moss, is the victim's drinking pertinent?' Huffman might just as well have been asking me if I'd driven to work today. It's LA. People who work at home drive to work.

'In and of itself, no, Your Honor. But the witness's reaction to it has bearing.' That's legalese for 'Just let me finish.'

'All right, Ms Moss. Objection overruled.' That's legalese for, 'Let's get this going. I have a pickleball game at six.'

The witness, who must have thought she'd been forgotten about by now, looked a hair surprised when I turned back in her direction. 'Francie, how often did you have to pick up your dad and make sure he got home safely?'

'Oh, just a few times,' she answered and the look in her eyes told me how to save her from prosecution again.

'You sure?' I asked.

Her mouth twitched a little. 'Now that I think about it, I guess it was more like a couple of times a week.'

I don't like to pace in front of the witness; it makes them nervous and there aren't a lot of times you want to unnerve a witness. So I stayed still. 'And in all those times, Lt Trench only spoke to you the one time?' I asked.

'Well, he'd say hello or something, but that was the only time we had a conversation.' I got the impression Francie had decided against lying on the stand any longer.

'Francie, I'm going to ask this one last time, and I want you to remember the oath you took when you were sworn in. Did Lt Trench *really* say that he wished your father would die?'

There was no hesitation. She looked me straight in the eye. She seemed as sincere as a person could be.

'Yes,' she said.

THIRTY-FOUR

'So the day didn't go quite as well as you might have expected,' Patrick said.

'Not quite, no.'

We had opted to eat dinner in the kitchen and were now considering going out to a movie. But Patrick was not much in the mood to be recognized, and he'd insisted on putting a complete state-of-the-art screening room into the house, so we were probably going to end up watching a film at home. First, we had to clean up the kitchen and have a conversation about how swell my first day at trial was (I'm from New Jersey, so you have to expect some sarcasm) and how he hadn't left the house today. This hiatus was going to be complicated, I saw. Because nobody knew how long it would last.

'If Francie says one thing and the lieutenant says another, how does the jury decide which one is lying?' Patrick asked as he hand-washed my dinner plate. There was no sense using the dishwasher for two people. I was clearing various items off the table and putting them away.

The mayonnaise – which we had not used for this meal – always goes in the door to the fridge. I don't know why, but the label is emphatic about it. So I moved the salad dressing on to the top shelf. 'Generally speaking, they believe the person they liked better on the stand,' I said. 'That doesn't bode well for Trench. Generally speaking.'

Patrick put the dishes in the dish drainer next to the sink. We don't dry dishes with towels in my house. We prefer the natural process. He turned and used the dishtowel to wipe his hands, because we do that. We're not barbarians. 'So how can you controvert what Francie said on the stand?' he asked.

'Controvert?'

'I'm British.'

'And very classy.' I was wiping down the table with a damp sponge. We'd given up on the antibacterial wipes left over from Covid because, well, a damp sponge is good, too. 'There's not much

I can do to *controvert* what Francie said, but I can make it look awfully unlikely that her story was accurate. Whether she was mistaken or lying will be up to the individual jurors to decide.'

'Who's next on the DA's witness list?' he asked.

'If we stick with the order he submitted in the witness list, it'll be the ex-wife, who I imagine will not testify for long, and then he'll get to the cops who were at the scene after Schaeffer was shot, and then he'll bring in the only physical evidence he has and talk to the ballistics expert from the LAPD, who will testify that the bullet in Schaeffer's brain matched Trench's gun. And I'd better have my own ballistics expert to say it doesn't when I get to call witnesses.'

Patrick looked a touch surprised. 'You don't have one scheduled yet?' He makes it sound like *sheduled* when I say *skeduled*. His way is cuter.

'We've been having trouble because the cops are being cagey about their own report on the bullet,' I said. 'They've submitted it in discovery, but only a summary, not the report itself.'

Patrick walked over as I put the sponge into the sink and scanned the room for unnoticed details, but found none that needed noticing. 'They can do that?' he asked.

'They claim they're getting us the full report, and they probably are, but they're dragging their feet.'

'Interesting?' Patrick asked.

'I'll let you know when I get the full report. Now, tell me about this script Angie wants you to produce.'

Patrick smiled his genuine smile, not one of the acting smiles. He gestured toward the kitchen entrance and toward the screening room, and I walked in that direction. He followed right behind. 'Angie has not lost her touch,' he said. 'It's a very funny script and it will make a good movie.'

'I hear a "but" coming.'

'You do. *But* I'm not sure the role is right for me and I'm not sure it's the movie I want to produce *now*. It'll take years to develop, then get to a studio for distribution and to actually film. I don't know if I have the passion for it that Angie does. She might do better with another actor to play the lead.'

We sat down on the cushy sofa we had in front of the absurdly large screen, but we weren't thinking about a film to watch yet. I reached over and took Patrick's hand. (I'd give it back later.) 'I think you've only been on hiatus for a couple of days and you're already starting to go stir crazy,' I said. 'Maybe plunging into a new project wouldn't be such an awful thing.'

Patrick laughed lightly. 'I love you, darling, but don't pretend you understand the film business any more than I understand the legal profession.'

Dem's fightin' words, pardner. 'What does that mean?' Patrick got his hand back sooner than I'd anticipated.

'It means that at the moment, having given up a fairly successful series after being fired – in the eyes of the industry – from a very successful one, I need to score a big hit to keep my name in the conversation for better roles.' Patrick took *my* hand this time. 'It's not that I think you're ignorant of what I do; you have a good grasp of it. But you tend to think of it from the artistic standpoint, or from the view of someone who loves me and wants me to do something that will make me happy, but not from the perspective of someone who considers the business end of the . . . business.'

'Like Patsy?' I asked. Patsy DeNunzio was Patrick's late wife, who had been a singer and was involved in the film business. I met her once, at the only hearing for the divorce she didn't live long enough to get.

'Stop being jealous of Patsy,' Patrick said. 'I was divorcing her when I met you.'

'I'm not jealous. I'm trying to determine what I could do to understand your work better.' OK, so I was a little jealous of Patsy. Patrick still spoke fondly of her, as opposed to having suggested he could kill her at that conference. It's a long story.

'I don't need you to understand my work any better than you already do,' he told me now. 'I think being in the same line of business was one of the things that drove Patsy and me apart. I need Angie to understand my business and she is doing a spectacular job of it, but she wants to choose my roles for me and I'm not letting her do that.'

'Isn't that what Josh is for?' Josh was Patrick's agent. He also had a business manager whose name I kept forgetting. Harry? Henry? Something else with an H?

'Josh takes offers and suggests my name to people he knows are planning a project that I might find interesting. He *can* bring my name up in conversations, but he has to know the film or series is being cast before he knows to do it, and often these things are conceived by an actor who has a production company.'

'Like you.'

'Like me, yes. But I'm not going "stir crazy," as you say. I just don't think Angie's passion for this script is the same as my own. But I do think she should produce it.'

Produce it? *Angie?* Things had come a long way since she'd taken a leave of absence from her job running Dairy Queen franchises to come to Los Angeles and save my life. Now she was a movie producer. I wondered if she knew that.

'You think Angie should be a producer?' I needed to hear him say it. The only way it would be better was if Angie were here in the room.

'I think she already is,' Patrick answered. 'She just needs to take the instincts she has and apply them. She likes this comedy. I think she'd be good at comedy and action movies. So this is a good project for her to use as a beginning.'

I squeezed his hand a little harder. 'You're a wonderful employer,' I said.

'And at the moment I am unemployed, but my company has five different projects in various stages of development. We can keep the lights on in the house for a while, Sandra.' I hadn't actually been worrying about that, but now that he'd brought it up I would for a bit. Once I got done with Trench.

'Patrick, how does an actor react – on stage, especially, when it's live – if someone does something they didn't expect?'

His eyebrows lowered, either thinking or concerned about me and my lack of ability to segue. 'This is about the lieutenant's case, isn't it?' he asked finally.

'You know me so well.'

Patrick put on his thinking face, all serious and mouth pulled in. Anyone else would have looked ridiculous. 'There are two keys to dealing with another actor who goes off book or forgets their lines,' he said. 'First, you have to keep in mind who *you* are and stay in character. React the way your character, not you, would react.'

'What's the second key?'

'It's the key to almost everything in acting,' he said, his eyes getting a little dreamy and unfocused. 'You've got to really live in the moment.'

Now there was a term I'd heard in any number of contexts.

Therapists, yoga instructors, mentors. OK, mostly therapists. I'd gone when my parents divorced and was sent home for being too sane. 'What does that mean, practically?' I asked Patrick.

'For an actor, it means not trying to remember your next line and not trying to think back to something you did in the last act or at last night's performance,' he answered. 'You have to deal with right now all the time, and this is key: You have to be conscious of all that's going on in that moment. Who your character is, who the other character is, what their circumstances are and what everybody wants. Then you can get through it and help your acting partner do the same.'

I let the sofa absorb me a bit. 'That sounds hard.'

'You start to have more respect for actors who make it look easy, don't you?' Patrick reached for one of the myriad remote controls he had on the table in front of us. 'Did that help you at all?'

It was a good question. 'Maybe. I had a plan I wanted to use with Schaeffer's ex-wife, but I think I'm going to scrap it. Someone convinced Francie to fabricate a story about Lt Trench and I can't be sure it wasn't her mother, or that Marcia hasn't also been corrupted as a witness. So I have to go at it differently.'

Patrick, probably already anticipating what I was going to say, smiled. 'How?' he asked.

'I have to think about what she wants and stay in the moment,' I told him.

THIRTY-FIVE

'I hadn't seen Wally in at least three months when I heard he was dead,' Marcia Sweeney Schaeffer Liebowitz Kendall said. 'He wasn't paying me alimony for years, and our daughter is an adult, technically, so we had no reason to talk to each other.'

There was a lot to unpack in Marcia's testimony and she'd just gotten started. But Barnett was not having any of it; he was focused on the line of questioning he'd no doubt rehearsed. And good for him. That's what I would have done.

'Who called to let you know he had been shot?' he asked.

Marcia was looking at the jury. She seemed to find them fascinating, like she was flirting with them. The jurors, for their part, were watching Marcia but didn't seem likely to ask her out anytime soon.

'Well, I wasn't his wife anymore and hadn't been for a long time, so the department didn't send anybody to my door,' she said. 'Actually a friend of mine saw it on Twitter and called to ask if this was the same guy I'd been married to, and that's how I found out.'

'You said you hadn't seen your ex-husband for a few months before he was murdered,' Barnett reminded her. He liked to use the word 'murder' whenever possible, as if the jury might forget why they were there and cite Trench for jaywalking. 'Had you spoken to him or heard from him online at all?'

'Yeah, he called me about a week before,' Marcia said. 'He wanted me to ask my husband if we could lend him some money. He said he had medical bills.'

'Did he say anything about being worried that someone was after him?' Barnett asked.

I stood up. 'I believe the prosecutor is leading the witness,' I said.

'Question withdrawn.' Barnett kept any irritation out of his voice. I was ruining his rhythm but he wasn't going to let it stop him. 'What else did Wally say when he called you?'

'He said he was worried that someone was after him.' The rules of the courtroom are many and various, but they quite often don't have the practical effect that was no doubt intended when they were written.

'Worried in what way?' Barnett asked. I wondered how many ways there were to be worried, and how one would make the distinction.

This seemed to stump Marcia as well, and she stared blankly at Barnett for a moment. 'I guess like he thought someone was trying to kill him,' she said, but it sounded more like a question, as if she were asking the DA if that was the right answer.

'Did he mention who he thought it might be?'

You had to see the answer coming. 'He was scared of K.C. Trench,' Marcia said.

Trench, as was his habit, did not react. But I think I saw his jaw tighten a bit. If he testified, he wouldn't be able to deny that he had some serious animosity toward Schaeffer, but he knew he'd never really considered killing his fellow detective, except for maybe a split second when he let the brake pedal on his car slip just a bit. But there was no one on Barnett's witness list who would be testifying to that point, so I felt a little better.

'Why was . . . did your ex-husband say why he was afraid of Lt Trench?' Barnett asked. That was a cute little signal to me that he had been annoyed with my objection. Tough. It was a good objection.

Marcia, having learned her lines, smiled a bit because she knew what to say. 'He said Trench blamed him for his wife's death, even though he had nothing to do with it. She was shot by a criminal in a supermarket.'

And suddenly there was a stranger in the chair next to me. That was not the Lt Trench I knew, and now he wasn't in the chair, either. He stood up and pointed at Marcia. 'That's a lie.' Even now he wouldn't shout. 'Detective Schaeffer deliberately sent Susan into that crime scene . . .'

I touched my client on the sleeve and he looked down at me, startled. 'You're *not helping*,' I said as quietly as possible. Trench sat down while Barnett failed to disguise the self-satisfied smirk on his face.

'Ms Moss, please instruct your client that he may not address the witnesses or speak out of turn, or he will be held in contempt of this court,' Huffman said, because stating the obvious was his new hobby.

'It won't happen again, Your Honor,' I said.

'I'm sure it won't.' Judges like to have the last word.

Trench looked as emotional as I'd ever seen him, which wasn't much. His eyes were open and clear. His mouth was closed, thank goodness. He was breathing a touch heavily, like the outburst had drained him of his usual energy. He was lightly biting his lips, perhaps to hold them in position. For anyone else this was a slight change in tone; for Trench it was equivalent to him singing an aria for baritone from Leoncavallo's *Pagliacci*. And weeping through it.

Barnett, meanwhile, was barely holding off his celebration while facing Marcia again. 'Did Wally say anything else of note?' he asked.

'Yeah. Instead of saying "so long" or "see ya soon" when he hung up, he said "goodbye."'

'Why is that significant?' the DA said, pressing his point.

'Because he thought he was going to be dead soon and this might be the last time we spoke.'

'Thank you, Marcia.' Barnett headed back to the prosecution table. Huffman looked at me, and I stood up and walked toward the witness box.

'Hi, Marcia,' I said. She didn't look at me. I think Marcia knew she was in the act of a small betrayal, based on our history of her drinking while I didn't, and us bonding through that. 'Tell me, how often were you speaking with your ex the past, say, five years or so?'

Marcia wrinkled her brow. 'Five years? Not too much. Maybe two, three times.'

'And in those conversations, did Detective Schaeffer mention Lt Trench by name at all?'

Marcia didn't hesitate. 'No.'

'OK. So there was no mention of the lieutenant until this final conversation you had with your ex-husband.'

Marcia still wasn't looking at me. 'Not specifically, no.'

'And even then your ex didn't speak Lt Trench's name, did he?'

Eyes at half-mast. 'No.' She wanted this to be over. But it wasn't yet.

'Marcia, did it strike you as odd that your ex-husband was suddenly worried about some threat, which he didn't detail, from Lt Trench about his wife's death, despite it being more than five years after she was killed in the line of duty?'

She was staring straight ahead, not at anything or anyone in particular. It was like watching an AI program testify, but with a little more inflection in the voice. A little. 'I wasn't paying attention to that. I didn't know how long it had been. What's the difference?' Trench's hands curled into fists but his face betrayed nothing.

'Marcia,' I asked, 'did your ex-husband say that Lt Trench had threatened him directly in any way?'

Now she did look at me and she appeared annoyed, as if I should just accept that Trench had shot Schaeffer and concede the point. How dare I ask questions that might put that hypothesis in doubt? 'No,' she said flatly.

'Did you ever hear Lt Trench threaten your ex?' I knew that Marcia was not present when Trench made his uncharacteristic pronouncement at the LAPD holiday party years before.

'No.' Now it was like we were a married couple who were having an argument and she just wanted me to go away.

Sometimes you improvise. 'Marcia, do you believe that Lt Trench killed your ex-husband?'

She was happy to answer that one. 'Yes,' she said, a little too emphatically (but not so emphatically that I would put it in italics).

'Why?'

That one startled Marcia. 'Because he thought Wally had done something to kill his wife,' she said.

'No, I meant why do you think the lieutenant is the one who shot Detective Schaeffer?' Now, Marcia had totally known what I meant by the question but hoped she could deflect it because she didn't have a good answer.

It hadn't been enough time for her to think of an especially convincing one. 'Because Wally said he was afraid of Trench.'

'When? You said he hadn't mentioned the lieutenant by name in five years.'

Barnett was up like a jack-in-the-box, but a well-dressed one. 'Your Honor, the witness has testified that Wally Schaeffer had said the defendant was after him and that he feared for his life.'

Huffman turned to look in my direction, so I obliged him. 'No she didn't, Your Honor,' I said. 'The court reporter can verify that all Ms Wallace said was that her ex-husband was afraid of the lieutenant, which was a subjective statement. Detective Schaeffer never mentioned the lieutenant by name at all.'

Huffman trained his eyes on Barnett. 'That's how I heard it, Mr District Attorney. Objection is overruled. Assuming that was an objection.' Oof.

I walked back over to Marcia. 'When did your ex-husband say that Lt Trench was threatening to kill him?' I asked.

Marcia had made her face smaller somehow. 'He didn't.' She wanted a divorce from me now. It would be her fourth.

'You said your ex-husband was calling to ask if your current husband could help pay his medical bills. Didn't he have the LAPD's medical insurance plan?'

Barnett gestured without standing up. 'Relevance, Your Honor?'

I looked at the judge. 'If she's lying about that, she can be lying about the rest,' I said.

Huffman looked irritated. 'Objection sustained. Enough, Ms Moss.'

I nodded at the witness. 'Thank you, Marcia.' I walked back to the defense table while the judge informed us we'd be in recess for lunch.

When people started to file out of the courtroom, Trench looked at me. 'She and her daughter were both lying,' he said.

'I know.'

'You'd spoken to both of them before, Ms Moss. Did you know this was what they would say on the stand?' Trench was interested in process; he wasn't castigating me for not being prepared.

'No. I would not have bet they'd change their stories like that.'

Trench seemed to regard that and looked straight into my face, which was his habit. 'What do you think it tells us?' he asked.

'That somebody got to them.'

He stood up to make his way out. 'Very good, Ms Moss,' he said.

THIRTY-SIX

I went back to my 'office' for a quick lunch and to check up on a few of the family law cases I still had on my desk. But my phone was loaded with texts and voicemails from Nate, so I called him back as soon as Holly was finished reminding me that the meeting about my becoming a partner in the firm would be held within a week of Trench's trial ending, one way or another. If I was in the midst of putting together an appeal of a guilty verdict, the meeting would still take place. I'd prefer to avoid that, so first I got back to Nate.

'Where you been?' he wanted to know.

'In court, defending our client,' I said. 'Why didn't you know that?'

'I've been busy. Found out a few things that you can use. To begin with, did you see which uniformed cops the DA has testifying for him?'

'Yup. Clifton Armstrong and James Clanton.' Our two friends from the pizza place and the set of *Torn*. Go figure.

'Somebody thinks they're credible,' Nate said.

'Who?' I asked. He meant someone in the LAPD.

'The same guy – sorry, *person* – who is playing fast and loose with the ME's report and the ballistics data,' Nate said. 'We haven't been able to get complete copies of either one, and that's awful clumsy for anyone above the rank of meter maid.'

'Meter *person*.'

'Of course. But I should be able to get you those files within a couple of days. When do you get to present your case?'

I looked over the list of witnesses Barnett had submitted. 'End of the week, earliest,' I said. 'This guy really wants to put on a pageant.'

'That shouldn't be a problem.' He must have turned away. 'I know, Angie; calm down!'

Apparently this was Angie's half-day to apprentice with Nate. And she was a movie producer now.

'Angie wants the phone,' Nate said before it was clearly snatched out of his hands by my shrinking-violet best friend.

'We've solved the case.' Angie gets right to the heart of the matter, and she's rarely wrong, so my heart beat a little faster.

'Tell me,' I said.

'Schaeffer was on drugs,' Angie said.

OK, sure. I didn't know why that was important, and it had no bearing whatsoever on whether Trench had shot him, but it was sort of an interesting fact. If we had the name of Schaeffer's dealer and found out he'd owed a lot of money, maybe there'd be something to hook into. Right now, I didn't see the point.

'OK,' I said.

'No. You don't get it. Schaeffer was on something called Krazati.'

Well, she was right about me not getting it. 'I've never heard of that one,' I told Angie.

'No. You haven't. Because you don't have lung cancer.'

Well, that had taken a quick left turn. 'Schaeffer had lung cancer?'

Nate must have wrestled the phone away from Angie again, because he responded. 'It looks that way. He was on an oral medication called Krazati. It's a pretty new drug that helps some people with certain kinds of lung cancer. I haven't seen the ME's report, but I'll bet that's in there. I got it because he was using the union's pharmacy plan and they do mail order.'

'Isn't that against all sorts of HIPAA laws?' I asked.

'It's best that you don't ask questions,' my investigator told me. That wasn't especially reassuring.

My mind was racing but I still didn't see how this information cleared Trench. *Somebody* had shot Wally Schaeffer, and whether or not he was ill, even dying, at the time seemed irrelevant. 'I'm not seeing a way to help the lieutenant with this,' I told Nate.

'Frankly, neither am I. But I bet there is one.'

A topic for another day. 'What else have you got?' I needed something just to raise my own spirits. I didn't have to raise my client's spirits. I wasn't sure Trench *had* spirits.

'A theory about the fire,' Nate answered. 'I think it was set hours before it started burning, maybe the night before, and ignited remotely. We need to see some of the other security footage.'

The fire. I guessed that could help lead to a shooter, but at the moment it was delaying my return to my own real office for a ridiculous period of time and should have been out of my head weeks before. 'That's something,' I said.

'I'll call you later.' Nate didn't hand the phone back to Angie and he didn't wait to hear if I had any further instructions. He was busy being Nate.

I sat in my little prison cell for a bit and tried not to think about Trench being in a similar, but locked, space for a number of years. That wasn't going to help me prevent it from happening. I did a couple of quick things to get a divorce and a custody (of a cockatoo) dispute out of the way, and then I was ready to dive back into Trench's case.

But I didn't.

Instead, I called Patrick. 'Do you think you could come to the trial to lend some moral support tomorrow?' I asked. It had turned out that exactly what I hadn't wanted was exactly what I had needed all along.

'Certainly,' he answered. 'But first I'm going to give you an address. You should be certain to get there by seven.'

Ooh. 'What'll happen when I get there?' I asked.

'It's a surprise.'

It was, but not the kind I had been picturing. And somehow, Angie had beaten me to the address and had a margarita before I even walked through the door. She must have been watching because she sidled over to me almost immediately. 'Welcome to the *Torn* wrap party!' she said.

Sure enough, the soundstage to which Patrick had directed me was decorated for a very elaborate celebration. I'd been to wrap parties with Patrick before, but they were not this large. Maybe it was because this was the last one this group would celebrate together. Wrap parties are weird; groups of people who have worked together intensely for months and found all different kinds of closeness (some of them *very* close indeed) gathered and over the course of an evening realized they wouldn't be seeing each other regularly – or in some cases, at all – anymore. What started out jubilant often sloshed over into maudlin depending on how long the open bar was, you know, open.

Neon signs had been hung with the *Torn* logo flashing. There was, and I'm not making this up, a bounce house in the center of the cavernous space. There were pinball machines lining the walls (and people playing them) as well as stations with virtual reality goggles available. People were wearing those and wandering around aimlessly. One area all the way on the other side of the stage had a very (in my opinion) ill-advised water slide. I saw one man in a business suit getting wet so he could be behind a woman wearing considerably less. But she was still dressed for this celebration.

'Is this the Feldstein bar mitzvah?' I asked Angie.

'Come on. I planned it myself. The idea is for everybody to break out and have some fun for a change!'

'That's the goal at the Feldstein bar mitzvah too. Except most of the people there have broken out already.'

'Have a drink.' My friend always has the best advice. 'Patrick's over there in the cluster of people.'

She spoke the truth; my boyfriend was at the center of a small, but growing, klatch of people who had worked with him for months and in some cases years, but were coming to the conclusion that this was *it*. 'Looks like he's going to be held up for a while,' I said.

'Wait until everybody else gets here. Come on, I'll get you a drink.'

This wasn't everyone? Maybe I did need that drink. I let Angie herd me to one of the bars (there were six) and order me something other than the glass of white wine I actually wanted. I was busy taking in the sight of people in the television business enjoying themselves and trying to line up a new job at the same time.

'I hear you're a movie producer now,' I told Angie as we left the bar for a table near the bounce house. It was loud there, but that helped us be unheard by the rest of the growing crowd.

'Patrick told you? I'm not sure it's going to happen. I'm not sure I can do it.' Angie was drinking something the color of a Smurf. It wouldn't have any effect on her. I've never actually seen Angie drunk. Alcohol is afraid of her.

'Of course you can do it,' I said. 'You can do anything. And I know, because I've seen you do anything.'

Angie waved a hand to indicate that I had been joking; I hadn't. 'This is a skill set that I've never trained for,' she said. 'Three years ago, I was managing two Dairy Queens.'

'And managing them beautifully. But you've been studying this business since Patrick gave you a job, and every time I see you, you've been promoted again. You'll be in charge of Hollywood within five years at this rate. They'll all just accede to your brilliance and line up.'

Angie took a healthy gulp of whatever blue substance that was. 'You're a nut,' she said.

'I'm drinking something with a color that occurs in nature,' I said. 'Who's the nut?'

There were about twenty security guards, in outfits that wanted to be police uniforms, scattered around the soundstage. So far they'd done a grand total of nothing because there had been no disturbances. Even the guy in the wet suit had behaved himself with the woman in less than that. So it was a little disconcerting when I saw one of the guards headed our way.

'Ang,' I said.

'Relax. You weren't going over the speed limit.'

'I wasn't the last time, either.'

My anxiety was only heightened when I saw Judy, who had been keeping a discreet distance, walking purposefully toward me. I stood up to intercept the security guard, or at least to be on my feet when he reached me in case running was going to be included in the evening's activities.

Judy got there first because she's Judy. She looked at me, sensed my tension, and said, 'Don't worry, ma'am.' Then she did the last thing I expected her to do: She turned toward the security guard, who was just coming within earshot, and reached over to embrace him. 'Terry,' she said.

'Judy. Good to see you.' The guard had an avuncular voice and when the hug broke up it turned out he had a friendly smile as well. 'What are you doing here?'

'Working,' Judy said. 'Just like you. Are you still on the job?' That's what cops say about being cops.

Terry's eyes darted back and forth. 'Maybe there's someplace we can talk,' he said.

Judy, the guard and I ended up on one of the sets of *Torn*, which had not been taken down yet but would be the next day. Turned away from the crowd was the office of Patrick's character (or one of his characters, since the show was built on a somewhat-outdated 'multiple personality' premise that Patrick had grown to hate), so we could sit down in that 'room' without the danger of being heard or even fully seen.

Angie, the unofficial hostess of the party, had understood this was a private conversation and went off to attend to the celebration, probably by playing a lot of pinball. She's great at pinball, too.

'I'm taking this on the side just to make some extra money,'

Terry told Judy. 'But I came over to talk to you, Ms Moss. You're defending Lt Trench, aren't you?'

I acknowledged that I was Trench's lawyer.

'How is the case going?' Terry asked.

I didn't know where Terry was coming from. He seemed to be friendly with Judy, likely from her days on the LAPD, but every active officer I'd run into so far had some gripe with Trench and wanted him to go to prison for the rest of his life. That was a sentiment with which I disagreed, so it wasn't clear how to approach Terry's question. 'It's still early in the trial,' I said. 'But we maintain that the lieutenant did not shoot Detective Schaeffer.' I had established where I stood without requiring Terry to do the same.

He looked at Judy. 'She doesn't trust me,' he said.

'She never met you before,' Judy pointed out.

'That's true.' Terry turned to face me. 'I stand with Lt Trench. But I've heard some things in the department that worry me about his case. Somebody wants him in prison, and maybe they want that because they know someone on the inside who could silence him for good.'

OK, that took a while to sink in. 'If the lieutenant gets convicted, there are already plans to have him killed in prison?' I said, my voice rising more than I wanted it to. 'Who's behind that plot?'

Terry shook his head with what I guessed was frustration. 'If I knew, I'd tell you. But here's the thing: I know something funny happened with the test on the bullet that supposedly killed Schaeffer.'

'*Supposedly* killed him?' I said. 'Are you saying he's not dead?'

He held up his hands as if surrendering. 'No, no. I'm saying it's not certain that the bullet they're showing to you is the one that actually killed him. I know a guy in ballistics, and he is afraid for his life.'

I felt the hair on the back of my arms flutter. Luckily I was wearing long sleeves. 'Who is he afraid of?' I asked Terry.

'Even he doesn't know. But orders are coming through unusual channels and he doesn't know what to believe about this homicide.' Terry hadn't stopped sweeping the room with his eyes and I noticed Judy doing the same thing. So far they hadn't spotted anything disturbing, or had chosen not to say anything about it.

I leaned forward and rested my elbows on my legs so I could speak forcefully but quietly to Terry. 'What was he told to do?'

Terry shook his head. 'That's the wrong question. It's really what he was given to analyze. My friend – and no, I'm not giving you a name, no matter how much I want to – said the bullet he was given to compare to the one they test fired from Lt Trench's gun didn't go through the usual channels. And he was told in no uncertain terms not to question anything that was going on.'

I'm not an exponent of conspiracy theories. Any decent investigation into most of what you see presented as fact on the internet can be disproven in less than ten minutes. But the idea that an exhibit in a murder trial might not be what it was being presented as meant that someone in the LAPD, and possibly someone fairly high up the chain of command, was deliberately committing any number of crimes in order to get Lt Trench convicted.

He wasn't kidding when he said he wasn't well-liked among the ranks.

'You won't tell me who your friend is,' I said. 'If I found him on my own, do you think he would testify?'

Terry looked at me as if I had suggested he simply grow an extra arm to use in emergencies. 'Not a chance,' he said. 'Like I said, he's afraid for his life. He knows someone is keeping an eye on him and they don't want this information to come out.'

So this was a major breakthrough that was going to yield me a grand total of nothing I could use in court. Even if I got Terry (assuming he had a last name) to testify, he'd be able to offer nothing except hearsay and that would get thrown out of the record in seconds. The jury would be instructed to ignore it.

So that was a non-starter. Probably. 'Terry, if I asked you, would *you* testify?'

Judy actually registered surprise, which I didn't think was possible. Her eyes widened and then went back to normal, as if embarrassed they had left their initial expression to begin with. She gave her head a shake, I think trying to convince Terry and me that her momentary lapse had been the result of a sudden chill or something heavy she'd eaten for dinner. If Judy ever ate.

'You're asking a lot,' Terry said after he could look me in the eye again.

'I know. And I'm not sure I'm going to ask you, but if I do I need to know whether you'll do so willingly. I could ask the court to issue a subpoena, but I don't need you in the witness chair feeling hostile toward the defense. If you won't do it, say so and I'll find another way. If you will testify, I might or might not contact you and ask you to do so. What do you say, Terry? I know you want to help the lieutenant.'

He dropped his head down again and seemed to nod it like he was doing a workout routine where he had to do pulses with his neck. 'If you need me, I'll be there,' he said without looking up. 'But don't need me.'

'I'll try not to,' I said. 'But you are going to have to tell me your last name.'

THIRTY-SEVEN

T he rest of the party, Angie would like me to tell you, was a huge success and everyone had a fantastic time. I was mostly on the phone to Nate from outside the soundstage, where the music and general din was too loud for my poor little iPhone. The parts I saw were just lovely.

The next day in court, the issue of the ballistics test was raised immediately when Barnett called J Middleton Powell (I'm not making that name up), the head of the Firearm Analysis Unit of the LAPD. J, a gray-haired man of indeterminate age (anywhere from late 40s to mid-70s because I really can't judge such things, especially in Southern California) carried himself like minor royalty. I sort of expected him to be carrying a scepter as he walked to the witness box. But he wasn't.

Sworn in and looking solemn and official, J looked at Barnett as if assessing a peer, which technically he was, and gave up no facial expression. He was a statistician and a scientist and wanted you (particularly if you were on the jury) to know that he had no skin in the game. He dealt with facts.

'Mr Powell,' Barnett began.

'Technically, it's Dr Powell,' J told him. 'I have a Ph.D. and am employed by the Forensic Science Division of the LAPD.'

'My apologies, Dr Powell,' Barnett said.

J then waved a hand as if shooing the smallest of flies. 'It couldn't matter less.' Except he'd gone miles out of his way to bring it up.

'*Dr* Powell.' Barnett was anxious to get on with it and cut this nonsense. 'Did you perform a number of tests on the bullet that was removed from Wally Schaeffer's skull after he died?' A couple of jurors winced, like they hadn't already known Schaeffer was shot in the back of the head. Barnett was making them uncomfortable just when he wanted to do exactly that.

'My unit was tasked with that analysis,' he said, which told us nothing.

'Did you perform the tests yourself?' Barnett asked.

'I did not,' J said, 'but trusted members of my team did perform them, and I reviewed them before signing off.'

'And what conclusions did you reach after the tests were conducted and confirmed?' Like anyone thought he'd ask if they didn't seem to substantiate the prosecution's case. So much of court is theater.

'That the specimen . . .'

'The bullet,' Barnett corrected.

'Yes. The bullet we received from the victim was fired from the weapon that had been retrieved from Lt Trench's home,' J, the little rat, said.

'There was no room for error?' Barnett asked, because he was really enjoying the moment.

'No. The markings on the . . . bullet taken from the body matched the ones from another bullet we fired as a test in the lab.' J had no doubt testified in court before, but was still mostly used to speaking to and with other lab rats who knew all the nomenclature. It's like getting a group of lawyers together to talk, something I don't recommend if you're not a member of the bar.

'If it pleases the court, may we see prosecution exhibit E?' Barnett asked the judge. Huffman nodded and pointed at the bailiff, who spoke quietly into his communication link to the audio/video officer. Screens where the judge, the jury and the attorneys could view them lit up with what I'm sure J thought were fascinating images of spent bullets. 'Dr Powell, could you point out for us on the tablet computer by your seat how these two bullets can be identified as having been fired from the same gun?' A lot of words for 'show us the lines.'

J then went on for an extended period of time showing us lines in bullets that at least to the naked eye appeared to match. I had no doubt they did and therefore planned not to challenge that particular part of J's expertise. It was his ability as an administrator I found questionable.

'So there is no question that the bullet that killed Wallace Schaeffer was fired from Lt K.C. Trench's gun. Is that a fair statement, Doctor?'

Surprisingly, J took a moment to think that over. 'I think it is a fair statement,' he said. 'But in every case there is the possibility for error or misinterpretation. So is there no question? I would say there is very close to no question.'

Barnett looked like he wanted to throttle his star witness, but that would look bad and looking bad was Barnett's worst nightmare, so he controlled himself. 'Thank you, Dr Powell,' he said, and walked back to his table.

I stood up at mine. 'Dr Powell,' I said. 'You have testified that the bullet that was fired from Lt Trench's gun as a test in your facility matches the one you received from the medical examiner's office as having been removed from Detective Schaeffer. That's correct?'

J was happy I had acknowledged his genius. 'Yes,' he said, trying to suppress his eager grin.

'Can you tell us the process that goes into the delivery of a bullet from a homicide victim to get it to your unit?' I asked.

'The process of delivery?' J asked. The grin had been replaced with a look of some confusion.

'Yes. How does the bullet that a medical examiner removes from a body end up in your lab for testing? What has to be done for it to get there?'

Barnett had no doubt figured where I was going with this, and he stood up. 'Objection for relevance,' he said. 'Who cares how the bullet is transported from one office to another? It still matches.'

'Of course it matches,' I said. 'The defense concedes that point for the time being. The question is really whether the bullet Dr Powell had to examine was actually the one that was fired into Detective Schaeffer.'

Patrick was probably thrilled at that moment that I'd agreed he could come to court today, because he thinks I'm a stunning legal mind and no doubt thought I had just turned Barnett's case on its ear. I glanced at him quickly, a row behind the defense table next to Judy, and he had almost applauded. Patrick lives for applause and thinks everyone else does, too.

'I'll allow this line of questioning, but I don't want it to take up the rest of the day,' Huffman said. 'Make sure you get to a point in a reasonable period of time, Ms Moss.'

I assured him I would and then looked back at good ol' J. 'Please, Dr Powell. How does the bullet make it from the ME's office to you?'

He had been given enough time to compose himself, sitting straighter in his chair and puffing out his chest a bit. 'The item, in this case a bullet from a police service weapon, is marked by the medical examiner immediately after removal and placed in a similarly marked container, in this case a sealed plastic evidence bag, then addressed specifically to our unit. Someone in the ME's office will deliver it to us in a very short period of time.'

I had been nodding along to indicate I was following everything he'd said, which was partially true. I was also planning my next question. 'What precautions are taken to ensure that the bullet isn't removed or tampered with?'

'The container, in this case—'

'The resealable plastic bag, yes,' I said. Because I just had to.

'Yes. It is marked with a code created by our security software and must match when we receive it. We are also sent an email with the codes for all that day's items and their corresponding evidence numbers.' J looked quite officious now, folding his hands in his lap and keeping his face impassive.

'And the bullet from your lab tests? How would that have been secured?' I asked.

'In much the same way. After a round is fired from the weapon being tested, the technician collects and bags it for comparison. The same codes, that is, the same kind of codes, are used in identifying the specimen.' He forgot to use the word 'bullet' there. No doubt Barnett would scold him later. I hoped J could stand it.

I tried to look blank, like I was just starting to understand. 'So in this case, the technician in your lab who fired Lt Trench's gun would have generated an identification code for the bullet they had fired as a test. Then they would have attached that code to the spent bullet and isolated it from other test cases. They would have bagged the bullet and done what with it? At what point would the two bullets have been in the same room at the same time?'

J had listened very carefully during the question, and it showed. He looked professorial, even more than when it had been announced that his name was J Middleton Powell. The bow tie he was wearing added to the persona. 'When it has been established that the exhibit from the ME's office is in house, that is, when our unit is in possession of it, it will be matched with the test exhibit from the weapon we were given by the police. Then our analysts will examine the specimens to see if they are indeed identical. In this case, they were.'

'Who did those comparisons, Dr Powell?' I asked.

He examined me a moment, seeming to wonder how such a stupid woman had been trusted with this case. 'As I said, they were performed by trusted members of my team.'

'Names, Doctor. Names. Who were the people who performed

these side-by-side comparisons that you claim prove the bullet in Detective Schaeffer's skull had come from Lt Trench's service weapon?'

J blinked a few times. 'I would have to consult the report,' he said.

'Consult away, Dr Powell. Your report is part of the record and has been entered into evidence.' I looked up at Huffman. 'Can we have that exhibit . . . document . . . shown to the witness on his screen?' I asked.

'Objection, Mr District Attorney?'

There was no way Barnett could object to his witness reading a document he himself had entered into evidence. 'None, Your Honor.'

'So ordered.' Judges like to order things. He could just as easily said, 'OK,' and been done with it.

I saw the iPad on J's knee light up and he picked it up gingerly, as if wondering what this odd magical artifact might be. But he scrolled expertly through his own report. 'The tests were performed by Evelyn Woodruff and Marshall Gianinni,' he said. 'Both well certified and trusted members of my team.' At this point I thought J might have trusted members of his team too much, or trusted too many members of his team.

'Would it be possible, Dr Powell, for anyone – either the people who did the comparison tests, or the couriers who brought the two bullets to the lab – to have switched the items in those sealable plastic bags? How do we know those are the right bullets?'

There was one of those murmurs throughout the courtroom that you hear on TV courtroom dramas. I hear one about every 17 cases. And they're barely audible. But you know you've struck a nerve when you hear it.

'They were definitely the right bullets,' J said with a huffy tone. 'The identification codes matched and there was no evidence of tampering on either of the evidence bags.'

'How many stickers with the identification codes are created when the technicians number the items they're sending along?' I asked.

'I don't have that information at my fingertips.' J slipped a little on the word 'fingertips.'

'OK, we'll let that go for now.' I figured I was being magnanimous, but Barnett's expression indicated he did not agree. 'Dr Powell, wouldn't a bullet taken out of a man's skull look different by nature than one fired in a lab?'

'Look different in what way?' J asked.

'For example, I assume the medical examiner would have to use surgical instruments to remove the bullet, right? Isn't it possible there would be some scratching or markings due to the use of, say, forceps to remove the bullet?'

'Yes, that is certainly possible.'

'I see,' I said, giving the indication that I might at least have cataracts when it came to this particular point. 'So how would the person making the comparison compensate for that? I mean, the two bullets wouldn't actually be identical, would they?'

'I understand that you have not ever worked in a firearm analysis unit, Ms Moss.' J was going to condescend to the little lady now, a classic mistake they still think will work out well for them. 'Of course, the analysts are well trained in such matters and would be able to determine the difference between a mark made when a bullet is fired from a gun and one created by a surgical instrument. It would not in any way prejudice the analysis.'

I took a few steps away from the witness box and toward the defense table to signal that I was almost through questioning this witness. 'What if the analyst wanted the comparison to be positive?' I asked. 'Would it be possible to manipulate the markings to match a predetermined conclusion?'

J looked like he might have a fit of apoplexy. 'It would be against every rule of my unit to do something like that,' he said through clenched teeth.

'But is it possible? Could a trusted member of your team possess the skills to make a comparison come out as identical, even if the bullets did not match?'

Barnett was on his feet in less than a second. 'Objection!' Yes, he actually yelled.

'I'm not saying it happened,' I told Huffman. 'I'm asking if it's possible.'

The judge gave me a look to indicate he did not find this entertaining. 'Objection sustained. Strike the question from the record.'

I waved a nonchalant hand. 'No further questions, Your Honor.'

THIRTY-EIGHT

Huffman had given us Friday off so everyone involved, jurors mostly, could have a three-day weekend and think he was a hell of a humanitarian. So I spent the day trying to wrangle a meeting with Captain Bruce Moran of the LAPD's robbery-homicide division, because the city of Los Angeles believes it's just as bad being murdered as it is to get stuff stolen from you.

Once Moran ran out of excuses (meetings, lunch, probably a prostate exam), he deigned to speak to a defense attorney, of all people, and I showed up in his office with my trusty iPhone set on record.

He was a broad man, almost rectangular in shape, seemingly too wide to be proportional to his height, which was just below average. He had a neatly trimmed mustache. He wore a dark blue suit, not a dark blue uniform. Moran was his own man, his superior officers told him.

'I wasn't present when Lt Trench threatened Detective Schaeffer and I obviously wasn't there when Schaeffer was shot,' he told me right up front. I'd foolishly thought I might get a question in first. 'I don't know how I might be able to help you, Ms Moss.' As if helping me was even on his Top 100 Things to Do list.

'Part of my defense for the lieutenant is about the bullet that your forensic division says matches one fired from Lt Trench's gun,' I said. 'How is that traced back to the medical examiner's autopsy of Detective Schaeffer?'

'Everything we get from the ME is tagged and bagged, and everything is given a unique filing number so we know where everything went,' he said, as if that explained anything. 'And the markings on the bullet matched the markings from Lt Trench's service weapon. They match.'

Where had I heard this before? Oh yeah, in court from J Middleton Powell, bon vivant. 'How do you know that's the bullet from Schaeffer's body?' I asked. 'How do you know it wasn't exchanged for another bullet along the line?'

Moran stared at me like I'd said that Peru was invading Santa

Monica and we were going to need a bigger boat. 'I just explained that,' he said. 'There was a unique filing number.'

'But doesn't that assume that everyone dealing with the bullet is honest? Couldn't another ID tag have been printed for an empty bag and then another bullet would be substituted?'

'That's impossible.' Moran nervously played with his mustache. Luckily he'd been neat at lunch.

'Why?'

'Because there is never just one person dealing with something like that. There's always supervision. Nobody was ever alone with that bullet.' Except Schaeffer, but I didn't mention that.

'So at least two people who wanted to see Trench in jail would have to have been involved at the same time. Is that what you're saying?' I asked.

Moran opened and closed his mouth three times, fast. 'No!' he said. 'I'm saying that couldn't have happened.'

That was as much as I was going to get. 'Do you like Lt Trench, Captain?'

Of all the questions I'd asked, this appeared to be the one for which he was best prepared. 'Lt Trench is one of my best detectives,' he said.

'Why, after years of not putting them together, was Lt Trench partnered with Wallace Schaeffer on the Darren Wharton case?' It wasn't going to be part of my defense itself, but it might lead to something.

'I thought that the lieutenant's expertise might help with the case.' That said nothing, but luckily it didn't take long to not say it.

'Did someone request it?' I asked.

'Actually, Wally asked me for Trench, said he needed the help. Trench was too proud to say no just because he didn't like the guy.'

I stood up and nodded in his direction. 'One last thing.' Because I've studied my Columbo. 'How are Officer Clifton Anderson's gun range scores?'

Moran started to look it up on his computer and then stopped himself. 'That's not information I think you need to have,' he said. 'Now, please leave. I have duties to perform.'

And that was when I started to get an idea of what had actually happened.

THIRTY-NINE

'The lieutenant said, "If you laugh again, I will kill you," to Wally.'

LAPD Officer Kyle Murphy, perhaps 40, was holding his hat under his arm and sitting in the witness chair as stiffly and uncomfortably as I could imagine a person doing. But he was not sweating, he was not shaking, he did not stammer and in no way was he betraying anything other than competence. And with every word he stared just a little bit more intently at Trench.

The jury, of course, had been told as far back as Barnett's opening statement that they'd be hearing exactly this testimony, so Murphy's statement had little-to-no effect on their outward behavior at all. They were paying attention, but they were not shocked. They were also well-rested after a three-day weekend and ready for this trial to be over. I could relate.

'What was the context?' Barnett asked Murphy. 'How did the subject even arise at a holiday party?' Barnett was doing the thing lawyers do where they pretend to be naïve and amazed at something they themselves have been encouraging a witness to say for weeks. He was better at it than most, but not the best I've ever seen. Of course, I've used that tactic myself and I'm not the best I've ever seen, either.

'I didn't hear the whole thing because I was about fifteen feet away in a different part of a crowded room,' Murphy answered. 'So I don't know how it got started.'

'Did the lieutenant just stand up and shout that out of nowhere?' Barnett didn't *want* to plant the words in his witness's mouth, but he wasn't above doing it.

'As far as I know,' Murphy said. 'Like I said, I was not right in that part of the room when he said it, so there might have been other stuff happening first.'

'How did the defendant look when he said that to Detective Schaeffer?' How did he *look*? Who cared how he looked?

The question appeared to stump the witness, too, because he looked at Barnett for a decent-sized moment before looking back at Trench. 'Pretty much like he does now, only then he was standing up,' he answered.

Trench, for his part, was bordering on stoic, of course. Apparently being a sympathetic defendant in a murder trial wasn't part of the school curriculum on Vulcan, where he'd grown up. I preferred him being basically unreadable to him looking sinister, but an expression of concern or sympathy for Schaeffer, at least, wouldn't have been an awful thing.

'How did Wally Schaeffer react?' Barnett asked.

Now, I'd spoken to a few of the people who had been in the room and I thought this was an error on Barnett's part because I knew the answer to the question. But Murphy seemed to search his memory, as if Schaeffer's response had not been memorable at all.

'The detective looked surprised, first, and then he seemed to get mad at the lieutenant,' he said after he was finished thinking. 'Everybody else thought it was weird that the lieutenant would say something like that out in front of the whole department.'

I stood up because I hadn't objected to anything in a while. 'Objection,' I said. 'The witness can't know what other people in the room were thinking.'

'I'll sustain that,' Huffman said. 'Do you want to rephrase the question, Mr Barnett?'

'No, thank you, Your Honor. I'll move on. Officer Murphy, did Lt Trench move toward Detective Schaeffer after he spoke?'

Again, that was an example of very gently leading the witness, but I didn't see the point to objecting when Murphy would have said the same thing whether I did or not. If his answer was especially damaging, I could always raise an objection afterward, but I was puzzling over why Barnett had asked the question because no one I'd spoken to – including Trench, who would sooner rip off his left arm than lie – had mentioned anything even vaguely resembling an altercation at the party.

'Yes.' Murphy was direct and, no doubt as he'd been instructed, waited for the next question. I looked at Trench, who didn't react facially but shook his head a tiny bit to indicate that what the cop was saying hadn't happened. Slowly but surely, the lieutenant's faith in his fellow members of the Los Angeles Police Department was being eroded, and it must have hurt him awfully. Not that you'd know by looking at him.

'What happened?' Barnett asked.

'The lieutenant took a couple of steps toward Wally and pointed at him, but they were too far apart and there were too many people between them so they never reached each other.'

'And those were his exact words? "If you laugh again, I'll kill you for what you did." Is that right?'

'Maybe not his *exact* words,' Murphy said. Maybe there was a little sweat on his forehead now.

'Thank you.' Barnett walked back and left the lane open to me. I was going to keep this brief. 'Officer Murphy, what you're saying is that you heard one sentence out of what might have been an ongoing conversation, that you weren't looking at the defendant when that sentence was spoken, and that he took maybe two steps toward the victim but no more, and maybe not. Is that accurate?'

'I looked at him when he started talking,' Murphy said. His honor was at stake.

'Yes, but it was only one sentence. Are you even sure Lt Trench was the person speaking?' It was a cheap trick, but sometimes those work.

If nothing else, it got Barnett out of his chair. 'Objection. The witness has already stated it was the defendant making the threat.'

I looked at Huffman. 'I object to the word "threat,"' I said.

'I don't see how "I'd kill you" could be interpreted otherwise,' Huffman said. 'Objection sustained.'

'Which objection?' I asked.

'The prosecution's objection is the one I'm ruling on and you know it, Ms Moss.' OK, he had a point.

'Understood, Your Honor.' I walked back to the witness stand. 'Officer, have you ever heard someone say the words "I could kill you" before?'

Murphy knew where I was going and so did Barnett, but instead of looking trapped they appeared irritated with me, an emotion I was happy to live with. 'Yes,' Murphy said without inflection.

'In any of the times when you heard someone say that, did they kill the person they were talking to at that moment?'

'No.'

'Have *you* ever said it to someone?'

Murphy's eyes narrowed. 'Not that I recall.'

'No further questions.' I headed back to my table as Barnett stood up. 'Redirect, Your Honor?'

'Make it quick, Mr Barnett.'

Barnett didn't even bother walking to the witness box. 'Officer, did the defendant say, "I could kill you" to Wally Schaeffer?'

'No. He said, "If you laugh again, I'll kill you for what you did."'

Barnett sat back down. I looked at the jury. They weren't buying what I was selling. 'The witness is excused,' Huffman said, and Murphy walked all the way out of the courtroom.

I don't text when I'm in the courtroom, of course, but I wrote myself a note for a text to Nate at the next break: *Medical records and list of cops*. Don't worry; I knew what I meant.

Having sat back down, Barnett launched himself out of his chair again. Maybe he thought the jury would be impressed with his athleticism. 'The people call Officer Clifton Armstrong.' The cop who broke my taillight. The president of the I Hate K.C. Trench Club. This wasn't going to go well, even given that I'd known he was on the witness list.

Armstrong strutted – and I'm afraid there's no other word for it – up to the witness box, took the oath with a smirk that indicated he considered it a guideline and not a rule, and sat down. Barnett looked at him like a proud father looks at his son.

'Officer Armstrong,' he began, 'in your duties as a police officer in this city, have you had the occasion to deal with the defendant, Lt Trench?' Why not ask him if his uniform was blue. Barnett was starting really generally in order to work his way down to the nitty-gritty, which was bound to get nittier and grittier.

'Sure, I've met Trench a number of times.' You could almost see him chewing gum and sticking it under the surface of his desk at school.

'And what is your opinion of the lieutenant?' Barnett asked.

I was on my feet. 'What possible relevance does the officer's opinion of Lt Trench have in this case, Your Honor?'

'I'd like to know that myself, Mr Barnett,' the judge said.

'It goes to the witness's objectivity and credibility,' the DA told him. 'The officer was present at a very telling incident and the jury should know why he is relating the story. His opinion of Lt Trench is central.'

Huffman rubbed his eyes for a second or two. 'I'll give you a little leeway, Mr Barnett, but not a lot. Proceed.'

Barnett nodded his acknowledgement. Big of him. 'What do you think of the lieutenant, Officer?'

'He has a very good record of closing cases and he is almost always polite,' Armstrong said.

Barnett raised an eyebrow. Trench stared straight ahead and might have been calculating his tax bill in his head. '*Almost* always?' Barnett asked.

'Yeah. I didn't even know he knew my name. I mean, he's a big-deal detective and I'm just a cop out on the streets.' Really? We're going to play this as a morality tale of the upscale detective against the salt-of-the-earth beat cop? 'But then we ran into him and his lawyer at lunch and he called me by name and threatened to write me up for being out of uniform. At lunch.'

Armstrong was burying the lede, but Barnett was happy to dig it up for him. 'That's not all that happened at lunch that day, was it?' he said.

I objected again. 'What does a lunch that took place well after Detective Schaeffer was shot have to do with this case, Your Honor?'

Barnett didn't wait to be asked. 'It goes to a pattern of behavior, a violent pattern, on the part of the defendant,' he said.

Judge Huffman looked like he'd had a series of long days that were all today. 'You have two minutes, Mr District Attorney, and then I will end this line of questioning.'

'Understood. Officer, what happened at the lunch when you and your partner just happened to run into Lt Trench and Ms Moss?'

'The lieutenant pulled a gun on us and threatened to kill us,' Armstrong said.

Barnett gave the judge a look that said: *That quick enough for you?*

FORTY

'It Trench threatened you with a gun? Why?' Barnett said.

'You'd have to ask the lieutenant,' Armstrong answered.

'I'd love to,' Barnett muttered in a stage whisper.

You and I know what happened at that lunch, so take it as a given that Barnett and Armstrong managed to paint it in the worst possible colors. Armstrong and Clanton just wandered into the same Italian restaurant as Jon, Trench and I did, made some small talk and then Trench, *completely* unprovoked, pulled a gun out of his pocket and said he'd shoot them if they didn't leave. Armstrong couldn't speculate but he assumed the lieutenant was having some mental issues (which I of course had stricken from the record immediately, for all that would be worth). Then Barnett, not even trying to hide his frat-boy smirk, handed the witness over to the defense, and we know who that was.

Jon Irvin.

Jon had returned to work today, wearing a face mask and feeling much better, so he and I had agreed that, since he didn't play a major role in the hilarity being discussed but had been present in the room, he might handle the questioning of this witness, and he jumped right in. 'Officer Armstrong, what were you and your partner doing right before the lieutenant produced a weapon from his pocket?'

Armstrong opened his mouth to speak, but Jon cut him off. 'And before you answer, please keep in mind that I was there at the time, as was Ms Moss, and both of us can testify later in the trial if it becomes necessary.'

Barnett just raised a hand. 'Objection. The witness is being intimidated.'

Jon looked at the judge with an expression of absolute innocence, something he does very well. 'Would it have been better if I'd reminded him that he is under oath and can face perjury charges if he lies on the stand?'

Huffman seemed to be using his right hand to erase both of them; he waved it back and forth. 'Enough of this. The witness will answer the question.'

Jon smiled. 'What were you and your partner Officer Clanton doing just before Lt Trench felt it necessary to pull a gun on you?'

Barnett thought about objecting again – you could see it – but then he looked at Huffman's face and sat still.

'We were just sitting at our table minding our own business,' Armstrong lied.

'Oh, not really,' Jon said. 'Let me ask it another way. Were you standing up when the lieutenant, admittedly, produced a weapon and pointed it at you?'

Armstrong, who had clearly thought he owned the place when he walked to the stand, now appeared to want another look at the deed. His shoulders were rounded now, rather than square, and he appeared to have found something fascinating to look at around two feet below eye level. 'I don't remember. Maybe.'

'OK,' Jon said. 'You don't remember. Do you remember pulling your arm back to try and throw a punch at the lieutenant?'

Armstrong looked angry. 'No. I didn't do that.'

'All right, but I have three witnesses in the courtroom who might disagree.' Jon was pushing his luck more than I was accustomed to seeing from him, and sure enough, Barnett stood and objected. I'll spare you the back-and-forth; Jon was instructed to refrain from such references and he said he would. 'Officer, was that restaurant a favorite of yours? Did you and your partner frequent it?'

'No,' Armstrong said. 'I don't think I was ever there before.'

'Then why did you go there that day, if it wasn't to confront Lt Trench and Ms Moss?' He was gallant enough to leave himself out of the equation.

'We just wanted some pasta,' Armstrong said. The jury was watching him trying to find a safe place to look in the courtroom and surprisingly he did not choose Barnett's table. He looked at the back of the gallery, where his partner Clanton was just leaving. Quickly.

'And is it true that earlier that day you had pulled over Ms Moss, broken her taillight with your baton and then cited her for having a broken taillight?' Jon asked.

Here came Barnett again. 'Objection. Relevance?'

'One more question will show relevance,' Jon assured Huffman, and was granted that question. 'Officer, didn't you tell Ms Moss that you were no fan of Lt Trench, you thought he had killed Detective Schaeffer, and you wanted to dissuade her from defending him?'

'I never said "dissuade,"' Armstrong said.

'Did you ever take a loan from Detective Schaeffer?' Jon asked. Armstrong stared at him. I'd seen that stare. If I were Jon, I'd be very careful about my taillights. 'He loaned me a little money,' Armstrong said.

'In fact he loaned you thirty thousand dollars, didn't he, Officer?'

Barnett: 'Again. Relevance?'

'Extremely relevant, Your Honor,' Jon promised. 'Detective Schaeffer was in the habit of giving out loans with high interest rates to his fellow officers, and Officer Armstrong was one of them. It goes directly to the homicide, as we'll see.'

Huffman looked skeptical. 'Let's not try Detective Schaeffer in this court,' he said.

'I have no intention of doing so. Officer, did Detective Schaeffer loan you thirty thousand dollars?'

Armstrong, hand over his mouth, mumbled, 'Yes.'

'Did you pay it back?'

'He died before I could,' was the answer.

'Was it still thirty thousand, given the interest that Schaeffer charged?' Jon said.

'No. I'm not sure what the final number was.' Armstrong was trying to dissolve into the floor.

'According to the records discovered in Detective Schaeffer's apartment, it was fifty-six thousand, but next to your name he wrote, "Forgiven." Any idea what that meant?'

'No,' Armstrong said.

'No further questions.' Jon had done an admirable job.

Barnett didn't even redirect because he was afraid his witness would lie some more, just as obviously. 'The prosecution rests, Your Honor.'

'Let's take a recess until tomorrow at nine a.m.,' Huffman said. 'Then we will hear from the defense's first witness.'

Whoever that was going to be. (Oh, I had witnesses, but I still had to decide what order to present them in. Yeah, I know that sentence ended on a preposition. I'm tired.)

Patrick, of course, showered me with praise as soon as the courtroom started to empty. Trench looked at him without obvious expression, thanked me dispassionately for my effort as he did every day of the trial, and left, still looking like someone had stuck a broomstick up the back of his suit jacket.

I let Patrick drive home because: 1. It was his car; 2. I was exhausted like I always am after a day in court; and 3. This way I could do the texting and possibly calling I needed to do.

First, I texted Emma and asked (OK, instructed) her to put together a request for a court order releasing Schaeffer's medical records, one of the possible exclusions to the HIPAA law. She didn't ask any questions and sent back a message saying it would be on its way before the end of business. I thought we'd already reached the end of business, based on how achy my feet were, but it was only 4 p.m. Go figure.

Then I got on the phone to Nate and told him what I was planning, which he immediately thought was a horrible idea. He was probably right, but I felt like the jury was getting away from me and it was far too late in the game for that to happen; I had to take a risk. And this was going to be a risk.

Nate, after he was done telling me how wrong I was, agreed to shift his focus to Schaeffer's loan shark side hustle and told me he'd get back to me within two days. I told him it had to be within one day and Nate hung up on me. It gave him plausible deniability in case he was late; he could tell me he'd never heard me say that. Nate is no fool.

I told Patrick I'd have to work most of the evening. He nodded his understanding, then asked, 'How will you get all this into the trial record if you implement this new plan? You seem to be cutting off a number of possible avenues to get facts to the jury.'

I snorted a sort of mini laugh. 'Do you think you're a lawyer again?'

'I never thought I was a lawyer. I thought I could help you with some of the expertise I picked up by *playing* a lawyer.'

'From scripts written by other people who weren't lawyers,' I pointed out.

'We have consultants.' Patrick was on the verge of pouting.

He pulled the car into our property and used the key card to open the gate, then drove through toward the garage. 'Let me answer your question,' I said. 'Things don't have to be said out loud in open court to be part of the record. I want to submit the exhibits so that I can ask about them when I question my witness.'

'Clever,' Patrick said as we got out of the car. 'But I'll be interested to see how it will work.'

'Or, if.'

'It'll work. You're brilliant.'

I loved him enough to wait until I was in front of him to roll my eyes so he wouldn't see. 'Did you enjoy coming to court today?' I asked. It was a clever way (I thought) to get on to the subject of his current jobless status, and maybe get Patrick to think about what might be next.

'You know I always love seeing you work.' And that was it.

I opened the back door with my key card because nobody has keys anymore and all these whippersnapper kids should get off my lawn. 'But?' I said.

'But?' As if he didn't understand.

'That was the shortest comment you've ever made on my work since I met you, Patrick. You think I did something unwise or ill-advised in court today and you don't want to say so. Now, out with it. If I can't accept criticism from my boyfriend, I will have no way of connecting with reality at all.' OK, so I was laying it on a little thick.

We walked in through the den and I flung myself on to the cushiest couch, which was all of them, but I selected the one farthest from the door. Patrick stayed standing and looked down at me. 'I'm not qualified to criticize your legal expertise,' he attempted.

'Nice try. Say what you aren't saying. I'm a big girl. I can take it. I'll still love you afterwards. Probably.'

'But will you marry me?' That old chestnut.

'When you're ready.'

He scowled because he knew I wouldn't explain that.

'I thought letting Jon Irvin question the cop was an error,' he said. 'You're the lead attorney. If you hand the cop off to your second chair, you're signaling to the jury that you don't consider him an important witness. But the prosecutor does and you're conceding the point. Why did you do that?'

I looked at him and tried to figure his reasoning 'You think I was afraid of Cliff Armstrong?' I asked.

'Not at all, and that's why it baffles me.'

'I thought Jon would be less angry and therefore more professional in questioning Armstrong,' I explained.

Patrick shook his head. 'That's not it. You can tell that to other people and you might try to convince yourself, but that's not it.'

'Then what is it, Mr Prosecutor?'

Patrick walked around the sectional sofa and sat next to me, then picked up my feet and put them on his lap. 'It's that you're desperate to win this case and you're trying anything you can think of to gain an advantage. You think you're losing, but you're not.'

I actually felt tears come to my eyes, and I never do that. 'I am losing, Patrick. I'm not doing my job and Lt Trench is going to go to jail for a very long time.' I sat up and he put his arms around me.

'You're not losing. You've been involved in the case, but I've been watching the jury. They *want* to acquit the lieutenant. All you have to do is show them how to do it.'

I lay back and let him engulf me. 'I don't know how.'

'Yes, you do. And tomorrow you will begin.'

I wished he was right. I cried for a while and then let Patrick's arms make me feel safe.

FORTY-ONE

*E*xcerpt from the court reporter transcript of The County of Los Angeles v. K.C. Trench

MS MOSS: Officer Ryan, are you acquainted with anyone who works in the Bureau of Firearm Analysis for the LAPD?
OFFICER TERENCE RYAN: Yes, I am.
MS MOSS: Did that person, or people, tell you anything about the way the bullet supposedly fired from Lt Trench's gun was handled on its way to the bureau?
OFFICER RYAN: Yes, that person said something was wrong and there was pressure to say nothing about it.
MR BARNETT: Objection. Hearsay.
THE COURT: Sustained. The jury will ignore what Officer Ryan just said.

MS MOSS: Dr Moskowitz, what is your current position?
DR MOSKOWITZ: I am retired from the New York Police Department's Forensics Lab, as its director.
MS MOSS: Did you examine the bullet that the LAPD said was taken from Detective Schaeffer's skull?
DR MOSKOWITZ: I did, and I consider it unlikely that is what happened.
MS MOSS: Why?
DR MOSKOWITZ: There are no markings from the skull itself. The striations on the bullet match the one that was fired from Lt Trench's weapon, but there are no markings that indicate it ever went through anything as hard or dense as a human skull.
MS MOSS: So, what conclusions can be drawn from that?
DR MOSKOWITZ: In my opinion the bullet was replaced with another.
MR BARNETT: Objection. The witness can't be led to a conclusion.

THE COURT: Sustained. The jury should disregard Dr Moskowitz's conclusion.

MS MOSS: Ms Lockhart, what is your current job?
MS LOCKHART: I am the chief of security for the building that houses the law firm Seaton, Taylor, Evans and Wentworth.
MS MOSS: The firm that Mr Irvin and I work for.
MS LOCKHART: That's correct.
MS MOSS: Ms Lockhart, did you review the security video from the night before a fire was set in my office?
MS LOCKHART: Yes.
MS MOSS: And what did you see in that video?
MS LOCKHART: A man identified as an LAPD officer was there at about three in the morning the night before the fire. He appeared to be setting up wires in your office, out of sight.
MR BARNETT: Objection, Your Honor. Relevance? What does this have to do with the murder of Wallace Schaeffer?
THE COURT: Objection is sustained. The jury should disregard all of Ms Lockhart's testimony as it is not relevant to this case.

'Ms Moss,' Judge Huffman said, 'you appear to have only one more witness on your schedule.'

'That's correct,' I told him. 'And did you receive all the documentation I submitted, Your Honor?'

Huffman nodded. 'It is being processed. Call your witness, Ms Moss.'

'Thank you, Your Honor. The defense calls Detective Lieutenant K.C. Trench.'

Trench stood and of course there was not so much as one wrinkle in his clothing. He and I had discussed his testimony three days earlier, before I'd decided not to call any other witnesses and let the lieutenant make his case. With my help.

And if you think that my heart wasn't pounding or my stomach wasn't in knots, then we don't know each other very well.

The lieutenant sat very straight in the witness chair and looked for all the world like he was about to discuss his favorite books or the best day of the week for him to arrest you. Calm, impassive, ultimately trustworthy but not very likable. I tried not to think about that last part as I assayed the jury. They were watching and their faces were almost as unreadable as Trench's.

'Lt Trench,' I began. 'How many arrests did you make in the last calendar year?'

'One-hundred-fifty-two,' he said. Not a moment's hesitation. 'Of which there were one-hundred-fifty-one convictions.'

'What happened to the last one?' I asked.

'It is still being processed.'

'Let's get right to it, Lieutenant. You did not like Detective Wallace Schaeffer, did you?'

Not a twitch. 'No.'

'Didn't you once tell me you hated him?' I asked. I needed this out there so I could stifle it in the jurors' minds.

'Yes, I did.' It was hard to tell if Trench was annoyed with me or keeping up with his stock portfolio.

'How many people have you hated in your life, Lieutenant?'

Again, there was no pause. 'One.'

'So you hated Detective Schaeffer and no one else. Why did you hate him?'

'He made advances to my wife, and when she rejected him, he got his revenge by sending her into an unsecured crime scene, which resulted in her being shot and killed.'

I figured I'd ask the questions the jury wanted answered. 'Did you want to kill him?'

'Yes.' One female juror in her 50s or so widened her eyes.

'*Did* you kill Detective Schaeffer?' I asked Trench.

'I did not. Someone else shot him.'

A thought occurred to me, and it's always a bad idea to embrace such a thing in real time, but when did I ever reject a bad idea? 'You're an expert detective, Lieutenant. Who do you think killed Detective Schaeffer?'

'I do not have enough factual material to make that determination,' Trench said. Somewhere in the mists, Leonard Nimoy was smiling. Or raising an eyebrow.

'The prosecution alleges that Detective Schaeffer was killed with your own service weapon,' I said. 'Can you explain that? It was kept in a locked safe in your residence. How could someone other than you have killed the detective with that gun?'

Trench drew in a breath, a sign that he was thinking harder than usual. 'I do not believe anyone could have,' he said. 'I believe that my own weapon was not used in this homicide.'

The woman with the wide eyes blinked a couple of times and dropped her eyebrows. I couldn't tell if she was baffled or angry.

'But the ballistics test indicates it was, according to Dr Powell,' I said. Butter would undoubtedly not have melted in my mouth at that time, which was fine with me. I had no bread.

'As you noted in your cross-examination, Ms Moss, it is possible that the ballistics data was compromised.' Trench looked at Barnett, expecting an objection, but the DA surprised both of us and held his seat.

'How?' I asked.

'I cannot be certain. It is possible the bullet from the victim was replaced before it reached the ballistics unit, or that it was substituted for another when my weapon, which was confiscated at the time of my arrest, was being tested. I suspect the former.'

That was too much for Barnett. 'Objection! The defendant is speculating on expert testimony given by the head of the ballistics unit and deciding it was tampered with.'

Huffman was clearly open to that argument, and I didn't blame him, but he definitely had respect for Trench and could bend just a tiny bit. 'Lt Trench,' he said, addressing the witness/defendant directly, 'on what are you basing that statement?'

'It is the only theory that fits the facts,' Trench told him. 'I know I did not shoot Detective Schaeffer and I know the gun was in my locked safe. There were no signs of tampering on the safe or the doors in my home, so it must not have been stolen and returned. The only logical conclusion is that it was not used for the homicide. That means the ballistics report was in error or tampered with. I do not believe the ballistics unit would have falsified its report, so my conclusion is that the bullet was replaced before they had it in their possession.'

Huffman seemed to digest all that, pursed his lips, moved his head to the right and looked at Barnett. 'Objection sustained,' he said. 'The jury should disregard the defendant's speculation because it is just that.'

Several jurors appeared irritated. I took that as a good sign.

'Very well, Your Honor,' I said, because you don't get to say 'Very well' all that often. 'Lt Trench, can you tell us where you were on the night Detective Schaeffer died?' I happened to glance at Francie Schaeffer, who was sitting near the back of the courtroom. She was avoiding my eyes by looking at the floor in front of her.

'I left Police Headquarters at roughly seven p.m. and stopped briefly at a supermarket before going to my home, where I stayed for the rest of the night. I would estimate that I arrived home a few minutes past eight.'

'But since Mr Barnett is going to ask you in his cross-examination, if the medical examiner placed the time of death between seven and nine p.m., wouldn't that have given you time to go to his apartment and shoot him before you went home?' I looked at Patrick, who like most actors is a great audience, and he was totally engrossed in the proceedings. I'd get a better review tonight.

'I suppose there was adequate time, but I cannot say that as a certainty because I never tested the theory,' Trench said. 'I did not go to Detective Schaeffer's apartment.'

'But at the holiday party in question, you did say you would kill him if he laughed, didn't you?' I wanted to get that out of the jurors' minds by letting Trench explain his outburst.

'I did say that. It was a few months after my wife's death and a list of officers lost that year was being read. Detective Schaeffer was having a conversation with other members of the department, and when her name was read, he laughed. I am embarrassed to say that my emotions got the better of me and I called him out.' Trench was not making the same mistake again. His voice had all the passion of a man asking which bus to take to Pasadena.

Now that he'd made his explanation, maybe I could punch some holes in the prosecution's case. 'Did you mean what you said literally? Did you really want to kill Detective Schaeffer?'

Trench actually appeared to give the question considerable thought. 'I doubt it,' he said.

There was no chance I was going anywhere near that. Stick to the questions I could rely on for helpful answers. 'Lt Trench, in the twenty-two years of your distinguished career with the LAPD, have you ever drawn your service weapon and fired it?' I half-expected Barnett to object at 'distinguished career,' but he was willing to concede that Trench was a pretty good detective, even if he thought the lieutenant was also a stone-cold killer.

'Yes, I have,' Trench answered. 'Two times.'

'Have you killed anyone in the line of duty?' This was in Trench's file and part of public records so there was no surprise coming.

'Yes. Once. An armed assailant was firing at a group of officers, and I shot him.'

'When was that, Lieutenant?'

'October the fifteenth, 2014.'

'One last question, Lt Trench. Have you ever, under any circumstances, drawn a gun on anyone facing away from you?'

Trench looked at me. 'Shoot someone in the back? No, Ms Moss. Never.'

'And yet Detective Schaeffer was shot in the back of his head.'

'I cannot speak for the person who killed him,' Trench said. 'It was not me.'

'Thank you, Lieutenant.'

FORTY-TWO

B arnett's cross-examination of Trench was brief and point-less. He asked why Trench would say he wanted to kill Schaeffer if he wasn't going to do it. Trench had already answered that. He asked if he could account for the fact that the bullet from his gun was determined to have matched the one taken out of Schaeffer. Trench had answered that, too, and Barnett had objected to it. Then, unexpectedly, Barnett asked Trench if he had been present at my office the day of the fire. So I objected.

'We're not trying anyone for arson today, Your Honor. What is the relevance?'

Huffman didn't answer but looked at Barnett.

'It is the prosecution's contention that there were files in Ms Moss's office that might have further implicated Lt Trench in Detective Schaeffer's murder,' he said. 'If the lieutenant was there, he might have had motive to set the fire.'

'That's patently ridiculous, Your Honor,' I said. 'There never were such files and, if anything like that had existed, it would have been on several hard drives in the office. Paper documents just wouldn't have made any difference. But the key here is that the prosecutor is making up documents that didn't exist.'

Barnett humphed a little, but Huffman found in my favor and after that, he was pretty much done with Trench. Huffman looked down at me. 'So is the defense prepared to rest, Ms Moss? You did say you would call just one witness.'

'I lied about that, Your Honor. I have two more witnesses and both of them are on the list.'

Huffman, his tee time completely blown out the window, did his best not to sigh. 'Proceed.'

'Thank you, Your Honor. The defense calls Dr Barry Mencken.' Mencken, because I'd known I was going to do this the whole time, was in the courtroom and made his way to the witness box. He was dressed neatly, clean-shaven, and generally looking like

Central Casting's version of a doctor. Sworn in, he sat and looked patient.

'Dr Mencken,' I said. 'Were you Detective Wallace Schaeffer's physician?'

'Yes,' Mencken said. 'I was his primary care physician for about seven years.'

Barnett was on a timer and about to object any second. I figured I might as well give him the prompt. 'What kind of health was Detective Schaeffer in on the day he was killed?'

Not yet; Barnett stayed seated. 'I didn't see him that day, but I had been in touch with him regularly for some months and had spoken to him only three days earlier,' Mencken said.

'Three days earlier.' Like I hadn't known that. 'Why were you in such frequent contact with the detective, Doctor?'

That must have triggered the spring under Barnett's chair because he shot up immediately. 'Your Honor, no one is disputing that Wally Schaeffer died of a bullet wound. What possible relevance does his overall health have to this case?'

It was, I'd admit, a fair question, but I had an answer. 'It goes directly to my client's innocence,' I told Huffman. 'It's about how Detective Schaeffer was shot, and why.'

'Quickly, Ms Moss,' Huffman said.

OK, quickly. 'Was Detective Schaeffer in good health?' I asked Mencken.

'No. He was suffering from stage-four lung cancer, and was in fact dying,' he said. 'He'd known that for months. He probably only had a few weeks left.'

'I see,' I said, because maybe I did. 'And what medications was he taking at the time of his death?'

'He was on a drug called Krazati for the cancer and had undergone chemotherapy and radiation treatments,' Mencken said. 'He was not progressing.'

'Are those the only medications he was taking?'

'For the cancer, yes,' Mencken said.

'But he was also taking other medications unrelated to his cancer, wasn't he?'

'Yes,' Mencken said. 'He had a prescription for Lexapro for depression. It's not unusual for terminal patients to fall into depression.'

I looked a little sideways at Mencken. 'You said he had a prescription for Lexapro. Was he taking it?'

'I would have no way of knowing. Detective Schaeffer had not been to my office in a month.'

'What form did his depression take? Was the detective reporting he was having suicidal thoughts?'

Up came Barnett again. 'Is the defense seriously suggesting that Detective Schaeffer shot himself in the back of the head and then hid the gun before he died?'

I let myself be seen stifling a laugh. 'Of course not, Your Honor,' I said. 'The defense makes no such claim. We are quite certain that someone else shot Detective Schaeffer and equally certain it was not Lt Trench.'

'Then what connection has Detective Schaeffer's depression, if he was diagnosed with such, to his murder?' Huffman asked.

'I can answer that with my last witness,' I told him.

'I look forward to it,' Huffman said. I tried not to think of what that meant specifically.

I let Mencken go after that because he'd established everything I was going to need. Barnett asked him if all patients with terminal prognoses developed depression, was told no, and dismissed the witness. He wanted nothing to do with this part of the case.

'The moment we've been waiting for,' Huffman said to me. 'Please call your final witness. It really *is* your final witness this time, Ms Moss?'

'Yes, Your Honor,' I said. 'The defense recalls Officer Clifton Armstrong.'

Armstrong, who shouldn't have been the least bit surprised, shuddered across his whole (seated) body as if someone had jolted him with an electrical charge. He sat and stared for a second or two, then struggled to his feet and walked very slowly toward the witness box, staring at me the whole time. I wondered if he might have benefitted from some of Mencken's medications, or some hallucinogens. He finally sat down, was reminded he was under oath, and composed himself enough that the jury probably stopped worrying about his health. But he didn't stop glaring at me.

'Officer Armstrong,' I began, 'we established when you testified the last time that you owed Detective Schaeffer fifty-six thousand dollars at the time he died, but his private records list your loan as "forgiven." Were you aware he had forgiven your loan?'

'Yes.' It's hard to talk without moving your lips. Perhaps Armstrong was taking lessons in ventriloquism.

'Did he tell you why he had done that?' Of course he had, but now Armstrong was presented with a choice: incriminate himself or commit perjury. I was glad I was on this side of the witness box.

Suddenly his gaze shifted around the room, but he wasn't finding many friendly faces. Barnett, of course, wanted his witness to come across well, but he was aware that Armstrong was not doing so. Even Clanton had abandoned him; Armstrong's partner was not present in the courtroom.

'He didn't say anything to me specifically about it,' Armstrong said. It was almost certainly a lie, but hard to prove. He wasn't as stupid as he looked but that wasn't saying much.

'Had you discussed terms of how your loan might be forgiven before Detective Schaeffer did so?' I asked. Armstrong looked confused, so I added, 'Did he ask you to do anything for him?'

'Like I said, I don't know why he gave up my loan,' Armstrong answered.

In for a penny, in for a pound. 'Officer Armstrong, did Detective Schaeffer hire you to kill him and put him out of his misery?'

Pandemonium. Barnett practically hit the ceiling. Spectators actually got up out of their seats. I thought Patrick was going to give me a standing ovation. Nate, leaning on a post near the rear of the courtroom, grinned like a madman. When did Nate get here?

Huffman, however, was not amused. 'Ms Moss, do you have any evidence that such a thing happened?' he asked before Barnett could even get his objection out.

'Your Honor, we've had testimony that Detective Schaeffer was suffering from depression and might or might not have been taking the medication prescribed. We know he forgave Officer Armstrong's very substantial loan and the officer himself can offer no explanation. We know Detective Schaeffer was livid with Lt Trench and might have exacted his revenge from beyond the grave by framing the lieutenant with Officer Armstrong's help. Captain Moran said Detective Schaeffer *requested* to partner with Lt Trench on a case he could have handled himself. Then Detective Schaeffer was shot shortly after, perhaps in an effort to put Lt Trench in exactly the seat he occupies today. I am putting those pieces together and asking whether something happened that would fit the circumstances. If Officer Armstrong, who knows he is under oath and subject to charges of perjury if he lies on the stand, answers truthfully, it is entirely possible we will be discussing this case in different terms. But we need to hear his answer to proceed, I believe.'

Huffman, doing his best to be fair, turned toward the DA. 'Mr Barnett?'

'Judge, there is absolutely no evidence that has been presented in this case that indicates the victim would have even considered paying someone, let alone another LAPD officer, to kill him for *any* reason. There is no physical evidence except that the bullet from Detective Schaeffer's body matched the one from Lt Trench's gun. I don't see any reason you should allow this outrageous line of questioning.'

'I see merit in both arguments,' the judge said. 'Ms Moss, you have no direct evidence that what you are saying is true, and you know it. But the possibility exists and I'd like to hear Officer Armstrong's answer to your question. But that will end this line of questioning. Understand?'

'Perfectly, Your Honor,' I said, then pivoted to face Armstrong. 'Officer Armstrong. Did Detective Schaeffer offer to forgive your loan if you would agree to kill him so he could end his suffering and put Lt Trench in jail?'

Armstrong, no doubt aware that the maximum penalty for perjury is four years in prison, as opposed to the lifetime sentence a murder charge could bring, said, 'No.'

'The defense rests,' I said.

FORTY-THREE

C losing arguments are, to be blunt, a pain in the ass. There's so much riding on them, particularly on the defense side, when your words are literally the last ones the jury will hear before the judge instructs them on procedure. The case, especially one like this, can literally rest on the strength of that last argument.

Usually, the defense attorney will recap all the evidence she or he might have presented, refute a couple of points the prosecution didn't make as well as they might have hoped, then make an emotional plea for justice, making sure the concept of reasonable doubt is mentioned prominently and often. But this wasn't any case and I was more wound up than I'd be otherwise. I'd never been at a trial in which the jury had so often been asked to disregard testimony from witnesses. And that trick seldom works. I was counting on it. I looked at Trench, whose face bordered on serenity, and stood to walk to the jury box and address them directly.

I did not refer to notes, because I hadn't written any.

'It seems like so much of the time we're told what we should be thinking,' I began. 'We read things online or in the newspaper or even in the crawl on the bottom of a TV screen, and even without noticing, we're being told what we should think. We're also being told what we *shouldn't* think. What's wrong. What we shouldn't pay any attention to. What we should disregard.

'But sometimes our own minds take control. Sometimes we pay attention to the things we think are important, the things that can make the difference in a difficult decision, even if someone else told us those things are trivial, or don't conform to the rules. We feel it and we think about it and we come to our own conclusion regardless of what we have been told is the case. We take into account the content of a person's character. Not whether we like that person, because we know that pretty early on and it doesn't always make the difference. No, we think instead about what kind of person they might be, what it makes sense for them to do or not do, and we go not just with our gut, but with our mind. Sometimes we don't need to see the proof to know it exists. Sometimes we close our eyes and weigh our feelings along with our thoughts, both of them equally.

'Do we really know what happened when we weren't there ourselves? Sometimes we do, because there is a clear path to that conclusion and no possible way it might have occurred in another way. But most of the time we have to fill in the gaps in our own minds because we just didn't see it happen. We can decide based on what makes sense to us personally. We don't disregard hard evidence, but we temper it with common sense and multiple possibilities. Can something have happened in more than one possible way? We often find that it could have.

'When we believe that, when we conclude that there is more than one absolute conclusion to be drawn, we can take stock in our own minds, put away the things we've been told to believe, and decide what we believe based on what we know and what we think. And when that happens, we are doing our best work as citizens. We are bringing a piece of ourselves to what can seem like a cold, impersonal process. That, ladies and gentlemen of the jury, is what I think we should be doing here today. We should be ourselves and bring *all* of ourselves to the task at hand. I trust that you can, and that you will. Thank you for all the attention you've paid during this trial, because I know it's not easy. And thank you for being here and being yourselves.'

I sat down, terrified I'd made an awful mistake. It was probably the most Los Angeles and least New Jersey thing I'd ever done, and the stakes had never been higher.

Trench looked over at me, did not change his facial expression, and nodded slightly in my direction. It was the warmest thing he'd ever done for me.

FORTY-FOUR

'How long is this going to take?' Angie asked.

Patrick, Angie, Emma, Nate, Trench and I were in a conference room a few doors down from the courtroom. Judy stood just outside the conference room door. She believed it was better to protect me from someone trying to get inside than to try and defend me in that small room with that many people. I defer to Judy on such matters.

The jury, having been charged by Judge Huffman, was in their room, deliberating. They had been for four hours. People always ask whether longer or shorter deliberations are more favorable to a defendant, and the fact is that lawyers don't know.

'As long as it takes,' I answered, which is the response nobody wanted to hear, including me.

'We got your medical evidence into the record,' Emma told me. 'The judge signed the order this morning.' She looked over at Trench. 'That might help,' she said. Trench favored her with a nod and she seemed pleased.

'I don't have much new for you,' Nate said, his eyes a little embarrassed.

'Just as well. I've already rested the case.'

Trench was sifting everything through that computer chip in his head. 'If Officer Armstrong did actually kill Detective Schaeffer, it would have required the knowledge and contributions from multiple members of the Los Angeles Police Department,' he said. He looked a trifle bewildered at the thought: 1. That his fellow officers would conspire to falsify key evidence; 2. That an officer would act as a contract killer to get out of debt; 3. That the whole operation of Schaeffer's loan side hustle could have existed at all; and 4. That members of his own department must have hated him, personally, that much. I'm projecting, because Trench expressed none of those feelings and betrayed remarkably little with his face, but with Trench a little says a great deal.

'Not everyone is as trustworthy as you are, Lieutenant.' Patrick has always wanted Trench to like him more. Patrick wants *everyone* to like him more. I'm his girlfriend. It can be exhausting.

Trench didn't answer. He just sat in his chair, looking like he was deep in thought.

'I should have talked about the evidence,' I said out of nowhere.

Patrick put his hand on mine. 'I think you did a magnificent job,' he said.

I smiled at him, but he always thinks I did a magnificent job, so I wasn't especially convinced.

'Everybody knew what you were saying,' Angie told me. 'And they looked like they wanted to agree with you.'

That was it. The jury *wanted* to believe Trench hadn't pulled the trigger. But was the bullet evidence enough to convince them he had? Had I convinced them *not* to disregard what the judge had told them to disregard? After all, he was an impartial jurist, and I was a slimy defense attorney who wanted her client acquitted whether he was guilty or not.

Perhaps I should consider therapy again.

There was a knock on the door and every head except Trench's swiveled in that direction. 'Yes,' I said, because technically I was in charge of the conference room right now.

'They're coming back.' It was the bailiff talking through the door. He did not open it. I didn't want to think about what he might have imagined we were doing in there.

'Thanks, Norman.'

We started to file out of the conference room, but Emma stopped, looked at Trench, and straightened his tie, which did not need straightening. Once Nate, Patrick, Emma and Angie were gone, Trench held up a hand to stop me. We were standing by the open door. 'Just a moment,' he said.

Was this going to be the admonition I'd been expecting for being so vague in my closing statement? I thought our strength in the case lay in the things Huffman had told the jury to forget, but that I wanted them to remember. Was Trench mad because I hadn't used the time to talk about physical evidence, his sterling record and the prosecution's absolute failure to place him at the scene of the crime? I braced myself.

'Ms Moss, I want you to know that no matter what the verdict is today, I think you have done an exemplary job in my case. I think you are a very good attorney and I am glad to have had you in my corner during this trial. If we lose, I would like you to represent me in an appeal.'

I stood there for a moment and stared at him. Then without thinking I reached over and embraced Trench, who must have looked astonished. I held him for a moment and then realized that he probably found this excruciating, so I let go. 'Sorry,' I said. 'But what you said meant a lot to me.'

He straightened himself and looked down into my face. 'It's all right, Ms Moss. I assume this means you would accept the job.'

'Let's hope it's not necessary, Lieutenant.' I walked out into the hallway, where Judy was naturally looking from side to side but not in our direction. Trench followed because you always let the lady walk out first.

People ask me if you can tell what a jury has ruled by looking into their faces as they re-enter the courtroom. Jurors, it has been my experience, betray nothing. What are they going to do, smile and wave for an acquittal or point their hands like guns and 'fire' for a conviction? Contrary to popular belief, the vast majority of jurors take their responsibilities very seriously.

This jury was no exception. They filed into the box and sat when the judge told them to. None of them exchanged glances with another. They did not make eye contact with Trench, Barnett or me. A couple of the women were staring at Patrick. A couple of the men were staring at Angie. One woman, too.

Huffman wasted no time. He called on the chair of the jury, a woman wearing a business suit and sneakers, to stand and asked, 'Have you reached a verdict?' If they hadn't, they were putting on quite the show. Hung juries look defeated. This one looked anxious to leave.

The forewoman acknowledged that they had. They did the thing where the verdict, written on a slip of paper, is brought to the judge, who lords it over everyone else that he gets to read it first. He passed it back. 'Madam Foreperson, what is the verdict of this jury?'

'On the count of murder in the first degree, we find the defendant not guilty.'

I'll save you the time: It was the same on all the counts. There was an audible sigh of relief from my crew and a few of the cops in the room. Others looked – let's call it annoyed. A few left the room immediately and there was a general air of disarray until Huffman banged the gavel and brought the room back to order.

Armstrong was nowhere to be seen. He was probably booking a hotel in Tijuana.

I almost put my head down on my desk from the emotional release and general exhaustion. I could feel Patrick's hand on my shoulder from the row directly behind me. Dear Patrick. Unless it was the guy sitting next to him in the brown suit; that would have been creepy.

Then I braved a glance at my client. Trench, of course, would not celebrate. He would not gloat. He would not move a facial muscle. But he did look at me and say, 'Thank you.' That was all.

FORTY-FIVE

'It's good to be home.'

I was finally back in my actual office, with the small desk, the inadequate client's chair and the faint smell of smoke. And I'd never been happier to be anywhere in my life. I was talking to Emma, who was taking some of my books and rearranging them on the shelves to group by subject matter. The guys who had reassembled my office, give or take, had arranged them by size. Aesthetically pleasing, but not very practical.

'It sure is,' Emma said. 'Do you think they kept you out as an incentive until the Trench case was finished?'

My chair felt both familiar and strange at the same time. I'd gotten used to the even-worse one downstairs. But the window in this office and the few personal belongings that had survived were enough to make the place feel right. There was the one exception, but there was nothing that could be done about that.

'So after all that, do you still hate Lt Trench?' I asked Emma.

She was working her way through the volumes on divorce, which were taking up less of my time these days but were still needed. 'No, but I certainly don't trust the cops more than before. Look what they did to him.'

OK, so Emma had a point. 'Everybody should be judged individually.'

'Sure.' Emma was going to be a work in progress, but I had time. Probably.

When I was leaving the courthouse the day before, I'd stopped into the restroom and three sinks down I found Francie Schaeffer just staring at herself in the mirror. She didn't notice me until I said, 'Francie,' and walked toward her.

She looked up, almost panicky. She took a step back, as if I were threatening her. 'I had to,' she said.

We both knew what we were talking about, but I hadn't expected her to be so direct. 'Why?' I asked.

Francie looked back into the mirror so she could see me without making eye contact. 'My mom,' she said. 'She's gonna get survivor's benefits on my dad's pension and insurance. If they proved it was a suicide, that money goes away.'

I wasn't sure if that was true or not because I hadn't seen a copy of the LAPD pension or life insurance provision, but I had to say, 'It wasn't a suicide. Another man shot him. That's homicide, no matter what the circumstances.'

Francie shook her head barely perceptibly. She looked about to cry. 'Couldn't take the chance. Now I dunno what she'll do.'

I thought back to my meeting on the porch with Marcia Kendall in Encino. 'She probably doesn't need the money,' I told Francie. 'She's living a pretty good life.'

Francie blew her nose into a piece of toilet paper in her hand. 'She'll divorce it,' she said.

Back in the office (hello, office!) I'd say my tearful (not really) goodbye to Judy that morning, given that Armstrong had been arrested and charged with Schaeffer's murder, even if Schaeffer had asked for it. That would be a tricky defense and I was glad it would be someone else's problem. I had enough going on and preferred not to work for people who had tried to burn my office down. There are some trust issues.

Marshall Gianinni, the lab tech who had handled the bullets in Trench's case, had also been arrested and charged with evidence tampering. He had, as you might expect, also been suspended from his job, and would eventually be fired after he had reached a plea agreement with Barnett and testified against Armstrong.

Judy had gone off without more than a nod at Trench, and I vowed never to think of their previous relationship again for as long as I lived. There are some things one is better off not picturing, and that was a number of them.

Trench himself had thanked me one more time and then gathered himself to walk, with perfect posture, out of the courtroom, but not before dropping a bombshell on me. 'I am going to take a little time to decide if I want to return to my current position,' he said out of nowhere. I knew the revelations about others in the LAPD conspiring against him had hit hard, but I hadn't known it had knocked him over. 'Perhaps I have other roads to travel.' He had left before I could come up with a response, which was fair because I'm still working on one. I'm sure it'll be a doozy.

'It was a crazy case,' Emma said. 'I'm not sure I understand everything that happened.'

'That's OK,' I told her. 'I definitely don't.'

Patrick and Angie had said they were heading back to the head-quarters of Dunwoody Productions, which had moved off the lot of the studio where *Torn* had been produced and latched on with another studio, where some of Patrick's television productions, *sans* Patrick on camera, were being 'developed.' I thought 'developed' had gone out with film stock, so now you know how well versed I am in the film business. Apparently, Angie had been wearing Patrick down on the western comedy and he was willing to read it again. He'd be starring in it in no time, with Angie as producer, and that sort of made Angie Patrick's boss, and that meant my head was going to explode.

There was a knock on the actual, physical door, and Janine, our receptionist, stood there with a small cardboard box in her hand. 'This came for you, Sandy.'

'Is it ticking?' Emma asked.

Janine looked at her blankly.

'Thanks, Janine.' I took the box from her and Janine wisely hightailed it back to her desk, where everything was neatly arranged and she controlled her own destiny. I looked at the box.

'What is it?' Emma asked. She stood up from shelving books and looked over my shoulder. Emma needed a little work in respecting boundaries.

'I don't know.' The return address was a company I'd never heard of before. I got out a letter opener from my desk because I had just put it away and knew where it was, so I could start slashing away at the tape holding the box shut. It took just a minute to open it.

When I saw the contents of the package, I gasped. 'You OK?' Emma asked.

I nodded, then reached inside. There was a note at the bottom of the box. 'Couldn't think of you without it,' it read. 'Love, Dad.'

Next to the note was a little stuffed bear, identical to the one that had been destroyed in the fire, wearing a tiny t-shirt whose legend read, 'LAWYER.' I petted the fur on the tiny head and tried very hard, and almost successfully, not to cry at all.

'Cute,' Emma said. Empathy, too. She could use some help with empathy.

'Let's find a very special place for it,' I told her. 'This is a very important bear.'

I looked up at the spot the previous bear had held and thought to put it there, but from behind me I heard Holly Wentworth say, 'Nope. You're not putting that bear up in here. In fact, stop unpacking and put all your things back in those boxes.'

Emma looked stricken because this had probably been the most manual labor she'd done in her life, and I turned to look as puzzled as possible at my boss. 'Am I fired?' I asked.

Holly laughed a truly amused laugh, not one that people do because they think they're supposed to be amused. '*No*, you're not fired!' she said. She got a grip on her response and stopped being hysterical with laughter, which I appreciated. There's nothing quite like someone laughing directly in your face to make a person feel just a little bit inadequate. Or maybe that's just me.

'Why are we packing up? You're not sending me back to the broom closet, are you?' Somehow being fired would have been preferable.

'Of course not. But you have to understand, Sandy. Partners in this firm need to have much nicer offices than *this*.'

Believe it or not, it took a second. This had been coming for months, and I had been aware the meeting to decide on my partnership bid had been pushed until after Trench's trial was over. But in all that had been going on, well, things like being a partner at a major law firm in one of the largest cities in the country tend to slip one's mind.

'I'm a partner?' It wasn't that I hadn't understood her. I was using a little time to let it sink in and all I could think was, *I owe Patrick a ton of money!* Luckily, being a partner would help me pay him back faster. 'That was quick.'

Holly looked mock-offended. 'When I put someone in for partner, they become a partner,' she said.

'Was the vote unanimous?'

Holly crinkled her eyes a bit and smiled with a wry expression. 'The partners can't agree on *anything* unanimously,' she said. 'You'll see.' It sounded ominous.

'I guess this means I can afford to fix the taillight on the Hyundai,' I said. It was a joke. I didn't say it was a *good* joke.

'You won't have to pay for that,' Holly told me. 'I got a call from the lawyer for the LAPD this morning. They're settling our lawsuit now that Armstrong is charged with murder.'

It took me a second. 'We actually filed that suit?' I said, apparently out loud.

'Nobody messes with one of my partners,' Holly said.
Even Emma seemed stunned. 'Can I have this office?' she asked.
'Pass the bar first,' Holly suggested.

WHAT HAPPENED NEXT

I was making an emergency grilled cheese sandwich (cheese on toast melted in the microwave and don't you dare judge) when I heard Patrick come in through the back door. He walked in wearing an expression of determination I hadn't seen on him since he'd had to deactivate a nuclear weapon in an action movie.

He jumped right in. 'I went to see Patsy.'

That caught my attention. I got a little queasy whenever Patrick mentioned his late wife. In the years since her funeral, I couldn't remember Patrick visiting Patsy's grave. 'Really,' I said. Best I could do on short notice.

'I needed to think about what her reaction would be.'

'Um . . . you know Patsy's not going to answer, right?' I asked. It was one of many questions I had bouncing around in my brain.

'Of course. But being there helped me think about what she'd say if she could.'

The 'grilled cheese' wasn't getting any warmer. 'Say about what?' I asked.

He knelt down in front of me and looked up into my eyes. 'This is the last time I'll ask, Sandra,' he said. 'Will you marry me?'

I forgot about the grilled cheese. I gestured for him to stand up, and he did. So I could reach over and put my arms around him. 'Oh, Patrick,' I said. 'You're ready.'

AUTHOR'S NOTE

Alas, this is where Sandy Moss's journey reaches its destination. I can't complain that we managed to tell six of Sandy's stories, but it would have been nice to see where things went from here. The realities of the publishing business make that impossible. There is no blame to be assigned because they *are* realities.

This is the last book in the Jersey Girl series, and given that I never thought there would be a Jersey Girl series at all, that's a lot to be thankful for. Unless millions of people indulge an urge to buy this one or it becomes the basis for a wildly successful television or film series (rights are available), this will be where we say farewell to Sandy et al.

But it's a fond farewell, and there will be other characters with different stories to tell, some of them coming quite soon. If you found Sandy entertaining and interesting, please be on the lookout for others. If you didn't, well, feel free not to tell your friends.

This book and the five before it reached your eyes because of editors. It reached your eyes with a semblance of cohesion due to Rachel Slatter. Copy editors and proofreaders contributed to that level of coherency and I can only thank them from the bottom of my keyboard. They make my work look, believe me, much better than it did when they received it.

Thanks indeed to Rachel for letting me adjust the book so it would be a satisfying conclusion to Sandy's travails. I hate cliffhangers.

Rachel got to see the first Sandy Moss book, *Inherit the Shoes* (available wherever books are sold) because of the dedicated and inspired team at HG Literary, in particular my indefatigable agent Josh Getzler, who is also a good friend. Thanks to him and all. I should drop by the office more often, if only because there's a good pizza place nearby.

As of this writing I haven't seen the cover of this book (because it hasn't been created yet) but I'm willing to bet it's amazing, and that's due to terrific artists and designers. If you judged this book by its cover, that's who deserves the credit. You can trust that no piece of the art was my idea; I'm terrible at that.

This book was written without the use of Artificial Intelligence. I find the regular kind hard enough to deal with. Insist your reading material be written by humans, folks.

Also, this might be time to note that I have no working knowledge of police procedure in Los Angeles. I make everything up. How evidence is handled is, I'm hoping, considerably more secure than I have imagined here. This ain't no documentary, folks.

Every year is a difficult year, and if you believe in what some people say is a Chinese curse, that's what makes life interesting. This year has not been an exception, but here we are and we're still kicking. I find it's other people who most get you through the rough spots, and I rather selfishly rely on my favorite ex-prosecutor Jessica, and our offspring, Josh and Eve, for that. They are the best in the business, but you'll have to find your own, if you have not done so already.

To the readers of the Jersey Girl series, you are wonderful and indispensable. I will admit I wish there had been more of you so we could continue with Sandy, Patrick, Angie and Lt Trench, but instead we'll have adventures with other people. I'm nowhere near done yet, and hope you are not, either. Thanks for trusting me with your minds for a while.

Jeff Cohen
E.J. Copperman
Deepest New Jersey
March 2024